Mistaken Identities

By

Andrew Gray

CHAPTER ONE

Edinburgh; the 1990s

"Time, gentlemen, please!" The barman sang out the ritual words to a chorus of groans from his habitués who swallowed the last inches of their drinks with parodies of abstracted despair on their faces. The Jug was an Edinburgh watering hole for the exhausted business executive set like a precious jewel in the splendour of the Georgian New Town. It nestled, hidden beneath the entrance to a select family hotel. An unusual bar, it was cherished by its clientele for its eclectic mix of contents and varied decorative styles. There were odd suits of armour rusting away in various corners of the rambling old place. Many walls were papered with ancient copies of the Illustrated London News of the previous century, varnished over long since and yellowing with age. Rather than carpets, the stone floors were covered with antique Persian rugs which were almost worn through. On the walls, old hunting prints peeped out from a plethora of strange exhibits. There were bags of golf clubs, cases of medals from the Boer War, photographs of soldiers from that conflict and odd duelling pistols, hunting rifles and Zulu shields collected from Isandhlwana and Rorke's Drift. Musical instruments hung from the roof and paintings of hairy Highland chieftains looked forbiddingly out from corner nooks. The beer was all hand-drawn by the fiercely-aggressive bartender, Rory. A flame-haired and bearded Aberdonian, he brooked no disagreement with his way of running things.

That evening, the usual mix of town and gown were finishing off their drinks, looking forward to the approaching weekend. It was Thursday night and most had finished their real ale and headed off into the chill night air. At a corner table, Berrick Kildrum lit another cigarette and leaned forward, talking energetically. His companion, Alan Cruickshank was looking into his beer glass, swirling the golden fluid contemplatively.

"...market's going through the bloody roof. You know it. I know it. If we take our chance now, we'll coin it in."

Alan laughed ironically." You and coins." He held up a placatory hand. "Only kidding, Rick. I know you think buying property's a good idea. I agree with you, honestly. After all, it's not as though we aren't estate agents, so who'd know better than us, eh?"

He swallowed a mouthful of beer and winked at the barman. "In a minute, Rory. We're just finishing up." He accepted a snout from Berrick and puffed at it, eyebrow cocked as his companion finished most of his beer.

"Thing is, I'm not so well up on the mortgage business," Berrick went on.

"Leave that to me," Alan grunted, swallowing the last of his beer. "All right! All right, Rory, damn it! I've finished, OK?"

Rory weaved his way past an old suit of armour and approached their table, his bearded chin thrust forward aggressively. "Time means bloody time you two. C'mon. On yer bikes. Ah've a bed tae go to, even if you dinnae!"

They lifted their hands into the air in mock surrender, earning a savage grin from Rory.

"That's the way Ah like tae see ma punters. Bellies full ae beer, wallets empty, contents in ma till, o' course an' headin' hame.

Go on! Bugger off. See ye in the mornin'....worst luck!" He growled.

It was a typical winter night in Edinburgh. The traffic hissed by over the cobbled streets of the city and a huge gibbous Moon loomed, impossibly large over the New Town. Silvered tendrils of cloud were blown, helter-skelter under the hard, bright stars that peppered the black welkin. Huddled groups of folk were hurrying by, heads bowed to the arctic wind which knifed through even the bulkiest of winter clothing. Bidding each other goodnight and agreeing to meet at the office the following morning, they parted and hurried home. Time was of the essence. Of that, they were sure.

The next morning, Berrick arrived at their office which occupied a corner basement by Royal Circus. Alan was already there, going through the mail with Tanja. He smiled to himself sardonically. Tanja: a raven-haired, half-Croatian girl who ran their office with a frightening efficiency. When she had joined them, Alan had acted as usual. He had ignored Berrick's advice and had chased her with his usual brand of focussed concentration. She hadn't stood a chance, poor girl, but, as Alan had found to his cost, success had resulted in Tanja dinning into him a very clear idea as to what going out with her was to mean. Responsibility. Not a very Alan thing at all.

Alan extracted himself from Tanja's possessive embrace and headed for the door with Berrick in his wake patting his pockets, a frown on his face.

"What is it?"

"I must have left my list of properties to visit at home. Have you got yours?"

Alan pulled a copy of the Property Pages out of his pocket and waved it under Berrick's nose.

"You're a dopey sod, Rick. It's all that collecting coins that does it. Mark my words: it'll get you nowhere. Get with it."

"And where do you think you're going, Alan Cruickshank?" Tanja asked with mocking grimness.

"Property hunting, Wicked Witch. Back soon! Ouch!" He exclaimed, as he ducked the rubber Tanja had thrown at him with deadly accuracy. It hit him on the ear. He dodged round the door while Berrick seized his post and hastened after him.

"She's quite a girl!"

"Whew! You can say that again!" Alan grinned at him, rubbing his ear.

"A face like an angel, lips like Kate Moss..."

"Legs like Claudia Schiffer...."

"Tits like Gina Lollobrigida...."

"Dream on, pal. It's the only way you'll see 'em. In your mind's eye!"

They turned into Royal Circus, home of Edinburgh's community of advocates and Alan cursed. "I don't believe it! A ticket! I've only been parked for five bloody minutes. Jesus!"

He tore the offending pink slip from the windscreen of his superannuated BMW and thrust it into his pocket. He unlocked the door and created a minor dust-storm in the ashtray. Berrick added to it as he opened his own door and climbed in.

"Don't you ever clean up this wreck?"

"D'you want a lift or d'you want to walk?"

The BMW roared into life and pulled violently away from the pavement, scaring a squirrel in the gardens on the other side of the street into a headlong dash for cover.

They careered up the steep incline leading towards the Southside. First stop Rufin Finkelbaum & Co, solicitors, in Morningside.

Mr Finkelbaum was a strange individual. He had long fingernails like a werewolf and breath that would have felled an ox, had one been passing. He gave them the keys to two properties which were in the Property Pages and noted their names and addresses in an ancient ledger.

"I would appreciate the return of the keys today, if you please, gentlemen," he peered over his half-rimmed glasses from beneath eyebrows of preternatural hairiness, "I have another client who has an appointment to view the property tomorrow. Isn't that right, Mr Widdicombe?"

His clerk, who had been busying himself with a knuckle-deep examination of his right nostril was caught out by the sudden, surprise question. Surreptitiously wiping the digit on his crumpled, shiny-seated trousers, he nodded, coughing in embarrassment. "Yes, Mr Finkelbaum. A Miss Melville, I believe."

"There." Mr Finkelbaum fixed them again with that stare. It was like a wild animal peering out from beneath a bush as though gathering itself for a final, desperate leap for the pursuer's jugular. Unnerving.

"By five pm, gentlemen, if you please."

They were parked near Morningside Station. Swift consultation with the map confirmed that they were in the right area, but two streets away from their destination. They walked the short distance, noting the general state of the properties they passed.

"Subsidence. Hmm. Not good news there. Look at that one. Ripe for redevelopment, wouldn't you say? There can't be anyone living in it who's less than ninety. Look at the colour of the windows. Green. Can't have been painted since the forties!"

"Ahh! There we have it. Balcarres Building. Well, it's a tad close to the railway line, but it has potential. Let's take a look."

They knew the moment they walked in through the door that they had made a mistake. The place reeked of human filth of the worst kind. Scrawled on the walls were slogans, "Save the Whales!" and "Free Nelson Mandela!" Somewhat more puzzling was "If God made Lesbians, why didn't He give us pricks?"

The stench of ordure was too strong for either of them to venture any further into the stair. They staggered back out hands over their mouths, gagging.

"Christ! They should pay us to see places like that."

"And provide Noddy suits to keep out the stench!" Berrick agreed. "Let's hope the place in the Old Town's a hell of a lot better than that."

"If it isn't, Mr Finkelbaum will enjoy the sensation of having his keys returned per rectum sideways on."

"And all at no extra charge."

"You said it."

The weather had been rather murky in the morning, but now, it became increasingly so, obscuring the surrounding buildings as they strolled back to the car. Berrick had turned his attention to his post in the belated realisation that he had completely forgotten about it. It seemed that the bulk of it consisted of fliers of one sort or another. He quickly screwed them up and lobbed them into a litter bin. The last item was a package. It was a Post Office padded envelope.

"Ahhah!" He grinned. "At last!"

"What's that, then? Dirty photos hot from your favourite pornographer?"

"Bollocks. Here."Berrick tore open the top of the envelope and delved into the package with a grin of pleasure as they reached the car. Alan unlocked the door and climbed in. Berrick joined him and swiftly put on his seatbelt.

"Well? Or is it a secret ?"

"Oh." Berrick shook his head. "No. It's just my hobby. Look. "He pulled a clear plastic envelope out of the package and showed it to Alan.

"Oh...that." The latter commented. "Is that all?"

Berrick turned the proof set of euros over in his hand and looked at them fondly. "They'll be worth a good bit in a few years. Y'see, Alan, what you miss is the pleasure of looking at the sheer craftsmanship that goes into making these coins. Especially when they're a limited edition like this one. The silver alone makes the set valuable enough, but the artwork is like a rare edition of a masterpiece in fine art."

"Art!" Alan lifted his eyes heavenward. "Art is for poofs."

They climbed back into the car and Alan started her up. As he pulled away from the kerb, Berrick turned round in his seat and gave him a puzzled look. "What are your hobbies and interests, Alan? You never mention any. I mean, outside of work and Tanja, of course, what do you like?"

"Who said I like work?"

"Touché. Seriously, though, tell me."

"Never gave it much thought to be honest. I like beer and women. I like a good conversation -"

"Argument, more like."

"I won't dispute that. It livens things up. And....um...."

"Run out of ideas already?"

Alan swerved to avoid a woman who had opened her car door without looking.

"Stupid cow!" Alan bellowed, sounding the land-train klaxon he'd installed as a horn. "They shouldn't allow women on the bloody road. Use your eyes, can't you?" He pointed significantly at his own eyes as he passed her shocked face, ashen at the deafening cacophony which had almost stopped her heart from fright as it let loose over one hundred decibels of volume.

"Y'see, it's blithering bloody idiots like that who really get my goat. I can talk endlessly about them. Doesn't leave time for much else."

"Except drinking."

"Right you are. Are the pubs open yet? I can feel a thirst like a dredger coming over me."

"Bloody hell, Alan. Dylan Thomas from you of all people! Where did you learn that expression?"

"In a pub. Where all the best things are learnt."

"Mmmmm." Berrick remained non-committal. "It seems very limiting and, indeed, limited. If you want my opinion."

"Well, I don't. You do all those poofie things like coin collecting and going to arty-fartie plays at the King's Theatre..."

"And you get pissed..."

"And fuck women. Yeah, I know. Who do you think John Stuart Mill would say had better quality fun, eh?" Alan looked sideways at him as he steered around a bollard near Greyfriar's Bobby on the wrong side in the near-impenetrable fog, his headlamps ineffectually carving two opaque paths through the still air.

"You must have been at the dentist's last week." Berrick responded inscrutably.

"Eh? Come again?"

"It's the only place you might have actually read something instead of leering at today's topless twosome in the Daily Shitforbrains. The Reader's Digest, perhaps?"

"So?" Alan grudgingly acknowledged the accuracy of Berrick's barbed tongue.

"It's true, isn't it?"

"So? Tell me something, then; when did you last make the beast with two backs?"

"Hell's bells! Now, it's Shakespeare! Literary allusions twice in one conversation? It must be some kind of record. It'll be Machiavelli next."

"Answer the question, smartarse."

"What question was that, then?"

Alan parked the car and sneered over. "I knew it. No tottie these days? No potholing with the old one-eyed trouser-snake, eh?" He tut-tutted. "You should get out more. Do a bit of chatting up of some of this wonderful city's varied and delightful crumpet. That's what you should be doing instead of collecting bloody silver coins. What a waste of time. It'll never do you any good. You mark my words."

They stopped the car and climbed out. The mist was blowing a little now, though the gloom was almost Stygian. They were looking for Blackfriars' Close and decided they must be nearby. They had parked by the Canongate Kirk and now walked back up the street . The mist was blowing like smoke and the banners hanging from the venerable lands waved their heraldic panoply in sad flutterings.

They had passed the Close twice before they eventually deciphered its name carved from an ancient stone archway, covered in bird-droppings and hidden between two gryphons. It was a narrow, dark passageway lit from further down by two inefficient orange streetlights They hovered, seemingly, in the pea-souper blanketing the Town. They crossed the deserted High Street and entered the Close, peering at the doorways they went by, their footsteps echoing hollowly in the still atmosphere of the place.

"This is it.." Alan studied his list in the feeble light. They stood outside a faded and battered main tenement door. Its colour may once have been blue, but time and the weather had made it into a dull, battleship grey, echoing the monochrome misty air. Alan took the key out of his pocket and turned it in the lock. He pushed, but, initially, nothing happened! Give us a hand, Rick, will you? Something's making it stick."

Berrick lend a sturdy shoulder and heaved hard. There was a grating sound, harsh on the ears and, suddenly, the door swung open. Berrick fell onto one knee, caught out by the immediate effect of his intervention. As he slipped down, the contents of his wallet fell out of his inside pocket and landed on the dusty floor.

"Damn!" He said without much force. Scrabbling about, he collected the items together and put them back. As he stood back up, Alan was already ascending the stairs and gesturing to him to hurry up.

"Coming." He said and, letting the door swing back on its returning spring, he hastened to follow. As his shadow was cast back onto the floor of the entrance by the grim blue light of the stair, it crossed the small, folded pink square of his driving licence.

Up the stairs they trooped, their shadows preceding them and the mustiness of the air increasing. By the time they reached the second floor, the air was stale.

"Phew! It's pretty ripe here. Is it worth looking at this place?" Alan asked, wrinkling his nose.

"Let's see the flat first and then decide," Berrick replied.

Their footsteps echoed off the walls as they climbed steadily past the first floor. Various doors were vaguely visible in the subaquaeous light, but all looked battered, seedy and unwelcoming. No sounds were to be heard.

"Must all be tenanted. See - they've all got names stuck on."

"Means they're temporary occupants."

Alan grunted. He was unimpressed, but reserved judgement. The air was stale and overlaid with a smell of boiled cabbage on the second floor despite it being only half-way up the stairs. Unused and anoxic somehow. Berrick studied the doors. There were three. Two had no names visible on their old wooden surfaces. The third said "Wyatt".

"This is the one." He muttered. "Is it occupied?"

"I doubt it. Probably just the odd ghost of a Covenanter, or some such. "Alan replied. He felt uncomfortable as though he was under close scrutiny. Berrick fitted the key into the lock. It was stiff and reluctant to turn . A shadow crossed the door, startling them both. Alan leapt as he turned, expecting something atavistic. It was a cat coming up the stairs. It stopped and stared balefully, its ears laid back and hissed at them, before turning and continuing up the worn stone steps. With a last grunt of effort, Berrick turned the key in the lock. Silently, the door swung open. An empty passageway, lino-floored and bare-walled gaped at them.

"Shall we go in?" He asked. Alan preceded him into the hallway. Berrick followed him, pushing the door to. It swung open again. "Damn," he said, without feeling.

"Oh, stuff the door. There's nothing to steal here anyway."

"Mmm."

"What's through here, then?" Alan pushed open a peeling door halfway down the hall. It was distinguishable only vaguely in the gloom of the flat by its faded colour. "Wonderful decor in this place - squit-green walls and turd-brown lino."

"Tasteful." Agreed Berrick. "What's in the room?"

"Kitchenette. Or was. It's just a six-by-six box, with a window looking onto ..." He disappeared from view.

Berrick moved past and pottered down the hall, his footsteps echoing on the floor. Pushing open a second door, painted purple, he paused. "Are you still there?"

"Yeah."

"So? What's the view?"

"Search me. Impermeable grime and grease, combined with impenetrable murk outside, make it rather hard to tell."

"Hey! Look at this!" Berrick had given up on the purple-doored bedroom. "A round room!"

Alan sauntered through to join him.

"Neat! Smells of mustiness. It's big, though."

The room was, indeed, round. It was also big. The walls were ochre and the ceiling had once been white. A large centre-rose had a Chinese lantern suspended sadly from it in flaccid surrender. On the other side of the room, a door stood resolutely shut. The only other door off the corridor was the one Berrick had already looked into. A small bedroom, it overlooked the Close. Pale marks on the faded wallpaper showed where posters had been pinned. One still remained. It showed a fierce figure with a clenched fist and said: "Workers of the world, unite!"

"Obviously let to Liberals," Alan mused, and peered out of the window. Despite the hour, the Close looked tenebrous, the cobbles gleaming slickly under the dim orange lamp as the mist eddied in the gentle breeze.

"It's just a haar." Berrick peered over his shoulder through the window." It'll be sunny in an hour, you mark my words."

Alan took a cigarette out and lit it from a Zippo. "It's a dump."

"You took the words right out of my mouth. Still - let's see what the other bedroom's like."

"What other bedroom?"

"The one in the bumph. It says it's a two-bedroomed flat. It must be through the door in the lounge."

"I must have missed it in all the excitement," Alan sighed, crushing the cigarette under his heel.

They hadn't noticed that the lounge was carpeted. It was a very deep pile. Almost hairy. The room felt warm. Berrick thought back to his student days. Yes, he thought, this room makes the flat worthwhile. If it were redecorated throughout, with a bit of half-decent carpet ? Well, it might have potential.

He opened the door. An empty room gaped at him. It was built under the eaves and, instead of the window he had expected, it had a large skylight, which cast a dim light across a threadbare Turkish rug, which had somehow escaped the removal men.

As he was about to cross the threshold, however, he felt a strange, prickling sensation, somehow alien to his normal perception. He could not name it and, for a second, hesitated.

Alan called to him from across the lounge, his voice sounding muffled. Frowning, he turned to ask him to repeat what he had said. Following Berrick's voice, Alan sauntered into the bedroom. Empty though it was, he could see the potential. This one could be a winner, if they just approached the proposition imaginatively.

Berrick, turning, saw Alan follow him in and closing the door behind him. "There's something funny about this room." Alan asked.

"What?"

"I said -"

"I heard. Funny? No. It is unusual just to have a skylight, instead of a window, I'll grant you." He glanced up at the large, slightly warped pane through which he could see the almost luminous haar which had silently embraced the Old Town, rendering every sound strangely muffled. Even as it made gloom, it also provided an odd kind of light.

"Hey, can you smell cigar smoke?"

Berrick sniffed tentatively, a small frown etched on his brow. "Funny, that. Yes. Old cigar smoke. The former resident must have preferred them to fags, I imagine. Not the sort of thing students smoke."

He turned. He could feel the hair rising on his arms and his head, as if a strong field of static electricity was developing. He looked at his hand and the hairs were, indeed, standing on end. His head was spinning.

"What the hell's happening?" He put his hand to his brow as he felt a rush of blood to his head. He put out a hand and leaned against the wall for a moment.

Alan looked at him oddly, his shock of hair rising up on his head. "You know, I feel as I've got ants crawling all over me." He gripped Berrick's shoulder and there was a crack of electricity. "Bloody hell!"

"Jesus..." Berrick jumped back at the sound.

They looked around the room. It seemed as if time had stopped. There was no sound to be heard. True, they had not heard anything in particular in the rest of the flat, due to the haar. Yet, somehow, there was a deadness of hearing in this room. No echo. No motion in the thick mist outside the room. It was opaque, white and luminescent and yet its dim light on the plain, off-white walls was fading. Everything was becoming dark.

"Let's get out of this place. Something is not bloody right!" Alan snapped.

"Come on." Berrick was as keen to get going and, disorientated in the vanishing light. he found the door. There was the crack of a static charge as his hand connected.

In desperation, wrenching it open, with relief, they fell through and slammed it shut behind them, closing it and leaning back with eyes closed.

Alan breathed deeply, leaning back against the door, his eyes closed." Phew! Thank God we're out of that!"

Berrick tapped him on the chest with the back of his hand. "We're out of it, sure. But where are we?"

CHAPTER TWO

Alan opened his eyes, surprised at the comment. They were standing on a low-ceilinged room with an exceptionally deep-pile carpet. There were no windows, but blue walls with an elegant design in a faintly Chinese style. The light came from recessed lamps near the ceiling and, more faintly, a pale daylight gleamed up from some hidden source below. Two balustrades, surrounding circular stairs, stood in the centre of what now transpired to be an otherwise empty landing. One stairway led up, the other down. Berrick looked at Alan with a troubled expression on his face.

"What the hell happened there?"

"God knows. Where the hell is this? It wasn't on the details of the flat."

"Well, it's a hell of an improvement on the rest of it."

Berrick patted his face and hair. "That place was alive with bloody static."

"We were lucky not to have been electrocuted. That place is an accident waiting to happen."

For a moment, they simply gazed about at the sumptuousness of the carpeted landing. There was no sound that could be discerned except their own breathing.

"D'you know what?" Berrick breathed, struggling to make sense of it.

" No. Can't say I do."

"It's the Old Town, y'see?"

"Eh?"

"The Old Town. Back twenty years or so, a guy owned a pub in the Old Town, just off the High Street. Just like this flat."

"So?"

"Knocked down a wall and -" He stopped.

"And?"

"And - ah - he found a whole suite of rooms that had been blocked off in the eighteenth century. You know, like Mary King's Close?"

"Got you! That street under the Royal Mile that was left in the 1660s when the folk all died of the plague and -"

"-and was built over in the nineteenth century when the City Chambers were constructed."

"I know the place! Been round it! Weird! Really odd. Everyone died and they left it as it had been all those years. Yeah!" He scratched his head." So, you think this is something like that?"

"Exactly. Except -"

"Except what?"

Berrick looked at the landing critically and shook his head. "Except, this place is still occupied. Look!" He pointed. "That's a gas lamp. And, it's lit. How many gas lamps have you seen in your life?"

They paused at that. Indeed, a gas light was burning, its soft luminescence giving a mellow glow to the scene. Less bright than electricity, nonetheless, it was more pleasant than a fluorescent light. Far more so, indeed.

Uncertainly, feeling like house-breakers, they pushed themselves away from the wall, Berrick looking back at Alan, who seemed, uncharacteristically, less sure of himself.

"Where's the door?"

Pausing, Alan turned. "It's there. No…..there, maybe. No, look." He stepped across to the wall. "It's here. See? The line of the doorframe, if you look closely."

For a minute, they looked about in a state of indecision. At length, Alan made his mind up.

"Let's take a look."

Nodding in acquiescence, Berrick followed him down the circular staircase. Their eyes opened wider as they reached the foot of the stair. It opened onto a large hall. The walls were wood-panelled and gleamed from recent polishing. A parquet floor glowed in honey-coloured tones beneath their feet demonstrating clearly that they had chanced on occupied property.

"Look!" Berrick pointed at several portraits which hung at intervals on the walls. They were original paintings. All were portraits of important men in old-fashioned costumes. There, at the end was a man in Restoration wig and heavy coat, a spaniel at his feet and an army in the distance behind him. Further on, were admirals in naval blue uniforms, soldiers in familiar red. The centuries passed and the wigs became smaller, the fashions more modern. As their eyes moved to the most recent, they found a man dressed in a wing-collar and a frock-coat, sitting and gazing at a sheaf of papers held in his left hand, apparently absorbed by its contents. They moved closer to study it. At the bottom of the picture was a name. Alan laughed.

"D'you believe it?" He pointed it out to Berrick who was still gazing at the painting.

"What?"

"I should have recognised who it is, but the costume fooled me for a moment. It's John Logie Baird! But see what it says." He read the small legend below the name." 'John Logie Baird: Inventor of the telephone, 1955.' Can you believe it?"

"Look at this." Berrick said. "A painting of King James X. Have you ever heard of him?"

Alan shook his head. "It never came up in any pub quiz that I can remember."

"Of course it didn't. The only way we could have had a King James X would be if the Stuarts hadn't been kicked out in 1688." He laughed. "Stuart kings, indeed!"

Despite his head still swimming, or, perhaps, because of it, Berrick felt a twinge of something wrong. "This has all the hallmarks of some kind of shrine - you know what I mean. One of those nut-cases who wants to make out that the world is being told a Big Lie. That there was never a Moon Landing by Armstrong. That it was all filmed in a studio. That the Earth is really flat. That the 'Origin of the Species' is all a lie - c'mon, Alan. Let's move. Something is very, very wrong!"

The words were barely out of his mouth when a door opened at the end of the hall. Startled, they swung round to see who had entered.

A young woman, dressed in a long skirt which reached almost to her ankles was smiling at them. Far from appearing bizarre, she merely looked like someone who had been at an evening do and was still dressed accordingly. A single strand of pearls adorned her neck and her handshake was strong and warm.

"Mr Cruickshank? Mr Kildrum?" I'm Sophie Hanson. I apologise for keeping you waiting."

They protested , weakly, that she had not. Glancing surreptitiously at each other, they frowned and raised eyebrows at her obvious knowledge of their identities.

"I know you must be wondering what this is all about," she smiled disarmingly, "But, don't worry. Sir Ralph asked me to make you both comfortable. He'll be with you in a few moments. Follow me, please."

Elegantly, her feet tapping lightly on the highly-polished floor, she led them through the door by which she had entered and out into a corridor. This was carpeted, though with rugs of Persian design and, obviously of great expense. She prattled gaily about the weather and the 'awful problems of keeping this place clean'. The man who 'did' for them was ill and the dust didn't let up just because he was away. Still chattering in a high, clear voice, she ushered them into a small side-room, comfortably-appointed, with Victorian furniture in a superb state of repair. Hunting pictures hung on the walls and a fire flickered welcomingly in the hearth.

"Do please make yourselves comfortable. Sir Ralph will be with you shortly. I'm sure he will answer your questions. If you need to ask me anything, I will be over there -" she indicated a room opposite "- in my office."

So saying, she left them to their own devices and closed the door behind her. For a long moment, somewhat bemused, they wandered about the room, peering at the pictures. Berrick, strolled over to the window, but the haar was still filling the street outside with dense opacity. The faint sound of a typewriter could be heard through the door which Sophie had closed behind her.

"Sir Ralph could do with getting the girl a decent PC. That's no keyboard she's banging away at. My Grannie used to make that clattering when she did her correspondence."

Berrick nodded in agreement. "It's in keeping with the decor, though."

The door opened at that moment, startling them. A man in late middle age entered and smiled at them both, individually, with an accompanying nod. A halo of snow-white hair sprang bushily from the sides of his bald head. Heavy side-chops joined a bushy moustache under which nestled a pleasant smile. The old man was dressed in a dark blue suit of very formal style, similar, Berrick noted, to that worn by the last Governor of Hong Kong. Obviously, this cove was some kind of mandarin. He stifled the laugh which the pun triggered and spoke aloud in his best, formal manner. After all, he thought, he had had to speak to a few notaries in his time. The Moderator of the Church of Scotland was one who sprang to mind. He had been a prefect at school at the time and the man concerned had been wearing knee-britches and a froth of lace at his neck. This was par for the course in Scottish matters of state, after all. All old-fashioned togs. A bit like the judiciary, when it came to it.

"Sir Ralph! I'm Berrick Kildrum. This is my colleague, Alan Cruickshank."

Sir Ralph smiled politely and gestured to them to sit down. He selected a comfortable armchair and settled himself with a sigh of satisfaction before speaking.

"I apologise for dragging you both away from your affairs, gentlemen. I'm sure you're both wondering what this is all about."

Alan glanced at Berrick. They both nodded. Alan was about to reply that they were more than a little surprised, but Sir Ralph spoke before he could open his mouth.

"You are both, no doubt, in the dark about the matter I wish to raise. Let me make two things crystal-clear at the outset. You must understand that I represent HMG." Seeing the puzzled looks, he translated. "That is to say the Government. I apologise for the infernal initials. We civil servants live by them, MoW, EO, RN and all the rest. I know," he waved an apologetic hand tiredly, "they mean nothing to you. I'm afraid that I have spent a lifetime in using them without thought. You, in your civilian lives have probably had no contact with any of the ministries I imagine?"

"No, Sir Ralph," Alan replied. "Only the normal things like the Inland Revenue, I suppose."

Sir Ralph laughed. "Oh, God, those vultures! I spend half my life trying to persuade them that I have been working outside Great Britain and that my income from India is exempt, but they still try to nab a large chunk of it. You probably have the same problems with your own incomes, I dare say."

They both laughed and agreed. The old guy was all right. Not too much of a stuffed shirt. Even so, they both wondered what the cause of this meeting might be.

"Gentlemen." Sir Ralph began. Before he could proceed, however, there came a knock at the door. "Yes?"

The door opened and Sophie Hanson appeared.

"I'm sorry to interrupt, Sir Ralph, but it's the FO."

Swearing under his breath, Sir Ralph heaved himself out of his armchair. "Excuse me. Another damned telephone call from the powers that be. I won't be more than a couple of minutes.

Make yourselves at home. Sophie will make you both a cup of coffee."

He stamped off through to the office and Sophie asked how they liked their coffee.

Ten minutes later, they were finishing their cups when Sir Ralph came back, a grave look on his face.

"Things are worse than I thought."

Berrick looked at Alan queryingly and mouthed 'what things?' and received a shrug in reply.

Sir Ralph sat himself heavily in the armchair. For a moment, he simply looked them each in the eye. Something, obviously, was troubling him deeply. He spoke, after, it seemed, some inward debate.

"You're both agents, I believe - and good at it." He waved down their agreement. They were about to tell him about the new Tollcross development they were handling. After all, something that came from the Government would be a feather in their caps, if that was what this was all about.

"Come with me, please." Sir Ralph rose to his feet. He paused, however and turned to look at them both again, his face now grim. "This is on the QT, you understand? No word to anyone at all?"

Uncomprehending, they nodded.

"I need your word."

"Of course, Sir Ralph. It goes no further." Berrick answered.

"Yes. Absolutely no word at all." Alan confirmed, mystified.

With no further comment, they were led through the great hall and off to the left, into another short passageway. A more spartan aspect defined this quarter. Rather than Persian carpets, there was a distinctly military look to this area of the house. Prints of military actions in parts of the Empire adorned the walls. There, India. On the other wall, somewhere in the West Indies.

Sir Ralph opened the door of a small room and ushered them in. It was simply furnished. Large maps hung on the walls showing Europe, the Atlantic Ocean and America. A telephone, fashionably shaped in the old-fashioned candlestick style, rang as they entered. Sir Ralph apologised to them, striding over to answer it.

"Yes? Yes? I see. Very well. Send him in." He returned the earpiece to the rest and turned to them.

"Sorry about that. My 2IC needs to speak to me. He'll be here in a moment ."

Footsteps sounded outside the door and a sharp rap preceded the entry of another man, probably in his late thirties. To the surprise of Alan and Berrick, he was wearing full dress: red jacket and kilt. Judging by the tartan, he was a Black Watch officer.

As he spoke in subdued tones to Sir Ralph, Alan leaned towards Berrick. "This must be something to do with the Festival. The Tattoo, I think. I can't see why they need estate agents though. It's all on Government property, isn't it?"

Berrick nodded and replied quietly, "It's getting bigger, though. Maybe they want it to move to another site. Buy somewhere bigger, perhaps? Christ, Alan, this could be our big break! Think of the commission!"

The officer nodded to Sir Ralph while Alan and Berrick whispered excitedly to each other. He turned as he spoke and seemed to ask a question about them, for Sir Ralph turned in their direction and nodded.

"Gentlemen. I'd like you to meet Major Andy Ramsay here. He's my ADC. I don't have anything to hide from him in this matter, so, let's sit down." He gestured them towards a comfortable settee. While they sat down, he and Major Ramsay took two of the deep armchairs opposite. Ramsay studied them carefully. He had a striking gaze, uncomfortable in its forensic scrutiny. Berrick found himself stir uncomfortably, trying to concentrate on Sir Ralph.

"We have a bad situation. I expect you both know the details." Sir Ralph nodded over to the wall upon which hung a map of the British Isles and, far to the west, the Eastern Seaboard of America.

"Situation, Sir Ralph?" Alan spoke up for both of them. He knew about the concern about the relatively weak position of the pound since it had been ousted from the ERM a year or two back. That could hardly be called serious, though. Was it the Iraqis, perhaps, or the Libyans? He looked at Berrick. He was the one who was interested in money, after all.

"You mean the ERM, Sir Ralph?" Berrick's words emptied out onto a puzzled silence.

"ERM? I don't follow you. What is the ERM?" Sir Ralph looked flummoxed.

Berrick flannelled. He collected coins, but, other than the gist of the Exchange Rate Mechanism, he was as ignorant of such matters of high finance as any Tom, Dick or Harry.

"Well, Sir Ralph...you know....ahem...currencies in Europe. Weakness of the pound against the others. Trade imbalance. All that."

Sir Ralph coughed. "No. None of that. Pound's not doing too well of course. No, gentlemen. I mean the SITUATION. I mean France and Germany."

"Exactly." Berrick replied." France and Germany. That's what I meant."

"Oh - I see! Thought you were forgetting the invasion for a moment."

"Invasion?" Berrick asked, stifling a yelp as Alan's shoe kicked his ankle. "Of course, the invasion. Sorry. Do go on."

Even as he bit his tongue against the pain of the unexpected attack on his person, he knew enough of Alan of old. He was saying, 'shut your trap and listen.' It was a lesson he had had drilled into him by Alan all too often. Don't offer information. Let the detail come to you. Play the client and let him tell you what he wants, before you tell him anything. When you do, let it be what he wants to hear. So, he bit his tongue and smiled at the old chap and waited to hear about the invasion. He was suddenly very conscious of the cologne the Major was wearing. Of his close attention. He smiled apologetically.

Sir Ralph coughed self-consciously.

"I don't want to beat about the bush."

Tiredly he pushed himself to his feet. The Major stayed where he was for a moment, before getting to his feet and joining him. Sir Ralph selected a pointer stick and wandered over to the large wall-map.

"As you will be aware, gentlemen, there is a drastic situation thanks to the ambitions of our two main continental rivals: France and Germany. They are old rivals themselves, of course, though more so since the Prussians used this excuse to unite the various kingdoms into one mighty empire."

Berrick frowned in puzzlement and glanced at Alan who shrugged slightly.

"What excuse, Sir Ralph?"

He felt distinctly lost. He seemed to be listening to a history lesson about the Franco-Prussian War and German unification and some present crisis which it related to.

Sir Ralph looked at him. "Eh? Oh! Forgive me, gentlemen. I was assuming that you have been away for some time."

" We have?"

Sir Ralph smiled and winked. "That's why you're wearing the unusual mufti. Eh, what?"

Major Ramsay spoke up, his voice a clear, cultured baritone. "What Sir Ralph is covering may be summarised in one sentence. The Frogs and Bosche have invaded and are now poised to strike north through Yorkshire."

Thus stealing the old boy's thunder, he turned apologetically. "Forgive me, sir. I'm a blunt soldier not used to beating about the bush."

"Quite. Quite, m'boy. No matter."

Despite his urbane comment, this interruption seemed to bemuse Sir Ralph.

"Where was I? Ah! Yes. The invasion. Hmmm. It's true, y'know. Johnnie Frog and his German chum are hell-bent on overthrowing our good king -"

Alan gaped and Berrick's stifled cry turned into a violent sneeze as he hid his confusion. Sir Ralph continued, oblivious to their expressions of surprise.

Pointing at the map, he continued. "The combined fleets of both nations are attempting to cut us off from supplies from America. If they don't succeed in their invasion, no doubt they will hope to starve us into submission."

"And what are the Yanks doing?"

"Yanks?" The expression was blank.

"The Americans. What are they doing to help?"

"The American colonies are forming regiments of volunteers to assist us, of course -"

"Sorry, Sir Ralph? The colonies?" Alan could not bite back his startled question.

"Yes, yes. The colonies. What other American settlements are you aware of apart from the colonies, Mr Cruickshank?"

Alan subsided, waving an apologetic hand. "Forgive me, Sir Ralph. Put it down to tiredness on my part. I was just thinking of Canada, that's all."

"Canada? Oh, I see what you mean. No. Despite a lot of our countrymen being subjects of the French crown there, I'm afraid they're more likely than not to be fighting against us if they come into this conflict. Now, where was I? Yes. The colonies are not likely to be able to assist us in any marked manner, except, perhaps with food and drink, for several months. You will be aware, I am sure, that our military forces over there have always been minimal."

He turned from the map and glanced at Major Ramsay.

The Major stood up and tugged his tunic down ruminatively, before turning to the two puzzled men.

"I know you two are agents. Don't approve of that sort of thing in normal circumstances. However, we live in changed times, what?" He took a little stroll about the confined space of the room, pausing before the fire.

"Sir Ralph has good reports of both of you. Frankly, I think you're both the scrapings of the barrel. If I had my way, we would simply fight this thing out man-to-man. Nonetheless, HMG has its own opinion. I do as I am told. I have made the appropriate arrangements. You will have a passe-partout in the areas which we control. We are on the attack, gentlemen.

He coughed, before looking up at them, his eyes still gazing at them forensically, as if he could see every sinew, each blood corpuscle in their beings. It was extremely disconcerting." HMG needs you." He paused, as if for emphasis. "Your country needs you."

He stalked over to the wall map, and pointed at the area covering the north of England. "Here and here, we have reports of a massive Franco-German force - at least eighty thousand men - poised to attack Leeds. They are armed with the latest military equipment: they have artillery, cavalry and aircraft! Imagine it! They are able to fly supplies across the English Channel! They use radio to co-ordinate their forces. We hear that they have some form of mechanical goliath with guns. It is a sort of moving artillery piece with heavy armour. We are defenceless against it. It can cross trenches. Only our 4.2 inch howitzers can destroy it and they are in short supply."

The Major sighed softly, before crossing the floor and standing to face them. "Gentlemen, you may be our only hope. Forgive my comments from before. I am not noted for my diplomatic skills. However, Great Britain faces its most deadly threat in recent history. Our freedoms, our union with England, are in peril. Your, admittedly unorthodox skills in working as agents, may be the only hope this nation has against foreign domination for generations to come."

There was a long pause as Berrick and Alan looked at each other in silent consternation.

Alan glanced quizzically at the Major, noting the earlier, sarcastic use of the word 'gentlemen', and smiling wryly to himself. They had certainly won no friend there in this place of lunatics, despite the impassioned plea Ramsay had just made. He felt it safer to agree with them and keep his own counsel. Berrick's earlier comment about 'nut-cases' forced itself to the front of his thoughts and, glancing to his right, he gave a brief smile.

The Major turned to Sir Ralph.

"Well, I've said my piece. I take it that you have no further need of me , sir?"

"No, thank you, Major."

With a nod, the officer left. Sir Ralph looked at the pair of them.

"You're a rum pair, if ever I saw one." He tugged at his bottom lip for a moment, before reaching a decision.

"Well, now you know. We know you have the experience for the job. It's very straightforward. You need to make contact with the French king. I'll give you the letter tomorrow. It's simple and requires no subterfuge, despite Major Ramsay's disapproving attitude. We only want you to go to Versailles and hand over the letter. You will await a response. One hopes it will be positive. Then, you return to the welcoming shores of this kingdom to a peaceful outcome."

He examined his fob-watch.

"Time, I think, for a little refreshment. Also, for you two to get into something resembling normal attire. Where on earth did you get those ghastly clothes?"

As he led them out of the room, they made non-committal noises about the provenance of their clothing as he took them away from the formal, polished surroundings through a small doorway and into somewhere more domestic.

Here, the surroundings became less formal. A small dog scampered out to meet them, sniffing inquisitively at their shoes.

"Don't mind Toby. Heel, sir! Follow me, gentlemen. I think you need to be kitted out in somewhat less outlandish clothes than the ones you're wearing."

They looked at each other as they followed the puffing Baronet. Outlandish? Well, maybe so, in this madhouse. Shrugging at each other, they followed him into a comfortable family lounge. The question which nagged both of them was why they seemed suitable for such a madcap scheme in such an obvious madhouse. The total incongruity of the twee domestic setting seemed answer enough in itself. They winked at each other and decided to play along.

"Excuse the informality, chaps." Sir Ralph interrupted their musings. "Perhaps a small beverage to warm you in these beastly northern climes?"

"Thank you, Sir Ralph. "Alan replied, feeling that he needed something to test the reality of this weird place. "A whisky?"

"Capital!" The old gentleman confirmed with obvious approval.

"Bang on! That'll do for me too, thanks," Berrick confirmed with a small wink at Alan. Best to humour the old duffer.

Relaxed, now he was *chez lui*, Sir Ralph barked with laughter. Crossing the soft carpet, he pulled an ornate bell-pull and a faint ring could be heard in the distance. "Singh'll be here presently. But, make yourselves at home gentlemen."

The next hour was spent pleasantly. The whisky Singh served puzzled them as it clouded when water was added. A problem that the distillers had yet to come to terms with, Sir Ralph explained. It transpired to be an excellent single Islay malt, however, and helped to loosen the old man's tongue.

He explained the status quo as a member of the elite of HMG's Foreign Service. Fluent in six languages, from Hindi, Urdu and Punjabi to French, German and Italian, he was a fascinating guide to the intricacies of a world far removed from the mundane post Cold War world with which they were familiar. Still feeling euphoric after their earlier disorientating experience, despite the attendant, pleasurable light-headedness, they played along. They learned of the status quo of Sir Ralph's private world. It was with polite interest that they learned that the ruling dynasty was that of the Stuarts. It seemed that the King was descended directly from James II with only a short break when the Hanoverians had occupied the throne. They evinced apparent acknowledgement of the truth of this fact without laughter. After all, he had others who were convincingly suffering from the same delusion.

Within half-an-hour, however, another character appeared in the drama. Berrick was peering around surreptitiously for the Candid Camera. It seemed that Sir Ralph had sent word ahead without their noticing, for, shortly, a tailor appeared. A wiry old man with a strong East End of Glasgow accent, he made them feel at home as he measured them for 'suitable attire', as Sir Ralph put it. The measuring was detailed and took a long time. Luckily, however, the old man was a fund of stories, most of them unrepeatable, but very funny.

After he had retired, Sir Ralph took a massive half hunter from his pocket and studied it myopically. "It's five-and-twenty past six. No doubt you are hungry, gentlemen?"

"Indeed, Sir Ralph," Alan replied, feeling his stomach gently rumbling. Privately, he was looking forward to getting a tandoori and a few pints at the Jug.

"Of course, in the ordinary way of things, I'd be only too happy to invite you to stay here as my guests. But I fear I keep a simple household here. So, I have made arrangements to have you put up, at full government expense, at the North British Hotel by Waverley Railway Station." He rang the bell once more. "Singh will hail a hansom and have you taken there forthwith. Your new clothes will be ready in the morning and I shall have a cab round to collect you at half-past nine tomorrow morning."

And, so saying, he ushered them into the black-and-white tiled hall where Singh waited, massive, bearded and watchful. As they appeared, he opened the solid, oak front door and snapped the fingers of a white-gloved hand. A horse-drawn cab appeared, as though by magic, and Sir Ralph courteously bowed them out.

"Until tomorrow, gentlemen."

They climbed aboard the horse-drawn cab with serious expressions on their faces, their insides quaking with suppressed humour. As their hansom cab drove up St Mary's Street, they released the suppression, collapsing in gales of laughter, tears starting from their eyes at the whole preposterous experience.

"It's amazing," Alan gasped weakly, holding onto the side of the cab as it bumped uncomfortably over the cobbled surface, "mind you, he's got that major and the Indian geezer -"

"And the Glaswegian -"

"- and the Glaswegian playing along. I'm almost tempted to go back tomorrow and play along." He saw Berrick staring out of the window, his mouth open in astonishment.

"What is it?" Sitting forward, he peered round the window frame.

"Look - there's the gap where the Scandic Crown Hotel should be! They can't have hidden that!"

"I know. But, John Knox's House is there. We just passed it. Ha! PT's! Who would believe it! Do you reckon we're both dreaming?"

"Your guess is as good as mine. Hang on, though. The street looks as if it's been set up for some jamboree. Wait till we turn the corner. Here we are - oh! - there's the NB. Bloody Nora! Look - it's all black - the way it used to be. He can't have done all this just for some kind of joke!"

Indeed, the well-known railway hotel, built over Edinburgh's main railway station, exhibited all the signs of being back in its comfortable coat of grime, rather like a black birthday cake, sitting at the north end of the Bridge. Amid a busy horde of other black, horse-drawn cabs, with the odd motor car honking its horn to get by, their hansom reined to a halt at the main entrance. In short order, they were greeted by a splendid, top-hatted doorman, registered and shown to their rooms. A connecting door enabled them to make a sizeable apartment from their two suites. They were luxuriously fitted in a style reminiscent of the fin de siècle hotel itself. It was one which they recalled from their youth. Rather than dowdy, tatty and out-of-date, here it had a freshness and gloss which showed that it was no decades-old fashion of generations past. It had been very recently applied.

They were given dinner in their room ("Sir Ralph's orders, gentlemen," explained the maître de when they registered) and enjoyed a three-course meal of surprising excellence.

Later, they sat in shirt sleeves and had whisky and cigars while they talked over the odd events of the day. Alan swept back the long, dark hair which was getting into his eyes and puffed at his Corona. "We don't belong here. Let's face it. We've stumbled onto...I don't know what. We'll probably wake up in the morning and find that Rory's been putting LSD in our pints. If we don't." He paused for a moment, squeezing the bridge of his nose between finger and thumb. "I'm lost. This Sir Ralph guy seems to want our help in their war as 'agents'. It's not our war. We don't have a war in our world. I mean....what the hell have we got ourselves into?"

"I've no idea, but it's incredible, isn't it? It's a world of might-have-beens come true. Look, " Berrick struck a match and lit up a cigar of his own, crinkling his eyes against the smoke, "if only from the intellectual point-of view, it's invaluable. Haven't you ever played the 'what-if ' game? You know - what if Stalin had been assassinated in 1940? What if Napoleon had won Waterloo?"

"No."

"God, you're a dullard, Alan. Consider it now. We're here in 1993 just the same as we are at home - look at the calendar there on the wall."

Alan stood up and strolled over to look at it, his look of puzzlement giving way to one of almost comic surprise.

"D'you recognise the face?" Berrick asked. Alan's silence spoke volumes.

" 'Miss Marilyn Monroe, the famous chanteuse from the Colonies, at the Odeon Leicester Square, with HM The King last year.' Do you realise the impact this could have on our contemporary views of genes versus environment? Have you thought what Einstein or Napoleon may have been in this world? Probably nothing. But some ex-Princes in our world who dabble in antiques or who are successful stock-brokers, for all I know, control an invading army which holds half of England and which is poised to invade Scotland!"

Alan pursed his lips and shook his head. "I - we, that is - have a business to run and livelihoods to maintain, unless you propose to stay in this museum of a time-slip. Besides - what has happened to our parallel selves? Eh? Have you thought of that?"

Berrick scratched his curly mop of hair and shook his head. "I've read somewhere that you can't have a meeting with yourself in this situation because you'd cancel each other out."

"I think the time-glitch that hit us in the flat was the midwife of our crossing into this world. And that it effected a simultaneous transfer of our doppelgangers to our world. They must think they've gone one hundred-and-fifty years into the future."

"So, you don't really know?"

"No. I doubt whether anyone does."

On that note, they finished their drinks and parted company for the night on the agreed basis of seeing whether they would find that it had all been a strange dream.

CHAPTER THREE

They awakened early. Their beautifully cut broadcloth suits had already been delivered, with a full valise each, for 'changes to their apparel'. They fitted perfectly. A little later, as they breakfasted in splendour in the magnificent dining room surrounded by a large number of other hotel guests dressed in turn-of-the-century costume, the reality of their position began to hit home. They had swithered for a good five minutes when presented with the choice of breakfast. After porridge with cream or milk, they could pig out on devilled kidneys, bacon, egg, sausage, fried bread and toast; kippers (Loch Fyne, no less); kedgeree; scrambled eggs, fried bread etc.; cod roe; Arbroath smokies; a selection of cold meats....They settled for tea and toast with marmalade.

"Do you know.....I think we should go back to the flat and check it out." Alan mused as they left the dining room. Glancing up at the enormous clock in the hotel foyer, they saw that it was still only 7.40am.

"C'mon," Berrick slapped him on the shoulder and they strode into the sunlight on eastern Princes Street.

"I wish I had a camera. Imagine colour photos of Edwardian Edinburgh? You'd make a fortune!"

"Like your coins?" Alan laughed.

"Mock not, you disbeliever," Berrick grinned, stepping aside to

allow a smartly-dressed man in a frock coat and topper to pass

by. The man touched the brim of his hat in acknowledgement

of the courtesy and Berrick momentarily wondered how long

it had been since he had seen anyone do that. Ever?

In a few minutes, they found themselves at the very close they had entered only the previous afternoon, though then it had looked like night.

The doorway to the tenement was fitted with a latch and getting in was no problem. Now, all they had to do was to climb the stairs and knock on the right door.

"What do we say?" He asked Alan's back as he ascended the stair.

"No idea. Play it by ear."

"How helpful!"

"Well, Have you got any bright ideas?"

"No."

Seconds later, they were standing outside the flat. Alan knocked loudly.

They waited, looking at each other as footsteps approached the door on bare boards. There were muttered imprecations as the key turned in the lock. The door opened a fraction and a bleary eye peered round at them.

"Aye?"

Alan cleared his throat. "We need to come in."

"Eh?"

"Your flat. We need to come in."

"Why?"

That was a ticklish point. Berrick leaned forward. "We're from the Council. Pest control. You know...rats?"

"Rats? Whit? Here in ma hoose?"

"I'm afraid so. There have been several reports from others flats in the stair. We have to check every one. We won't take a minute."

The eye withdrew for a second and there was a whispered conference behind the door.

The eye reappeared.

"You'll no' be long?"

"No. We won't. Just five minutes to check that you're all clear."

The door creaked open and a small man in shirt-sleeves and no collar ushered them in. His grey-haired wife stood beside him, drawing her shawl closer as they came in, bringing fresh air in with them.

The flat was exactly as they remembered it from the day before, but less awful. True, it smelled of boiled cabbage and damp clothes, but it was clean.

Berrick led the way in, with Alan following behind, a little uncertainly.

"Is this the kitchen?"

Berrick thrust his head into the tiny space. A small range provided both heat and cooking facilities. The bedroom required only a brief check, though Alan took care to knock loudly on the wall. To the occupants' puzzled look, he shrugged. "It can make the little blighters take fright. You can hear them scurrying away if they are surprised. We have to do it in every room."

Clearly, that seemed to make sense and the same routine followed in the circular sitting-room. Just to make sure that the point was driven home, they held a short conference in full hearing to compare notes.

"Have you noticed any reaction?"

"No. We look as if we are clear so far. Is this another room?" Alan nodded towards the small bedroom.

"Aye. It's just a box-room."

"We still need to check it. Rats can travel up and down between properties behind the walls!"

The room was painted white – or it had been once. Now, it was empty except for a couple of tea chests filled with bits of china and straw. Berrick crossed to the other door with a grin at Alan, which was missed by the lady of the house who had led the way in. She was a small and slightly-built, with her hair tied back in a bun. One long, grey strand had escaped and hung down. Impatiently, she brushed it behind her ear.

Alan rapped on the wall as Alan opened the door with a loud shriek of rusty hinges. An empty cupboard yawned at him. The bare wooden shelves were thick with dust. Only an empty tin of paint on the floor showed that it had ever been used.

Berrick's shoulders slouched in dejection. He made a perfunctory attempt to knock on the walls and the back of the cupboard, but they were solid. He looked at Alan who just shrugged. What can we do? His expression asked.

Berrick turned to the lady of the house. "Thank you. Thank you very much. That shows no signs of rats, you will be pleased to know. We can leave you in peace."

The front door slammed shut as they went down the stair.

"That means we're stuck in this weird place."

"God knows, Rick. Maybe…just maybe. Come on. Back to the hotel." Alan slapped him on the shoulder. "I have an idea."

Half-an-hour later, they were picked up in a brougham and driven past the trams and omnibuses, horse-drawn cabs and the occasional motor-taxi on what had turned into a wet and windy morning to Sir Ralph's mansion. Most of the buildings were loyally flying the Union Flag. A squad of red-jacketed Highlanders wearing bearskins were marching up the Royal Mile to relieve the Castle Guard, their drill immaculate. One or two street-urchins cheered them, though the average burghers were more intent on getting to work or obtaining a wet before the pubs shut.

Among the men, heavy moustaches and flat caps or tammies predominated. They all appeared to be wearing suits and ties, whereas the women-folk wore full-length skirts and shawls. At the corner of St Mary's Street, a more gaily-dressed woman, one of the Newhaven Fishwives of legend, with distinctive stripes on her hitched-up dress, sold fresh fish from an open basket.

"So. What's the idea you were muttering about?"

"I think that we did it the wrong way round."

"Wrong way round what?"

"The doorway. We came out in Sir Ralph's house. That's the way we need to go back in."

Berrick leaned back in the comfortable leather upholstery as the brougham turned the corner off St Mary's Street into the Cowgate.

As the brougham drew to a halt at Sir Ralph's elegant front door, they climbed down and told the driver to wait.

The bewhiskered diplomat came out, grim-faced, his Indian servant close at hand, armed with a service revolver. Clearly, there were security concerns

In his hand, he held a sealed letter and a smaller envelope which he passed to them.

"There's no time to lose, gentlemen. Your train leaves in thirty minutes for Plymouth via Glasgow. Here is the packet for King Louis." He pronounced the name as Lewis. "And, in this envelope, are your instructions and five hundred pounds in notes." He leaned forward earnestly and fixed each of them with an eagle eye.

"We're all counting on you two. I know you both speak French. But, don't worry. You'll be met by Monsieur Rodriguez in Plymouth. He's a dago, but a good chap, even so. And he's accredited to the French Court. Thus the title of Mon-soor. He'll guide you to Versailles. With God's blessing, we'll see an end to German George and his Merry Men. God speed!"

"Sir Ralph – look – there's some mistake."

Sir Ralph's eyebrows rose a fraction. "Mistake? What sort of mistake?"

Berrick sensed the question was not one of mere curiosity as the tall Indian doorman narrowed his eyes in interest at the change in tone. He could see that the man was gauging the distance between him and Sir Ralph. His pistol was already lifting when Berrick intervened.

"Alan was meaning that we originally entered your wonderful mansion from a different direction. Upstairs." He put a hint of a question in the last word.

Sir Ralph looked puzzled.

"Yes. Upstairs. We came through from another building next door and…"

"And we left some of our belongings behind, "Berrick went on. "We wondered if we could go back and collect them before we go?"

"No time." Sir Ralph hauled an enormous half-hunter from his waistcoat and peered at it myopically. "Anyway, never heard of any entrance to the house upstairs."

He peered at them from beneath wild and tangled eyebrows, like a wild beast behind a hedge. "Poppycock!"

Turning to the Indian, he spoke slowly and clearly. "Singh – these gentlemen (was there a slight sneer in the way he said, gentlemen?) are catching the train to Plymouth. Accompany them, if you please and ensure that they do not miss it."

Singh grinned and nodded.

Sir Ralph turned away, but paused as they climbed aboard the brougham.

"Gentlemen. Remember that you are engaged on a mission on behalf of this country. If you fail to complete your orders, you know the penalty?"

He mouthed one word, "Death," and nodded. The brougham jerked forward and, with Singh sitting across from the them, they sped back towards Waverley, racing to catch the Plymouth train.

"What was that you said last night about having a business to run?" Asked Berrick.

Formalities at Waverley were few. Buying food, drink and newspapers for the long journey ahead and attending to the calls of nature left them barely two minutes to climb aboard and tip the porter who loaded their valises, before a loud whistle indicated that they were off. Singh stood, expressionless as they boarded and only left as the train puffed it way out of the station and began the long haul to the South-West of England.

"You and bloody flats!" Alan muttered savagely.

"You were just as interested in buying them as I was. Remember?" Berrick rose to the bait. "You're the mortgage man, remember?"

Alan waved him back into his seat with a sour expression on his face. "Arguing isn't going to get us anywhere."

"Well, who started it, for God's sake?" Berrick grumbled.

They were in a compartment on their own. They sat, facing each other, without company, feeling rather like latter-day railway enthusiasts, discovering how their grandparents had 'enjoyed' travel on the railways. Indeed, each of them was of a sufficient age to have taken journeys as children on steam trains and in similar carriages, though theirs had had the benefit of corridors. Having no facilities, they merely sat and watched the strangeness of the landscape pass them by. Great factories belched smoke skywards and other steam-powered behemoths shrieked by out of nowhere, startling them. Few, if any, cars were to be seen on the roads. Those that were to be seen were early models, open-topped for the most part, with heavily-clad drivers and passengers drawn from the wealthier classes. By and large, though, transport was horse-drawn.

To pass the time, they talked about the oddness of being in a place that was so far removed from their own world. It was as though there had been some factor which had caused the disjointing of time so that the same year in parallel universes could be so far apart in technological terms.

"Turn-of-the-century Britain is alive and kicking under the Stuarts, I see. Strange how a different dynasty can affect so many things." Alan mused.

"Not really. With no King George III to aggravate the American Colonies, no American Revolution. No American Revolution, and closer ties with the French Royals - don't forget our mission, mind - and no example to French Revolutionaries. Ergo, no French Revolution, no Napoleon, no French conquest of Europe. Therefore, less cause for a Bismarck to arise. We're seeing the equivalent period now, in 1993. This is pre-First World War Europe without the historic excuses which helped start it. The French have not had Napoleon and his wars of conquest. Thus, they haven't put the Prussians' noses so out of joint that Bismarck welded Germany together to counterbalance her by fomenting war with Louis Napoleon. Equally, they haven't a Queen Victoria heading an empire which would arouse the jealousy of her deformed nephew Kaiser Wilhelm II and cause him to start an arms race which culminated in the outbreak of war."

"Thanks, Professor."

Glasgow was a black city, bustling with workers and obviously a major conurbation. Its factories were myriad and its folk as small and work-weary as both recalled from earlier times in another world.

Alan produced the envelope after putting the sealed missive in a large pocket of his frock-coat. "Let's see what our instructions are, shall we?"

"What else is there to do, except look at the view?"

"Okay. Let's see - blah, blah - you are hereby instructed by His Royal Highness James XII, King of Great Britain, Ireland and France - Christ, that'll go down a bomb at Versailles if the package has this bollocks in it - and the Dominions beyond the Seas - blah, blah - to ensure that the communication with which you have been entrusted be delivered to the Person of His Majesty King Louis at the Palace of Versailles. Failure to ascertain that His Majesty King Louis receives this communication will be upon pain of death - charming! - you will await such reply as His Majesty King Louis deigns to grant you. You will immediately convey such response as His Majesty King Louis offers and return forthwith to the Kingdom of Great Britain ensuring that His Majesty King James or His Majesty's faithful servant Sir Ralph Somerville receives said reply in person - blah, blah."

They were both sunk in thought at the implications of failure as the engine steamed south at a steady sixty miles per hour. They passed over the Border at around eleven-thirty and reached Preston and Liverpool in the same brown study.

They visited the Gents at Liverpool and bought copies of The Echo, before boarding the train, eagerly reading the leaders, as they headed south towards Crewe.

"Did you see how excited the people in the station were?" Asked Berrick, tossing the paper into the corner.

"I didn't think about it. Why?"

"They were saying that there had been a great battle near Leeds, against a combined Franco-German force. Rumour has it that we - the Brits, that is - won!"

"Did we, by God?"

"But, you know rumours."

Alan grunted and said he would get some shut-eye. Putting the paper over his face, he dozed off to the regular clickety-clack, clickety-clack, and whirled down a dark chasm into a more familiar world of cars, planes, TVs and computers. It seemed barely five minutes before a sudden jolt jerked him awake with a start.

"Where are we?" He croaked.

"Crewe. Wait here. I'll get a paper and check the news." Berrick opened the door and sprang out. The platform was a scene of bedlam with crowds of people rushing from the train towards the news-seller crying his wares unintelligibly by the footbridge across the track. Lots of red-coated soldiers were to be seen standing in little knots, smoking pipes and talking or dozing beside their stacked rifles and packs. A cacophony of engines puffing and whistles shrieking made the scene one of chaos. Clouds of thick smoke wafted over the platform, but the idly gossiping soldiers paid it no heed. They seemed phlegmatic enough, thought Alan. Then he saw Berrick's hair above the bearskins and shakoes as he trotted back, papers in hand. Panting slightly, he clambered aboard and slammed the door behind him, as the Station Master blew loudly on his whistle. Other passengers, who had also gone for newspapers, sprinted back to clamber aboard before the train gathered speed as it pulled out of the station.

Alan leaned forward eagerly. "What's the latest?"

Berrick, breathing hard, opened up the paper. It bore a banner-headline. "Enemy force crushed - thousands flee."

"Well, well. Maybe Sir Ralph was a bit premature!"

"Maybe they know the power of propaganda." Berrick replied crustily, his lip turned down.

"Whadd'you mean?"

"Don't believe everything you read in newspapers."

"Okay. So, what d'you know that's not in those pages?"

"I was passing one of those groups of soldiers on the platform when I heard one of them - a sergeant, I think - say to an officer: 'When do we pull out, sir?' "

"That doesn't mean they're retreating, though."

"No, but the officer said, 'before the Bosche get here.' That's plain enough, isn't it?"

"Hmm. The soldiers looked pretty calm to me."

"They're professionals. Not conscripts. Anyway, if they're being pulled out, what have they got to worry about?"

They chewed over the meaning of the chance remark overheard by Berrick and ate their sandwiches in silence as they watched more countryside pass. After another hour or two, Alan pointed out a tall plume of black smoke on the horizon as their powerful engine drove ever southwards. Estimating their location to be around Birmingham, they presumed it to be the site of some bombardment by the enemy if their main force was, as the newspaper stated, in Yorkshire.

Gradually, the light lessened, as heavy clouds drew in, scudding low over the dank fields and black earth. The sun was sinking fast, but was obscured, and a tenebrous gloom settled over the deserted landscape where only a mournful wind stirred the trees. The odd crow flew caw cawing from the naked branches to wheel resentfully away from the speeding black engine, sparks billowing in its wake. The mournful whistle of the engine was suddenly swallowed by a tunnel into which they hurtled in a cloud of smoke and steam. Coughing and with their ears popping from the change in air pressure, they closed the window and sat in a noisy darkness as the train gradually slowed to a crawl and then stopped with a loud hissing of steam.

For long seconds, they sat without speaking until a distant banging of doors could be heard, coming nearer.

"What the hell is it?" Queried Berrick, urgently, throwing down the window and cocking an ear. Distant voices could be heard. He strained to make out the words being shouted. The tunnel's acoustics distorted them and made them echo. He could see, however, barely fifty yards away, a lantern was swaying drunkenly. Alan had jammed himself into the window too.

"Shh! Listen!" Alan's eyes, wide open in the blackness, widened even further. "They're shouting 'Raus!' That's German for 'Get out!' We need to move now. Get the bags. We can't leave them!"

Luckily, the valises were readily to hand on the luggage rack. Alan was about to open the door when Berrick whispered urgently, "Don't open the door. Use the window on the other side. Quickly!"

Going first, he dropped the six or seven feet to the cinders on the track and gathered the bags before Alan too dropped down softly, muttering a muffled curse as he did so.

"Shit! I've twisted my ankle. Here, give me a hand."

Berrick supported him and, awkwardly, they picked their way over the cinder track down the line away from the approaching voices on the other side of the train. They heard plaintive queries from the compartments as they passed. "Papa, why have we stopped?"

"Nothing of importance, I imagine, Henrietta. I expect the engine has broken down. That'll be the driver telling us to wait for a relief train."

Nothing of importance? thought Berrick with a grimace, as they hobbled by. If only they knew!

Suddenly, Alan tapped him on the arm. "In here," he whispered. The banging of doors, as passengers were ordered out, was almost level with them now. They cowered in an alcove built to shelter railway-workers as trains passed. It smelt of coal-smoke and stale urine. Feeling about in the dark, Berrick found a pile of sacking from which the smell of stale urine emanated. Pushing Alan down, he pulled the sacking over their heads and the bags and hunkered down uncomfortably on the jagged cinders.

Not a moment too soon. A German guard, his pickelhaube helmet etched against the reflected light from his lantern in the carriage windows, strolled past, his boots crunching loudly and stopped right beside them. Their breathing slowed to a barely perceptible level and their hearts thumped in dread in the utter darkness beneath the cloth. Suddenly, something warm and wet dripped onto Alan's head. With a superhuman effort, he controlled himself as the German sentry continued to direct a seemingly inexhaustible stream of urine onto him, before, with a grunt of satisfaction and a pause to button his fly, he resumed his stately progress down the train. For hours, it seemed, they crouched uncomfortably in that small space as the last of the passengers were marched away, in anxious bewilderment, their cries of lamentation loud in the echoing tunnel. At last, an officer bellowed an order and the soldier who had relieved himself on them replied, "Jawohl, Herr Kapitan! " and crunched off down the line as the engine got up steam.

A minute or two later, with a "Chuff! Chuff! Chuff!" it started on its journey again and gradually pulled away down the line, leaving them both alone. With an oath, Alan threw off the soaking old sacks which had covered them. He stank of piss and his voice shuddered with emotion as he rose stiffly to his feet. "God rot those bloody Germans! They're supposed to be our allies!"

"Not in this world. Forget where we're from. This is our real world now and it's not a pretty one, for all its quaintness."

They argued the toss over which way to go, opting out of caution to go back the way they had come in, rather than the way the Germans had taken the train. They took their bags with them as they walked in silence towards the beckoning fresh air and freedom of British-controlled territory.

CHAPTER FOUR

Gradually, the faint, distant light of a starlit night became visible down the line, the twin steel rails gleaming faintly, like arrows pointing the way.

When they reached the mouth of the tunnel, they paused cautiously, peering about for signs of guards. Unusually, perhaps, they were not in a cutting, but in open countryside with occasional trees and distant lights. A faint engine noise could be heard. With no sign of sentries visible, they tossed their valises down the embankment, following stealthily themselves, not daring to speak until they were over a hundred yards away.

"What shall we do now?"

"Christ! This is an impossible position to be in." Alan almost spat the words out. "And I stink like a Prussian piss-house!"

Berrick couldn't help grinning and only stopped himself laughing with an effort.

"You're right - they're bastards. But I'll bet you our boys are no nicer. We need to keep moving, though." He cocked his head to one side, listening. "That engine noise."

"Yeah, I know. It's odd. What is it? It's not a car. Could it be a 'plane?"

Berrick shrugged, forgetting the gesture would be invisible in the dark. "Maybe. The lights over there look quite bright. Probably electric. Keep your head down. I think we need to do a bit of investigating."

As they drew nearer, they saw that the lights were indeed electric. They emanated from a large balloon which was tethered in a field. It was a Zeppelin, or, rather, a British version of that kind of dirigible, for a large Union Flag was painted on her side. Also, the small knot of men gathered together in conference were wearing red jackets in the style of the British Army.

"Should we make ourselves known, or scarper?" Asked Alan dubiously.

"Where would we scarper to?"

"Hmm. Fair point. Okay, lead on, MacDuff."

Gingerly, they climbed over a stile and with trepidation, approached the small group who seemed to be arguing over something. One wrong move could mean a bullet between the eyes for their troubles.

"Ah! Excuse me!" Berrick called as they trudged over the rutted field, thankful that here, at least, rain hadn't fallen. Wading through mud after their last ordeal would have been too much.

The group reacted in surprise and consternation. Breaking up and peering anxiously into the darkness, their night vision ruined by the bright electric lights, one or two drew pistols which alarmed Berrick greatly. The last thing he wanted was to die in a time and place which weren't even his.

"We're British!" He called. "Don't shoot! We're unarmed!" They came in with their hands up, abandoning their bags in the grass.

"How many of you are there?" Called one of the soldiers nervously.

"Just the two of us. We're civilians and we have our hands up."

As they entered the small pool of light, an officer ordered two of the men to recce and make sure there were no other surprise visitors. He was a smartly turned-out man with a curiously familiar face and a fabulous, waxed moustache.

"Who are you?"

Briefly, Berrick explained about their identities and mission. The officer looked unimpressed. "A special mission for the Government? I'll need proof of it. Otherwise, you're suspected enemy infiltrators and liable to the death penalty."

"God Almighty!" Alan exclaimed. "Is death the penalty for everything around here? Even our orders threaten us with it, if we aren't successful."

"Do they, indeed? May I see these 'orders'?"

The officer held out his hand courteously, but with the authority of command. Berrick, conscious of the revolvers pointed at him, slowly held open his frock coat and carefully extracted the two documents from an inside pocket. The officer looked carefully at the sealed document addressed to the King of France. With the nonchalance of a high-ranking officer, he strolled away from them, gesturing to another officer to join him. For several minutes, they examined the documents and spoke softly together before coming to a decision. The more senior officer, a colonel, strolled back as one of the men sent to check the area returned at the double, snapping to attention and delivering a textbook, quivering salute, "All clear, sir."

"Very good. Carry on."

"Sah!"

He held out the letter and the sealed packet to Berrick and half bowed apologetically, "How did you gentlemen come to be here, may I ask?"

"It's a long story," Berrick began.

"Then, let us adjourn to the cabin in our dirigible. We'll be more comfortable there. We're on our way south, anyway, so we can drop you off." He laughed self-consciously at the faux pas, "Not literally, of course. We stop next at Cardiff. We seem to have lost our bearings, though."

As the officer led them to the surprisingly large cabin suspended beneath the great looming bulk of the dirigible, Alan gave him the details of the railway tunnel from which they had recently escaped. He also explained the predicament he found himself in. He was given five minutes to wash and change after their bags were retrieved, before rejoining them. In the meantime, now sure of their bearings, there was a hustle and a bustle as the dirigible was readied for take-off.

Alan returned with a grin and nodded his thanks to the Colonel. He was dressed in a slightly more modern short Norfolk jacket and matching tweed trousers with brown brogues. Berrick wished he had changed as well, but it was too late. The officer showed them to comfortable chairs in the opulent Captain's Cabin and then, crossing to an exquisitely-made, wooden chart table, examined minutely a large map lying open upon it.

"From Crewe south," he muttered, his fingers tracing a line as he checked features marked upon it. "Aha. Here we are! Captain Trelawney!"

The door to the Pilot's cabin opened and the officer with whom he had conversed earlier came in informally.

"Sir."

"Here we are, Charlie. Our friends have identified the spot. See? Those lights over to the east are the village here." He pointed at the map. "And here is the railway line and the tunnel."

"Right-o, Harry. Shall we up sticks, then?" His round, jolly face looked pleased despite the imperial moustache which obscured his mouth in its luxuriance.

"I think so, old man."

"Excuse me, gentlemen," Berrick interrupted. "But there are enemy troops near here -"

"What! Froggies?" Asked Captain Trelawney, his blue eyes flashing angrily.

"No. Germans."

"Ah. The Bosche. Bit of a cunning devil is the Hun, y'know. Too like us for our own good. Thinks, you see. Not like Johnny Frog. They're all piss and wind - begging your pardon, gentlemen - pardon my French! "

"Thank you, Charlie," replied the Colonel, twirling his moustache absent-mindedly. "Point taken. I think caution is called for. Dowse all lights except those on the binnacle. And, Charlie?"

"Sir."

"Send in the steward, would you?"

He turned and smiled disarmingly at Berrick and Alan. "Forgive me. I haven't introduced myself. I'm Colonel Webb. That is Captain Trelawney with the wild views on our European cousins. And this - " he gestured around him " is HMDS 'Challenger', the latest craft in His Majesty's fleet of dirigibles. We have heavy machine-guns and bombs to undo the enemy.

Damn' ungentlemanly. But there you are. Modern war ain't what it used to be."

The lights went out, even as the steward entered. "Whiskies all round, Smithers, if that suits you, gentlemen?"

The Colonel felt his way over to a nearby armchair as the engines powered up to a deafening crescendo and, with a sudden release, the Challenger lifted off into the night sky. Gradually, the sound of the powerful aero-engines diminished to an ever-present, throb-throb, never absent, but sufficiently subdued to permit conversation. In the Captain's Cabin, deadening in the fabric reduced the roar to a mere background noise when the steward closed the door behind him.

"I've always felt a calling to the music hall, you know," the Colonel commented a little later, as they levelled out at around three thousand feet and their whiskies and cigars were served.

"Oh, then, let me teach you the words to a song. It's called, 'Fings ain't wot they used to be' " Alan replied.

For the next half an hour, Colonel Webb practised the unfamiliar song, while Alan accompanied him on the comb, before giving them his rendition, once he felt confident with the words. When he had finished, Berrick and Alan applauded. The Colonel hid his pleasure by swallowing the last of his whisky and calling the steward for more.

"I'd say you have a real talent there," said Berrick.

"And we're the ones to discover it," added Alan.

To the Colonel's puzzlement, they roared with laughter, slapping each other on the knee. The next hour was passed in companionable conversation as they flew south-west towards Wales.

Colonel Webb excused himself as they neared an area of bright flashes and smoke which reached even their altitude. A minute later, he returned and sat down with a smile. "I think we may see some action, gentlemen. It's the French in this sector. I'm told on the wireless that they've launched an attack into eastern Wales. Our boys are putting up a stiff resistance, as you can see. But the main army's up north. It's mostly local yeomanry around here. Regardless of their status, however, they're defending their homeland. I think Johnny Frog will have a hard time of it."

At that moment, the door blew in with a sudden blast, the concussion blasting them across the cabin in sudden darkness. An icy wind tore through the ragged gap as Alan struggled to find his bearings.

"My God! Artillery!" Croaked Colonel Webb, lifting himself from the swaying floor. With a muffled cry, Alan found Berrick's unconscious form lying crumpled in the corner under a coating of debris. A small series of explosions on the ground gave him some dim light to see the injury Berrick had received to be a nasty gash on his forehead. He breathed stertorously even as Alan was bent over him, checking for signs of life. Satisfied that he was, indeed, only unconscious, rather than dead, he looked at the appalled officer in the faint near-darkness.

"No. Not artillery! Listen!"

Webb turned, incomprehension on his face.

"What? - "

A sudden blast of machine-gun fire removed all doubt.

"A night fighter - I've heard of them, but - "

"We have to shoot it down! Now! This balloon is an accident waiting to happen. Come on!"

Half stumbling in the wreckage of the unlit room, Alan dragged the stunned Colonel with him onto the flight-deck.

It was a scene of utter carnage. Bodies lay everywhere. bloodspattered, in the relaxed attitudes of sudden, unexpected death. It was as though they had simultaneously fallen asleep and hit the deck without flinching. Captain Trelawney lay on his side, a strange smile on his face, his left hand still holding a cup of coffee to his lips, the contents splashed over himself and the pale boards of the floor. The wheel slowly spun, back and forth, idly, as fierce winds dictated the direction the rudder should take.

"Where are the guns? Through here?"

Alan barged open the door and stopped in horror. A scene of even greater devastation met his eyes. The small crew of men had been mown down by the same murderous fire as those at the wheel. Such had been the surprise of the attack that the guns had not even been manned. Blood literally washed over the floor in that place of death. As Alan looked at the lifeless faces and blank stares of the corpses which, only minutes before, had been living, breathing men, he heard a small whimper. Could there be anyone alive in that charnel-house? None of the bodies showed any sign of life, but the whimper was clearer now. He turned back.

"Colonel - take evasive action - take us all over the sky. It'll confuse the bastard."

He settled his breathing for a minute. trying to ignore the horror before him.

"Who's there?" He demanded.

The whimper was repeated.

"Who is it, dammit?"

Gripping a stanchion, he reeled along the freezing gun-deck, his feet slipping in the gore while the icy winds tore at him, making his eyes water. The Colonel was following his advice and was hurling the dirigible around the sky to confuse the pilot of the night-fighter.

A sudden, twisting turn threw Alan down into a dark recess he could barely see in the blackness. He collided with something soft that shrieked in pain and fear. The smell of spilt coffee made him realise, suddenly, that this was the kitchen, all ten square feet of it, and that the terrified man crouched in the dark was the steward, Smithers. The noise of the wind made normal speech inaudible. Shouting as clearly as he could, he shook the cringing creature that once had been an RFC orderly.

"It's me. Alan Cruickshank. Do you remember? Colonel Webb's guest. You served us whisky a little while ago ... before this." He gestured invisibly at the carnage of the gun-deck.

"You must help me! If you don't, we may all die. We must get the plane that killed all those men!"

"Die?" The voice was weak and tremulous. "No. I'm safe here. Safe! Safe!"

Alan resisted the impulse to slap the terrified little man. Instead, he forced a coarse laugh out.

"Safe, you bloody coward? Safe? In this ruddy balloon? Whaddyou think keeps us up in the air, eh? Hydrogen. That's what. It's one of the most inflammable things there is. One chance shell from that plane and the bag burns and we burn with it, all the thousands of feet down to solid earth."

He had Smithers' attention now.

"Have you ever seen what happens when you hit the ground from this height? No? Well, let me tell you. You bury yourself a foot deep and not a bone unbroken. And you scream - all the way down!"

The little man literally threw him off in his frantic efforts to get to the guns, jabbering with fear.

With a fierce grin, Alan picked himself up and raced to the other Vickers machine-gun on the starboard side. Smithers had seized the port gun and was swinging it from side to side, searching the black night-sky for the fearsome killer stalking them.

"Release the safety-catch!" Alan bellowed, searching the sky on his own side of the dirigible, noting that they were now passing west of the great battle being waged far below them. Nothing. He turned to glance at Smithers who was squinting out into the dark also.

"Where in blue blazes is the bugger?" He demanded of the cold night air and shivered involuntarily. For a moment, he wondered if the fighter had been forced to quit the attack due to fuel shortage or a lack of ammunition. Then, a small movement in the distance caught his eye. An enormous explosion on the ground lit up the sky for a few precious seconds. There it was. A small speck, clearly identifiable as a triplane. German, Alan thought, in a detached manner, as he sighted carefully just ahead of the propeller.

The triplane was banking hard to get around in a steep turn. He could see its shape clearly. An ante-deluvian shark to him, but deadly nonetheless. Urgently, he squeezed the trigger, surprised at the kick of the Vickers which writhed in his hands like a thing alive.

"Here!" He bellowed. "He's here! Help with the belt!"

Accustomed to barked orders, Smithers sprang to his side, deftly managing the passage of the belt of shells through the machine-gun.

Almost lazily, the tracer marked the course of their fusillade, weaving through the cold night air and passing over the aircraft. The pilot, seeing the shells whizzing past, used every ounce of his strength and skill to pull the roaring machine round in the tightest turn he could effect. Still, no shells seemed to have hit the canvas-covered fuselage and the profile of the Fokker narrowed dangerously as the path it was taking edged into a closer and closer convergence course with the dirigible.

Biting his lip so hard that he could taste the blood, Alan watched the track of the tracers, noting how they were swept past the sweeping wings and edged the gun more to his left. For a long second, nothing happened. The fighter was now almost nose onto them and a twinkling indicated that their fire was being returned. Again, baring his teeth in a mad ecstasy of fierce battle joy, his fears forgotten in the fierce hatred of the unknown German pilot, Alan kept his finger jammed down. He couldn't see the course of the tracers. Were they passing the fighter and vanishing impotently into the night?

Now, the deadly machine was head-on, jinxing even as the dirigible swung ponderously. The stench of cordite was stinging his nose.

"Keep the ammo coming!" He bellowed at the steward feeding the long belt of shells to his Lewis gun. He barely spared the man a glance. The Fokker was dangerously near now, barely half-a-mile away. How could he possibly miss them? Alan's tracer was now arcing in towards the 'plane and he bared his teeth in a rictus of battle joy, exultantly. Yes! Surely the shells must be striking home - a sudden, blinding flash dazzled him and he threw up his hands to shield his eyes. Blinking, he stared through spots of light to see the tri-plane heeling over ablaze, its fuselage torn into pieces as it plunged earthwards.

"We got him, Smithers! We got the bastard. D'you see ?" He turned exultantly, pointing at the dying machine as it spiralled down, spewing flame and smoke behind it in a glowing trail.

Smithers lay propped against the ammunition box, a puzzled expression on his face. In the centre of his forehead, a large hole slowly leaked dark fluid down the white, white face.

CHAPTER FIVE

It took them an hour to reach Cardiff Aerodrome. Colonel Webb kept control of the huge balloon, despite damage to the rudder. In a rising wind, his uniform mere tatters, a graze on his left cheek and smoke blackening his features, an iron will urged him to control the behemoth in which he would ordinarily have commanded thirty men or more, now managing purely on his own. Alan checked for any survivors. To their relief, half-a-dozen men were found to be alive and Berrick had come round groggily half-an-hour after their desperate action.

As they were tied up to the anchor-mast, the Colonel switched off engines and pushed his dark hair out of his eyes. "I think Music Hall has it in trumps over this business," he commented drily, casting an eye at Berrick who was now awake, though ashen.

"I think we need to get a medic to look at you, Berrick. You look as white as a ghost. As for the other poor fellows ... "

They were greeted by the Station Commander who tut-tutted at the whole business, insisting that they were welcome in the Officers' Mess and that Major Blood would see to Berrick's wounds.

"Major Blood?" Berrick asked, dazed. "Is that a joke of some sort, like the rest of this place?"

"I don't follow you, old chap," replied Colonel Webb. "What joke do you mean ?"

Alan stepped in apologetically. "Nothing, Colonel. He's just disorientated, that's all."

"Of course. Can't have our chaps getting LMF *, can we?" He smiled and patted Berrick on the shoulder. "Join me for a whisky in the Mess when you're both cleaned up and we'll talk about getting you to Plymouth tomorrow."

Alan nodded his thanks and helped Berrick to the Medical Inspection Room.

The doctor, Major Blood, was a highly professional man who took one look at Berrick and immediately set to cleaning up the gash on his forehead, before stitching it as neatly as a seamstress.

"No drinks for your friend tonight, I'm afraid. No flight tomorrow either. I'm keeping you in here for observation. Head injuries can be funny things. Better safe than sorry." And, so saying, he firmly ejected Alan and closed the door.

Alan, for want of anything better to do, crossed the Parade Ground to the elegant, turn-of-the-century-style house which the Colonel had indicated earlier was the Officers' Mess. Inside, far from the stuffy formality he had expected, Alan found a junior officer attempting to circumnavigate a large room, which was thick with cigar-smoke and loud with cries of support, without touching the floor.

Alan ordered a whisky and water and watched the cavorting officers and gentlemen making bets, laughing and slapping each other on the back, while unobtrusive Sikh waiters moved among them, wiping table-tops and emptying ashtrays.

To a loud cheer, the young Lieutenant achieved his circumnavigation and was rewarded by a major with a bumper of champagne.

"So, you see us letting our hair down, Alan."

Turning, Alan noticed Colonel Webb at his elbow, now cleaned up and smartly-dressed in a borrowed uniform, a glass of whisky in his hand. He was suddenly aware of how scruffy he must appear in his smoke-stained mufti.

"Is it always like this in the evening?"

Webb lifted an inquisitive eyebrow, a mischievous smile on his face. "You haven't heard, then?"

"Heard? Heard what?"

Webb threw back his head and laughed. It was a relaxed act for a man who had been dicing with death barely an hour before. Still smiling and wobbling slightly, Webb lifted his glass.

"We've beaten the Frogs, m'boy. Thrashed 'em soundly. Even now, their infantry is pelting pell-mell back to London and their cavalry," he gurgled his whisky," their cavalry is food for worms." He lifted his glass unsteadily in a toast. "Damnation to the French!"

Alan pursed his lips thoughtfully, before tossing back his drink. "That could work both ways."

"Sorry, old boy, you've lost me."

Waving at the bar steward to refill their glasses, Alan gave the Colonel a glance. Drunk or not, his enquiring look was direct.

"All right, Colonel. You know the score - our mission," he translated, seeing the incomprehension at his slang on Webb's face. "If we go to the French now, they may decide that they cannot change sides. They may feel humiliated. You know how stiff-necked they can be."

"Aye. Proud lot. the Frogs. Damn fine soldiers too. See your point. Hmm."

"On the other hand, they may think they're onto a loser and go for the offer. I'm dubious, to tell you the truth. The battlefield may be the only place this conflict can be decided."

Several more whiskies did no more to decide Alan on the likely outcome of his mission. He found himself drawn to the celebrating soldiers as the hero of the hour, when they discovered him in their midst, and, despite protestations, was dragooned into singing a song or two for the rowdy officers. He complied with a rendition of "The Ball of Kirriemuir ", before passing out under a table.

Berrick awoke with a fearsome headache. He felt as if a train had hit his head, but a cool cloth was gently pressed against his forehead, easing the agony somewhat.

"How are you?" Asked a gentle voice. Gradually, a pale shape resolved itself into an oval face surrounded by a frame of white and two very blue eyes that looked him with concern.

Consciousness fled and he spun down a deep well of unconsciousness.

The next day, Berrick was more awake and was able to drink some soup. The owner of the gentle voice could now be seen quite clearly and he was immediately drawn to her blue eyes and sweet smile.

Nurse Melville admonished him, "You should be resting, Mr Kildrum, instead of blethering to me!" She had no other patients to care for. Clearly, Berrick was much more interesting than the usual cases she attended to.

Gently, she patted his brow with a damp cloth, her bright blue eyes concerned. "You may have concussion. That gash on your head is nasty. You may have strange ideas about things, but they will soon go away."

Berrick looked at her and laughed softly. "Let me tell you something, in that case. It's a long story and you may say that I am mad, but it's the honest truth. Just one thing?"

"What is it?" She smiled and he saw a dimple at the corner of her mouth. It enchanted him.

"You can't tell anyone else. It may not be safe.

"Oh? Not safe, is it?" She smiled again and her eyes crinkled in amusement at him. "Mr Kildrum —"

"Berrick. Please. And….what is your first name?"

"My first name? Oh. You mean my Christian name? It's Candice."

"What a lovely name. Very suitable, if I may say so." He paused. "Candice…..Alan – that's my friend who was on the dirigible with me – he and I are not from this world."

He held up a hand to stem her questions. "No, please. Hear me out."

He took a sip of the strong tea that Candice had brought him and started to tell her where they called home and how they had ended up where they were. Candice Melville sat and listened, shaking her head from time to time, as if in disbelief at what he was telling her.

After half an hour, he had said all her had to say and the tiredness won. His head lolled to one side and his breathing became steady and deep.

Nurse Candice Melville looked at him for a long while, before standing up quietly, so as not to wake him. Slowly, she bent down and kissed him on his cheek. He stirred briefly and then settled once more, but he had a smile on his face.

For four more days, Alan kicked his heels at the aerodrome while Berrick recovered. The news was still coming in of the pursuit of the fleeing French forces. The High Seas Fleet had moved south from Scapa Flow to reinforce the Channel Fleet. A sense of jubilation was in the air.

On Wednesday morning, he dropped in to see Berrick who was sitting up in bed with a turban of bandages on his head.

"Boiled eggs and bread-and-butter soldiers, eh? Some nurse must like you."

Berrick coloured slightly, an embarrassed smile coming to his face. "Oh, you know ..."

"No, I don't. Who is she? All the crumpet I've seen around here looks like younger versions of my Great-Aunt Edith."

"Not this one." Berrick scooped up the last of his egg and finished it with a satisfied grunt, licking his fingers clean.

"I'll take your word for it. Now to business. Have you heard how things are picking up?"

Berrick nodded. "Do you think our mission's still on?"

"I'd be surprised if it weren't, put it that way. Look, the French are on the run. But no word on the Germans. I see them as the greater threat. They're the further north of the two."

"And I, for one, don't believe the newspapers in this dimension. Remember the soldiers who were pulling out after the 'victory' at Leeds?"

"You think the defeat of the French is a lie?"

"I think it's probably ninety per cent hogwash. They may have been held, but no more."

"The people here believe it."

"They haven't been through the twentieth century we've experienced. They're naïve, I think. They believe everything the papers tell them. But, if it were true," Berrick leaned across and tapped Alan on the knee, "wouldn't there more activity around here? Wouldn't you see more troops coming and going? But, what's happening?"

"Bugger all, that's what."

"So, on we go to La Belle France?"

"Yep."

It was at that moment that Candice Melville entered the room. Alan stopped himself from whistling, though it took punch on the arm from Berrick to stir him to his feet.

Candice was a tall, elegant blonde girl in her mid-twenties. Although she wore an extraordinary outfit more akin to a nun's than that of a nurse, her elegance could not be disguised . Apart from an inelegant apron, she wore a puffy-sleeved blouse and long white skirt, her headgear an elaborate concoction of stiff white linen with wings and a red cross in the centre. It lent her the air of a medieval religieuse. However, her expression was sweet and her eyes had a crinkle of amusement in them as she looked at Berrick. In a mock-severe manner, she shooed Alan from the room, relenting long enough to tell him his friend would shortly be released.

Alan had barely left the room when Berrick pulled her to him, crushing her protests with a passionate kiss. For a moment, he thought that she would fight off the embrace that he had wanted to give her since he had first begun to recover, then, with a soft moan, she melted into his arms and her lips surrendered to his.

How long they remained in that passionate embrace, Berrick could not tell. It felt like centuries and yet only moments too. Her scent – was it lavender? – made his head spin as, indeed, did the experience of kissing her. He felt as if he had taken some extraordinary drug that made him float above himself, as if in an out-of-body experience and he felt himself saying the most foolish things to her about planning for the future and what they could make of themselves. She smiled and smoothed his hair and kissed him gently again.

"First, you must do what you must do…whatever that is. Then we can plan. Then – " She stopped for a second.

"Yes?" He asked.

"Then, you may tell me whether the world that you say that you come from really exists."

He drew her to him again and kissed her once more. "Oh, my love, my love. It exists. It really does exist."

That afternoon, indeed, Berrick was released from the care of Doctor Blood. Alan met him at the Medical Inspection Room, in time to catch another brief glimpse of his guardian angel. Alan could see why Berrick was smitten.

"Phew! Some ministering angel, me bucko."

"Hmm. Her name's Candice Melville. I've said I'll contact her when we get back."

Alan's brow furrowed. "I doubt if we'll have time, old son. We'll be hot-footing it north to Edinburgh, I rather suspect."

Berrick nodded reluctantly. "Well. I think that Candice and I have a future together."

As requested by the Station Commander, Colonel Jones, they reported to the Operations Room in the Staff Building, a smart Victorian-style country house near the Officers' Mess. A subaltern, with a transparent blond moustache and acne, asked them to wait, once they announced themselves, and marched crisply away to notify the Colonel of their presence.

They were ushered into a pleasant office cluttered with comfortable armchairs. Set around a roaring fire which reflected off the rows of photographs of earnest groups of young soldiers, with trophies held self- consciously before the camera's gaze.

Jones was a small, rotund, red-faced Welshman who bustled around them, making them comfortable and ordering coffee, before settling himself into a chair on the other side of the fire and scrutinising them.

"So, you're our two diplomats, then?" The voice was very Welsh and sing-song. but they both recognised the shrewd directness behind the appearance. A charming host nonetheless. They each nodded.

"Very well, gentlemen. I understand, from my superiors, that you are to be conveyed to Plymouth and thence to France."

"That is correct, Colonel," Berrick answered.

"Yes, indeed, boys. Unfortunately, however, due to the current situation, we will have to send you there by sea. From Swansea."

Alan exclaimed, "But, surely, we can go there by land, since the defeat of the French army."

Jones looked apologetic and shook his head. "I'd love to. The truth is, though, that the Frogs did a damned good job at demolishing all our railway lines into England. It's slowing the advance right down. Bloody infuriating, it is."

"So, it's 'Hearts of Oak' and 'swab down that deck, you lubbers', is it?" Berrick asked with a wry look.

"Aye, I'm afraid so. But - a word of warning - the sea isn't such a friendly place these days, see? I know the High Seas Fleet is heading south and all that. But there are several 'privateers', as they used to call them, operating in the Western Approaches and most of 'em are enemy."

Alan looked perturbed and pulled at his bottom-lip. He lifted a quizzical eyebrow at the Colonel.

"What are to trying to tell us, Colonel ?"

Jones squirmed uncomfortably, his face becoming redder. To cover his confusion, he pulled a pipe out of his pocket and started to pack it with rough shag, a slight tremor in his fingers betraying his anxiety. Tamping it down in the lengthening silence. Broken only by the crackle and sputter of the coal fire, he struck a match and puffed energetically. The clouds of smoke utterly obscured his face for moments before he seemed satisfied with the small bonfire he had lit.

"Colonel. We have seen a surprising lack of activity around here for all the song and dance that's been made about the great victory we've achieved over the Frogs. Frankly..."

"Frankly, Colonel," Alan interrupted, "I think it's all balls. I think you've all been spinning us a line." He stared at the

Welshman, his eyes unwavering. "Please tell us, sir. We'd appreciate a little candour."

Throwing the match into the fire, the Colonel spoke out of the corner of his mouth in a low voice.

"Listen, lads. This is gospel. And it doesn't go beyond these four walls. Understood?"

They nodded, breath held.

"I have your word?" His sharp eyes looked keenly at each of them, taking in the puzzlement clearly recognisable on each open face.

For a moment, Jones squeezed the bridge of his nose between the fingers and thumb of his left hand, his expression one of pain.

"You heard, the night you arrived, or the next day - I've lost track of time - of the rout of the French army that was invading Wales? Yes, of course you did." He puffed again, his eyes glistening slightly. "It's all," he paused, his jaw quivering, voice now gruff, "it's all a bloody lie! There. You have it."

They sprang to their feet. "What? A lie - whaddyou mean?"

Weakly, Jones waved them back down and waited until they had settled. "Look. I've been briefed, see? I know the importance of your mission. I am in the confidence of … certain important personages … certain personages," he repeated more firmly, "who stand to lose a lot - everything, dammit - if the Frogs and Huns win this damn' war!"

He took a visible grip on his emotions and, taking the pipe out of his mouth. stabbed the air with its stem. "The truth, if you can take it, is this …

"We held the French that night. And we made them pay dearly for every inch of Welsh soil. But we lost five thousand men. Five thousand of our best. The cream of our young men. The next day, the French were reinforced by their Guards. Big ugly brutes from Normandy. All huge moustaches and no brains. Since that day, we've been on the retreat. They'll be here within thirty-six hours and in Cardiff before the end of the week."

"And no-one knows."

Mutely, Jones shook his head. "I'm going to tell the people shortly, once you've gone. And, " he swallowed, "the reason I mentioned the privateers is simple. The only ship we have available is an unarmed trawler. We've been abandoned. gentlemen. We're all alone. His Majesty's Government has given us up for dead. "

Suddenly, fiercely, he looked at them. "You are our only hope! We'll fight here on the landing-field. We'll fight in the city and in the mountains. We'll never give up. But, we need you to help us. We're relying on you!"

There was a sombre silence while Alan and Berrick absorbed the information Jones had imparted. He was puffing jerkily at his pipe, fingers drumming silently on the arm of his over-stuffed chair.

Berrick cleared his throat. "Thank you for you candour, sir. A great man in another place once said much the same as you, in an hour of great danger to his nation."

"And what happened to him?"

"He beat his enemies into a cocked hat and lived to be the greatest man in his country. And he lived to a ripe and honoured old age."

"Well, then," said Jones, with a sparkle in his eye, "then, there's hope for us all yet." Pulling himself out of his chair, he shook them both firmly by the hand. "God speed you, gentlemen, and may He guard over your great enterprise."

⁇

BOOK II

A SLIGHT CHANGE OF PLAN

CHAPTER SIX

Union Flags hung limply in the damp air of Swansea as the bronchitic lorry wheezed through deserted, echoing streets down to the empty harbour. Or almost empty, for one ancient trawler, blackened with soot and scarred by a rusty acne, sat apologetically at her moorings, oily smoke trailing from her battered funnel.

The lorry trudged unwillingly to her, sliding to a halt on the greasy surface of the pitted concrete. Picking up their bags, the two descended reluctantly, and, without ceremony, the lorry chugged and spluttered away to an unknown destination.

"You the two for Plymouth ?" Called a deep, West Country voice from the deck. A bearded man with a mop of thick, grey hair under a dirty-blue peaked cap, thrust his head out of the wheelhouse. "Chuck the bags down. You'll 'ave to jump. Git moovin'. Oi 'aven't got all day."

As they complied with his command, he bellowed at a half starved-looking waif at the stern.

"Cast off! An' at the fore, you dumb arsehole!"

The wretch scampered along the quay and performed the task, before dropping like a monkey onto the deck. Not a moment too soon, for the Skipper was already turning the high prow of the smack towards the harbour mouth where a pale line of white horses could vaguely be seen.

"Ever been at sea in one o' these beauties? Oi'll bet you 'aven't, neither!" He laughed unpleasantly, but, seeming to relent, gave them a big wink and a cheery grin. "Don't mind

81

me, lads, it's just my way. I'm Captain Good. Welcome aboard. There's a bottle of rum below. Pour yourselves a tot. Leave me some, though. There's a sou'wester comin' on. It'll be rough tonight and Oi reckon there'll be some as'll get wet."

They dropped down into a tiny cabin furnished with a table, two benches and two bunks. A single electric bulb illuminated the scene.

"So - they have progressed to electricity. Marginally," Alan commented.

Berrick found the rum and, surprisingly, some clean glasses. Looking around, he realised that the cabin was as clean as a whistle. Not a speck of dirt anywhere.

"Funny, that," he muttered. He poured them each a tot and they sat in silent contemplation of the length of the journey in store, as the trawler met the first of the Atlantic swell. The rum in their glasses began to swirl in a wild manner, forcing them either to drink it or lose it on the floor. In decidedly heroic gulps, they swallowed most of their measures and held on as the swaying motion became more regular, though no less pronounced.

"Ever been at sea, Berrick?"

"Luckily, I'm a fair yachtsman. I used to do the odd bit off the East Coast."

"Thank God for that! The last thing we need is a Technicolor yawn on this impeccable floor!"

"What the hell are we doing here?" Berrick grimaced into his glass.

"How the hell do we get back home is more to the point?"

There was no answer to that except to complete their mission and return home

"If we can just get into that old bugger's house –"

"Without Gunga Din with his pistol."

"Without Gunga Din, then we can retrace our steps and get back into the real world."

They sat in silence, their thoughts a universe away.

For hour after hour, the trawler slugged her way seawards as the half light gave way to darkness. Both dozed in the bunks unable to settle fully due to the wildness of their passage. Gradually, from a point in mid-Atlantic, the tail-end of a hurricane in the West Indies stirred the mighty power of the ocean. From regular peak and trough, the sea began to flex its foam-flecked, glistening muscles. The little trawler struggled against the awesome power of the waves, always somehow avoiding being overcome by the waters. Sturdily, she shrugged aside the great, green sheets of Atlantic bile that threatened to engulf her.

For hour after hour, they chugged south-south west, eyes peering into the darkness lest any of the raiders which had been sinking or capturing British ships were in the neighbourhood. With any luck, on a night like this, they would manage to slink by, unnoticed. The weather was a worry. The glass had been falling steadily, hour-by-hour. Now it stood at a level which invited Good's concern. He was a seasoned trawler-master with over thirty years as man and boy behind him. Never could he recall such a bad indication of foul weather to come. Puffing at his pipe, he grunted to the cabin boy to make him a mug of tea.

Behind the small cabin, there was a small alcove in which stood a gas burner for conditions like this. A small boat like a trawler cannot risk her captain losing his concentration in bad weather. Sometimes that occurs when the crew have been fishing for one or two days at a stretch. If they cannot obtain strong coffee, the ordeal becomes a nightmare as tiredness fights against adversity. The addition of caffeine can make a considerable difference. Captain Good had made sure that his vessel was well provided for in that respect. As he awaited the drink, Good scanned the horizon. It did not look promising.

For a start, the sky was not only cloudy, it had a strange hue he had never seen before. It was almost yellow in colour. Had it been the aurora borealis, he could have identified it without question. However, it was not. Moreover, it moved in a strange way, as if circling over the ocean some distance ahead of them and to starboard. He was man enough to admit that the unknown terrified him. He had lost his father to the sea when he was only sixteen. The small town had been shattered by the awful events of that dreadful autumn and it had taken him all his working life to obtain this old tub to make up for the loss. His father had not trusted to insurance and, at the time, it had not been mandatory. So, he, the eldest son, had striven to climb over the backs of other men to succeed in keeping his aged mother and younger siblings. He was proud that he had done so. Now, however, he was seeing something which gave him inklings of his own mortality. Something up ahead.

Below, Alan and Berrick tried to sleep. The motion of the smack was unsettling, however good a sailor either of them might, or might not have been. It was ragged, buffeting the tiny vessel severely, almost throwing them to the deck on many an occasion, Nonetheless, they managed to attain some semblance of sleep as the night wore on and the trawler made slow headway against the forces of nature which were arrayed against her.

In the wheelhouse, Captain Good chewed hard on his unlit pipe as he wrestled with the wheel. Scrivens, the hand, kept him company, since stepping onto the deck was to invite instant self-sacrifice to the waves.

"Tell Ted to make more steam!" Good grated, as he heaved the rudder once more into a wall of terrifying proportions. Obediently, Scrivens bent to the speaking-tube and shouted the Captain's orders. A faint voice echoed back an acknowledgement.

Scrivens turned to the Captain and stopped, his mouth open. The enormity of the approaching wave eclipsed everything in view. Massive in size, it was the product of forces which resulted from the titanic storm now petering out in mid-Atlantic. Some vortex here and another there met, egged on by winds in excess of one hundred miles an hour. An eruption of a sub-sea volcano on the Mid-Atlantic Ridge exacerbated the enormity of an otherwise sizeable wave-form to make it assume proportions which only a large ship-of-the-line could hope to survive.

It was Scrivens who, lifting his head from the speaking-tube, saw the awesome scale of the approaching wall of silent, green water. No sky was visible above its sixty-foot height. And, in its silent approach, it sucked everything in its path into its mighty maw.

"Captain - the wave !"

Like a giant hand, the wave crushed the tiny trawler, smashing her wheelhouse into matchwood and sweeping the two men away like rag-dolls. In the Engine Room the stoker was hurled headfirst into the blazing heat of the boiler his mouth barely opening in a silent scream, before the red-hot coals incinerated him in a quiet 'phut'.

Even as her plates split asunder, Berrick and Alan were hurled back onto the rear wall of the cabin, stunned into startled wakefulness as the light blinked out.

For long moments, the tiny ship appeared to hang in a water-filled limbo before, seemingly slowly, she began to slide down, down, down to a grave on the ocean floor as the mighty wall of water passed over her, oblivious. Berrick gasped. It was the blackest dark he had ever experienced. The eldritch scream of tortured metal filled his ears above the distant roar of the sea. In an instant, he realised what had happened.

"Alan!" He roared. "Where are you?"

"Here. Over here," came the muttered reply.

"We have to get out through that porthole, wherever it is, or we're dead!"

Perhaps it was a slight gap in the clouds that caused a faint moonbeam to glance on the wave at that moment. Perhaps it was due to the faint luminescence, often ascribed to seawater at night, that the slightest glow in that direction, showed that there ... there! ... lay their only hope of escape.

Searching blindly about him, Alan felt the hard shape of something metal. An ornament, perhaps. It was hard to hear, difficult to speak in the din which assaulted their ears, which popped from the pressure. The boat span and rocked wildly in the wake of the passing wave, hurling them about like ninepins.

Struggling to regain his balance, Berrick bellowed again.

"Kick off your shoes! When I smash the porthole, we'll have to wait until the cabin's full of water before we get out. Then, swim like buggery, or we'll be sucked under!"

He groped his way towards the faint and fading gleam, finding he had to stand on tiptoe to reach the porthole, and smashed the glass hard. "Hyperventilate while you can!" He yelled and hit again with all his strength. A coldly glittering torrent swept his arm aside as it poured avidly into the cabin, swiftly filling the small space with its frigidly boiling lust, to swamp the last tiny bubble of air that kept the trawler semi-buoyant.

Panicked, they hyperventilated. even as the water overreached them, plunging them into a foul, salty soup that numbed them for long moments. In a sudden panic, Berrick plunged forward, colliding with Alan's legs as he thrust himself through the opening.

Berrick followed to find himself rising, as he struck out frantically to escape the dying ship's suction. His lungs ached with pressure and, unwillingly, he exhaled slightly as his exertions demanded oxygen. He was toiling. Stars flashed before his eyes.

"Stupid fool! " He cursed himself. "Idiot! This is all your fault. You will both die in another world, unknown and food for fish and all because of a ruddy flat ..."

Moments or, maybe, minutes later, he found himself afloat on a wild sea. A wave had slapped his face and awakened him from his stupor. He retched up salt water, gasping for breath. Fleetingly, stars could be seen between the scudding clouds. Real stars! He could see the Plough!

Where was Alan? He yelled his name but the wind and waves tore away the sound and hid it. In sudden fear of the bitter cold and the sea, he struck out, searching for something to hold on to. The waves threw him about in jest as his last ounces of strength were swiftly depleted. Something hard banged into his head and he blacked out.

Alan had waited until the small air-pocket in the corner had shrunk to almost nothing before he plunged through the port-hole, unaware that Berrick had not gone. As he swam down and through the narrow port-hole, though, he became aware of something entangling itself with his legs. In unconscious reaction to the suppressed fears of the unknown deep, he kicked himself free and rose to the surface. An enormous blackness hung terrifyingly over him as he gulped in air. Suddenly, a blindingly white light struck his eyes painfully.

"*Wer ist da*? " Demanded a voice through the howling wind. Alan could only cover his eyes and wave. Any port in a storm, he thought, even if it is German.

It was near dawn when Berrick came to. He was in a bed. Once again, his head was aching. There was a strange motion to the room which he put down to giddiness. Turning his head carefully, so as not to exacerbate the pain that threatened to split his skull in two, he peered muzzily around. Alan lay snoring softly in a bed a couple of feet away. At that moment, the door opened and someone came in. He was tall and had cropped brown hair and a carefully waxed moustache. Seeing Berrick awake, he smiled briefly.

"So, you have awakened, *Mein Herr*."

"*Mein Herr*?" Berrick answered. "You're German?"

"Even so. I am Doktor Klein of the Imperial German Navy. Both you and your companion were rescued from the sea last night. Regrettably, you cracked your head against the prow of our motor-launch whilst it was searching for you. So, you are a lucky man. You have escaped being food for fish twice in one night."

He checked Berrick's eyes and took his pulse. "Your head injury is not bad. In two, maybe three days and you are - what do you British say? - as right as rain. *Ja*?"

"*Ja*, " Berrick answered. "*Herr Doktor*, how is my friend?"

"He is as strong as an ox. Just sleeping. However," the Doktor lifted an eyebrow, "my Captain wishes to speak to you. He wishes to know what you are doing at sea in such a tiny boat at this time of year. You are not fishermen, *nichts* ? "

Fifteen minutes later, the Captain himself` was asking the same question. A vastly corpulent man with hard grey eyes above a trimly-bearded face, he gave every impression of not brooking any avoidance of` his direct questioning.

"Well, Mein Herr, what were you doing at sea, at this intemperate time of year, in a fishing-boat?"

"Trying to get to the South-West of England, " Berrick replied wincing at the infernal throb in his temple.

The Captain's gaze never left his face, searching with a disbelieving look. "Why?"

"I'd have thought that was obvious, Captain," Alan replied. He had awoken as the Captain entered the room. Though tired, he was awake now and sitting up in bed. "We're civilians. 'The French army is poised to take South Wales. There's no place for us there."

The Captain chewed this over in silence. "Civilians, eh? Well, we of the Imperial German Navy do not make war on civilians."

They both gave a silent sigh of relief. The Captain's look hardened, however. "But, we shoot spies."

Alan pictured the sealed packet in his frock-coat. Had they found it? His stomach turned while he maintained a bland expression on his face. "I shouldn't think that spies would find much to interest them in the Bristol Channel, *Herr Kapitän*."

The Captain grunted, his keen eyes scrutinising them shrewdly. Abruptly, he stood up. "It is of little consequence," he said, tugging his jacket down over his bulging belly. "Where you are going will keep you out off action for the duration. Good-day." So saying, he left the cabin in an echoing silence.

Wary off eavesdroppers, Berrick turned, smiling, and muttered, "Haud yer wheesht*," before continuing in a normal voice. "Seems a decent chap, the Captain."

Cottoning on to Berrick's use of Scots to throw any eavesdroppers who spoke English off the scent, Alan played along. "Absolutely. Salt of the earth. Be glad to be out of the damn' war, what?"

"Quite so, old chap. Tak tent*. I think they've been playing the white man, what with rescuing us from that storm, don't you know?"

"Couldn't agree more. Dinnae fash*. I'd say they'll probably drop us off behind their lines on the South Coast, where it's safe."

"More likely than not. Excellent! We'll be away from those damn' Stuarts and their ruinous policies. Dammit! Look at what they've done to the country. Bide a wee*. What we need is a strong king like the Germans have. Order. Discipline. Gods! What it is to be able to speak freely at last!"

Alan nodded sagely, then winced, and cradled his head. "Sorry old man. Head's a trifle sore. A bit whaur's ma sark*, if you get my drift."

"No, no. I shouldn't keep you talking in Davy Jones' Locker, you poor devil. You rest up and our allies will deliver us safe to friendlier shores."

So saying, and each understanding from the brief interpolations in Scots vernacular that the letters to the French King had been lost in the sea, they lay back in their beds and attempted to rest.

Half an hour later, Able Seaman Otto Kremlinger, who had listened to the whole discussion, was standing, as stiff as a ramrod before the Captain, giving his report. When he concluded, the Captain grunted and stuffed a chocolate into his mouth, chewing it with a thoughtful expression on his face.

"Pro-German, you say?"

"Most definitely, *Herr Kapitän*. They wish to be away from the faction supporting the usurper."

"Hmmph." The Captain swallowed his chocolate. "Any indication that they might have thought we were eavesdropping?"

Kremlinger looked puzzled. "No, *Herr Kapitän* . Just - relief, I think - that we had picked them up." He wilted under the Captain's fierce gaze.

"You had best be right, Kremlinger. You had best be right. Dismiss."

The Able Seaman saluted and left, like a startled rabbit, as the Captain's next appointment came in. He, by contrast, was relaxed in the extreme. Tall and wind-burnt, he wore a sardonic smile on his face. Dressed in civilian clothes, he evinced every sign of being a very self-contained and confident individual. A little over six feet in height, with dark, thinning hair and warm, brown eyes, he made a strange comparison to the stiff, uniformed Prussian Captain. Unbidden, he sat in the chair opposite the Captain.

"Okay, Bruno, what's the score?"

"I am Kapitän Bruno Von Landau, you Yankee troublemaker," he rumbled, before bursting into a bellow of laughter. "Get me a drink, you damn' rebel."

Leaping to his feet, the American complied with alacrity. "If there's booze, I'm your man, Cap'n."

"Ach, Hank, if only the world were made of people like us."

He accepted a brimming glass of schnapps and downed it in one vast swallow, proffering it for more. Hank poured him another, without comment, and passed it over.

"You know, if you Americans declare independence from your King and need help, then we Germans will offer you all the help you need to kick those damn' Stuarts out and then -"

"And then, ol' buddy, we'll be stuck with German soldiers in all major cities and a Prussian king instead. It won't wash, Bruno. Dammit! Half our people are Germans who came to America to escape from Prussia, an' Hanover an' wherever else. They ain't gonna want another king. No, sir! What we want is a republic an' no foreign domination whatsoever."

"Ach, Hank!"

"Don't Hank me, you ol' goat. Sure, we booze together an' damn the British together. But we don't share a political outlook. I'll help you kick this Stuart King out, but only to help us be free. Not to enlarge your country's dominion by including us in it. D'you know how many Americans there are now? No? Okay, I'll tell you. There are seventy-five million of us. That don't include blacks an' injuns, o' course." He bit the end off a cigar and stuck it in his mouth, before striking a match on his boot. "We'll help you here, sure." He lit the cigar and dumped the match in the ashtray. "But we'll take care of our own patch. Period."

The Captain shrugged hugely as though this argument were no big or new matter to him. Indeed, it wasn't. Hank always led off on this vein.

"Hank, I need a favour."

"Shoot."

"Shoot? I'm sorry -"

"Fire away. Get it off your chest."

"Ach, so. Well, I have a problem. Two problems, in fact. They are a pair of Britishers we rescued from the sea last night while you were sleeping off that excellent schnapps we had at dinner."

"Don't remind me! My head today! Oh, boy!"

"Ha, ha! I did warn you, Yankee. Anyway, these Britishers claim to be supporters of our cause. But their circumstances smack of something not quite right."

"You smell a rat?"

"In a nutshell."

"Okay. So, what do you want me to do?"

"Very simple. We will stage another 'rescue'. Tonight. From a boat that's been broached by last night's storm. You, the sole occupant, will be ... what? ... a smuggler?"

"No. Too thin. How about a rebel escaping from the clutches of the Brits in the confusion. A bit like your friends claim to be, huh? I was held in ... oh, Liverpool ... due to be evacuated north, when the German Army struck west. I hit my guard over the head and ran for it. Stole a yacht or motorboat and headed for Ireland. But the sea swamped the engine. Best if it was diesel. And you guys found me in distress. How does that grab you?"

"Excellent, Hank! Until tonight, then?"

It was the change in the steady 'thub, thub' of the engines that stirred Alan in his sleep. He glanced blearily at his watch, before going back to sleep. It was 0245. At 0330, the door of their ward was thrust open: the lights went on and two sailors led in a bedraggled-looking figure, his hair wetly plastered to his head, his face pale with cold. He was shivering violently, despite the large blanket they had thrust over his shoulders. In their wake came Doctor Klein, bleary-eyed and muttering crossly under his breath. He ordered the sailors to strip the man and to get hot-water bottles.

Alan and Berrick, half awake, sat up to watch the goings-on as the man, shivering convulsively and blue with cold, had his temperature taken. Klein grunted as he studied the thermometer. *"Kaffee* "' he ordered, adding, *"Heiss*! " He motioned the sailors to dress the man in warm pyjamas, before disappearing for a short time.

When he returned, he carried a glass of something amber-coloured in his hand. At a nod, the burlier of the two seamen lifted the man to a half-sitting position. Klein placed the glass to his lips. "Drink!" He commanded in German, pouring some of the fluid into the man's mouth. He coughed, but swallowed it and, gradually, some colour came into his cheeks. His eyes fluttered open. "Where am I?" He croaked, before another fit of coughing choked off the words.

"Ah! *Englisch*. Here," Klein took a steaming mug of coffee from a steward who had silently entered the ward. "Drink zis slowly. It is very hot."

Berrick looked at Alan and lifted an eyebrow. Alan's nod was almost imperceptible. The understanding was clear. Are we being had?

In the morning, they were allowed out of bed, although Berrick was advised to sit, which he did, impatiently.

The new patient slept like the dead until nearly ten. The Doctor came by to rouse him and gave him a brief check. "You're as strong as a horse, young man!" He announced, after checking his pulse. "Of course, the Captain will wish to speak to you."

Blearily, the man raised himself on one elbow and spoke to him in a distinctly American accent. "What ship is this?"

"Why, she's His Prussian Majesty's Ship 'Gneisenau'. A battleship," Klein added, somewhat unnecessarily.

"You're German?"

"Yes, and you are a prisoner of war, unless circumstances dictate otherwise."

"A pr - listen, buddy, I'm American! "

"Americans are still subjects of the British Crown, *Mein Herr*. You're all the same to us, I'm afraid." Klein stood up apologetically. "If you are a non-combatant, the Captain may look on you with a less-prejudiced eye. Good day."

As the Doctor left, stiffly formal, the American sat, mouth open like a village idiot, for several seconds. Then, seeming to recover himself, he looked across at the other two for the first time.

"Say! You two guys! Do you speak English?"

"Er, yes, after a fashion," Berrick replied.

"With an accent like that, you gotta be Brits. You sound like Lord Albemarle." Seeing blank looks, he continued. "He's Governor of my colony. Maryland? You know it?"

"Heard of it," Alan replied. "Never been there."

"Yep. That's just what Lord Albemarle said when he got asked a question about it in the House of Lords a coupla years ago. So. You two are English?"

"British. Not English. The latter is a subset of the former," Alan replied stiffly.

"Hey, buddy. I ain't trying to be abusive. Some of my best friends are Brits. Not many are English, though."

"So. What brought you here, then?" Alan asked. "Oh. And I'm Alan, by the way. This is Berrick."

"Pleased to meet you. I'm Hank Stuyvesant," he grinned. "Descended from the Dutch guy who founded New Amsterdam. What we call New York." He leaned back in the bed, cradling his head on his crossed forearms and looking to the white ceiling.

"I guess I can spill the beans, as we say, seein' as how we're out of reach of the long arm of British justice."

"Meaning what?"

"Let the man say his piece, Berrick," Alan admonished. "Go on, Hank. We're all ears."

"Okay. You've heard of the Patriots, I guess. You know, the movement for America to become a dominion, like Australia? It's been almost as century since that place got to rule itself. New Zealand too. But North Americay? No, sir! They say we're too much of a problem with the Injuns on the Great Plains. Hell! We've pushed a railroad right across to California. There simply ain't enough white folks to settle there. We've demanded that more Europeans be allowed to immigrate. But, no. It's a British colony an', with precious few exceptions, only Brits can settle there." He sat up, eyes bright with conviction and shrugged slightly. "O'course, we've got some Germans there too, now. Thanks to some marriage King James or his dad had. But anyone else? Forget it. D'you know that the Russian Tsar actually offered to sell Alaska to Britain and they said no? Have you any idea how much gold and coal and iron there is over there? God Almighty!"

He breathed heavily for a moment, then resumed.

"So, we got together. Some of the Irish, some of the Scots, and the Scotch-Irish and the English. We've had it up to here with Britain. We want to open up the West to bring in other white folks and make a proper country out of it. We petitioned Parliament an' they ignored us. We wrote to the Governors. We even wrote to the King. They all ignored us.

"In the end, we got together under a leader. A man of vision who welded us together. You may not have heard of him, but he's a great man. He's the leader of the revolution. It started two months ago, but it's spreading like wildfire."

"Who is this man?" Asked Berrick.

"He's what we call our President - Mr John F Kennedy."

"JFK?" Berrick leaned forward with sudden interest. "You're kidding! He's been dead for over thirty years, hasn't he?"

Hank sat up suddenly, his look hardening. In a soft voice, he said, "Who the fuck are you guys? This isn't that world. In this world, he's alive. And so is Marilyn Monroe. So, how do you know about the other JFK?"

In the tense silence that followed, no-one spoke. Hank looked shaken.

It was Berrick who, eventually, breached the silence. "You've come through like us. From the world of JFK's assassination in Dallas in '63? Of Monroe's suicide? Of space travel?"

"Yeah. To all the above."

"So, what are you trying to achieve? You're not a shipwrecked sailor, are you? You're with the Germans."

Hank shrugged, irritatedly, and nodded. "Have you looked at this world? It's backward, for God's sake. We still have slaves in the States! Slaves! Can you believe that! Whatever happened to William Wilberforce? Or John Brown? Can you guys live with that?"

Embarrassed, they looked away. "Maybe each universe has its own life to lead." Berrick muttered.

"And maybe each universe has a right to decency and human values? Have you thought of that? No. You haven't, have you? Did you know that your Army 'disciplined' some of the soldiers who were routed at Leeds by tying them across the muzzles of cannon and then firing them ?" Exhausted, Hank lay back.

"We were told that Leeds was a victory for the British."

Hank blew a raspberry.

"What do you think, Alan? Is he putting us on?"

Alan turned and walked over to Hank's bed and sat down. He looked squarely at the American. "Do the Squareheads know where you're from?"

"Nope. They'd think I was nuts. It's easier for them to accept me as a rebel. And I am, by the way. There'll be no Valley Forge this time! The Governors are toothless. There are no fresh troops available. They're all here. But there may well be a Civil War over slaves, just like the one in our world. There are too many vested interests. But old JFK's a cunning fox. He knows the South won't give up slaves. If he tried to force 'em, they'd be on th'side of the Brits.

"So, he's saying sweet things about self determination. I reckon he's planning to tax 'em out of existence. You know the idea. They're a luxury commodity, so you pay so much for each one to help the U S of A expand west. Add that to New Technology- we can bring guys through. They'll give us tractors, power plants, combine harvesters, weedkillers. Slaves'll be too expensive to keep."

"And, then what? Ship them to Africa?" Asked Berrick, with an edge of sarcasm to his voice.

"And what's wrong with that? In this world, JFK is operating in a vastly different culture. If the slaves can be freed and income increased by trade with a prosperous Europe, we can educate the blacks and make them a Peace Corps. Do you think Africa's civilised? Hell, man. They still eat people there. It's still the Dark Continent to the White Man. And, believe me, Africans still don't have liberal white values."

"Do the black slaves?"

Hank chewed his lip. He nodded. "Fair comment. Maybe I'm running away at the mouth. But, you get my drift? Something a whole lot better could be made of this world than exists, either here and now, or even in our world. It's hardly even polluted! Its rain-forests are virgin. Think of the potential, man! Think of it!'" He was visibly excited, having risen from his bed, pacing up and down as he talked.

"And what about the British?" Berrick's sally broke in harshly upon Hank's flow.

He blinked in surprise. "Why - they'll get a Hanoverian or Prussian Royal Family."

"And what benefit would that be to the people of Great Britain?"

"Well, they couldn't be worse than this lot, could they?"

Alan shrugged, "I suppose not. Not that I know a lot about this lot in the first place. You spout forth about American freedom to trade and expand in a free society. What about our people, though?"

"Well - " Hank struggled.

"I thought so, good buddy. It's all good and well freeing the Americans but, aren't you consigning Britain to vassal status in doing so? Look at the Prussians and the Hapsburgs too, for that matter. What freedom will they have? Christ! I need a cigarette. Do you have one?"

They were still sitting, pondering, when the Doctor came to examine Berrick's head again. He grunted approvingly and said the Captain was prepared to allow them on deck in three hours' time to watch them dock at Plymouth.

"Can we disembark?" Alan asked.

Doctor Klein laughed. "Unless you wish to become members of the Kriegsmarine!"

Roaring with laughter at his joke, he left.

"Does that mean we've passed whatever test the Captain and you were putting us through? You were testing us, weren't you, Hank?"

"Guilty as charged. But, I haven't spoken to the Cap yet. But, you just hang loose. I'll okay you with him."

They dressed in their cleaned and ironed clothes before climbing onto the slick deck beside a vast armoured turret, its capped guns pointing forward over the white horses to the dark wedge of land that was lifting clearly over the horizon. The bitter wind bit into them, knifing over the sea.

Hank had left them to speak to the Captain. They suspected it was also a good excuse to get out of the cold. They tried to shelter in the lee of the turret, but the wind gusted and swirled around them. By the time they passed the harbour mole, they were both shivering and blue.

⁇

CHAPTER SEVEN

Later that day, they were sitting in a pub on the waterfront, savouring pints of the local, hoppy beer. German sailors were enjoying the local brew also. It felt very strange. The three of them were at a corner of the bar, chewing over the same problem of reconciling the benefits to America of a new regime in Britain against the loyalty felt by Berrick and Alan towards the establishment, even though it differed from their own. Local civilians were playing darts idly or passing the time with a game of dominoes at the worn and scuffed tables around them. A constant hubbub of background conversation meant that they could not be overheard.

"It's fundamentally the same problem that you have, Hank." Alan continued. "Freedom or foreign domination. You see what we're getting at?"

"Alan, I understand. But, we've got to make a decision. You agree that this isn't exactly a town under a reign of terror. Am I right?"

"Well ..."

"Aw, come on, man. The bobbies are on their beats. Shit! We all saw the drunk Kraut sailors being bundled into the local jail like any ordinary piss-heads. Do the people look cowed? No. An' I'll tell you for why.

"Back five hundred years or so, there was a certain man named Martin Luther. He stood for what he saw as clear Christian values against the corruption of the Roman Church. Okay? Now, go forward two hundred and fifty years an' what happened? Go on. For Chrissakes. You're Scots! Where's your history?"

"The Forty-Five?"

"Exactly."

"Hang on a sec," Berrick butted in, "you mean they had the Forty-Five here too?"

"You bet your sweet ass. That's where the temporal dichotomy took place. Y'see, in our time, Bonnie Prince Charlie stopped at Derby. He wasn't stopped by soldiers. More by caution. But here - "

"Hang on, hang on," Alan butted in, "Yes, I remember now. George II was all packed and ready to leave for Hanover, wasn't he?"

"Exactly. There's little to separate the two events excepting one lord on Bonnie Prince Charlie's staff. Was it Lovat? I forget. It's difficult to remember two strands of history and who did what. In essence, he got well plastered the night the Jacobites took Derby. That was as far as Charlie got in our time. As you know, there was only slight support for the Stuart cause in the English towns. That, strangely, was the cause of the whole thing. It was a dare. When His Lordship was in his cups with his men, an Englishman named Terry - George Terry, in fact, that I do remember - who was also well gone, bet His Lordship that he and his men couldn't reach Warwick in three days. Now, that was not an impossible feat at the time but it was quite a dare.

"His Lordship tottered to his feet and said, 'Are you challenging the fleetness of my horses or the courage of my men, sir?'

'Both, sir,' replied Terry. 'for your horses are nags and your men are cowardly papists!'

"Now, Lovat, or whoever he was, almost burst a blood-vessel at that."

"He bet his castle in Scotland against Terry's wager of twenty-five pounds. It was a lot of money at the time, don't get me wrong. But paltry by comparison with the value of the castle. So, Lovat and his men, like stewed prunes, staggered out, ordered their horses and set off.

"His Lordship, due to his drunkenness, sent a message to the Prince. It was one of those great lies of history, like Nolan's orders to Cardigan at the Charge of the Light Brigade. He wrote: "Your Royal Highness's vanguard is advancing on Warwick. The road is open to London. God save the King!" Stirring stuff.

"Now, Charlie was a romantic fool and no general. But, when he awoke and received that, he made the greatest decision of his life. He moved his army south. Word spread. Lovat, or whoever he was, found no opposition. The Jacobites advanced and George decamped to Hanover. Thus, victory was achieved!"

"And all because of an English drunk!"

"And a Scottish drunk!"

"Touché!" Alan took a swig of rum and smacked his lips. "Judging by this stuff; we took the West Indies."

"Yep. An', it was during the same historical period. Not much to choose, really. You let the French keep Canada, mind you. But India's British."

"Still?"

"Still."

"So, we Post-Imperialists are in a time-warp. I mean, how can I put it? We're here and now, but, in most ways, we're back at the turn of the century."

"I don't get it. Why is that?"

"Search me. Perhaps the particular monarchy was the cause. I put it down to the Stuarts themselves. They were a decadent bunch. You remember how Queen Elizabeth had an age named after her? All those swash-buckling adventurers? An' all those great inventors of the nineteenth century? Well, the conditions weren't right, so....zip. Seems the 'phone here was invented by John Logie Baird in the '50s.

"You see, there's been a lethargy here. Europe's still streets ahead of the rest of the world. Hell! Japan is still an isolated empire. No Captain Perry because no USA. Equally, no Little Big Horn and no Hiroshima. It's all virgin territory."

"Is it for us to play with? Do we want to visit our ills on these people?" Berrick mused.

"Well, we'd better decide. "Alan replied.

"Hell! this is hard. We've met decent people on the Stuart side. They've been kind to us. They weren't cruel or callous. Just rather old-fashioned. Whaddyou reckon, Alan ?"

"The trouble is that we haven't seen or met anyone here who can show support for the Hanoverians or whoever they are. Is this a conquest or is there a measure of popular support? If there is, then why?"

"Damn' good question, Alan. Let's put it to the test."

"How?"

By way of an answer, Hank waved over the landlord. He was a ruddy-faced man with a moustache which joined his broad side whiskers. He strolled over to them, drying his hands on his apron.

"Landlord, we've just got down here from up north - Wales and the North-West. We're like fish out of water here. Up there, it's all confusion and we don't know the score. Between you and me," here Hank became conspiratorial, " I come from America, an' these guys were over there with me, so we're out of it. Is this just the Frogs and Huns fighting our boys or what?"

The landlord's laugh was surprisingly deep and genuine. "You're jokin', zur. Our boys, y'say? Well, I own some of the soldiers fightin' for James are Brits. From what I hear, they're doin' their best not to."

"Sorry?" Asked Berrick. "You mean they're running away?"

"Not good British soldiers. What? Run away? Not bloody likely, even if they don't support James and his crew. No, an' I'm speakin' as a former Sergeant-Major of the Royal Devon Regiment, mark you. Mind if I sit down, gents? Let me refill your glasses. Jenny?" He roared. "More drink for these gents and one for me." Turning back, he produced a cigarette and lit it, inhaling deeply and exhaling a long, satisfied breath.

"You fellows have been away from the Old Country for a long time, I reckon. Am I right?"

"Absolutely," replied Alan and Berrick.

"An' you are an American gentleman from the Colonies?"

"Correct," replied Hank, too polite to point out that he had just been through all this.

The landlord nodded fatly, looking pleased with himself. "I'd better fill in the details then, I reckon, because if I'm not mistaken, this old country seems like a foreign land to you, if you'll pardon my repeatin' the expression."

Jenny arrived with the drinks and smiled at them demurely before a hefty smack on her rump from the landlord sent her away with a scandalised expression.

"Where was I?" The landlord wiped the foam from his whiskers as he put down his tankard. "Well, first off, my name's Bill Tarbert. I'm the landlord of this pub an', let me tell you, I'm glad of the custom we've been gettin' 'ere of late. It's been lean pickings for over ten years, I can tell you. Back in '85, it was about average. Navy boys on an' off. Frigates off to the West Indies and Americay. Some off to Australia. Good consistent stuff. Then, there was that scandal. You may not've heard about it in the New World. It was that Prince Arthur.

"Now, Prince Arthur was a good lad. He was the prince the common folk liked. Good looking, a sportsman and a ladies' man. And there lay the problem. He'd gallivanted a bit - more'n a bit, actually. He was a golden-haired boy of twenty-five-odd, I suppose. Well, he wasn't worldly, if you get my drift. Not a drip, mind. A good horseman an' a damn' fine shot. But he didn't understand the ways of the world.

"Well, as I said, young Arthur was a ladies' man. Absolutely worshipped the little doxies. A bit like old Charles the Second. Upstairs, downstairs, in my Lady's Chamber. So his pa, the King, packed him off on the Grand Tour. Paris, Rome, Berlin, Stockholm. He had his wicked way with more ladies than all of us in this pub, I'll wager. Then, he met his match. It was in Hanover. She was the youngest daughter of King George. He was smitten, as they say. And she," strangely, tears came to the publican's eyes "she were the loveliest young lady you could imagine.

"The Hanovers were quite reconciled to being a continental Royal Family," he continued, dashing the tears from his eyes with the back of his hand," after all, it's two-hundred-and-fifty years since the '45. But, Arthur was ever the romantic. He declared publicly that he wanted to marry her. My God! The rumpus! Old King James had a fit. A real one. Confined to his bed. Reason bein', o' course, that they're Protestants and the Stuarts are Catholic. The Act of Succession states that no Monarch or Heir to the Throne may marry a Protestant. An' here was the Heir to the Throne of Great Britain sayin' that, not only was he goin' to marry a foul Protestant, but a member of the exiled Hanoverian monarchy."

Alan and Berrick exchanged glances, eyebrows raised. Hank looked equally surprised.

"We hadn't caught up with that back home."

"Oh, they tried to hush it up, y'know and it was nigh on thirty years ago now. But the European press were on to it and word crossed the Channel. So, there was sharp note sent to Arthur, commanding him to return forthwith and to abandon the lady. But Arthur and his father had never seen eye to eye. Arthur was no prating Catholic. He believed in God and Christ, he said. Man was the cause of religious disagreement and in God's House, all were equal, whether Papist or Protestant ."

"What happened?" Berrick butted in.

"Oh, well, they married. James disowned 'im and named the Duke of Buckingham as his successor. Arthur denounced his father and Buckingham. In time a child was born. A boy called Henry. Another, William, was next. And then, the worst thing possible happened." Here, the landlord had to dab his eyes again and then take a comforting draught of beer. Wiping his whiskers, his voice now low and husky, he continued. "The people here were for Arthur. He was every woman's ideal son or husband. Every man's role-model. He wasn't sunk in dissipation like so many of his family. He was the flower of European monarchy. But his father was jealous and fearful.

"I don't know the ins and outs of it, but, eighteen months ago, a truly evil deed was done. Prince Arthur addressed a meeting of Hanoverian industrialists at Hamburg stressing the need for us to move forward into the future. To seize the opportunity of making a better world out of the one we had. And he was shot. Murdered. In front of two thousand people!"

"Good God! Did the King do it? I mean, did he order it done?" Berrick stammered.

"I doubt it. They may have been at loggerheads but word had it that James was distraught. A week of public mourning was ordered. However " the landlord paused, "they didn't bring his body back because his wife insisted on being present at the funeral. The old King wouldn't have that. Said she wasn't his wife in the eyes of Rome and had no legal right to be there "

"Christ Almighty! That would rub the Hanoverians' noses in it!" Hank exclaimed.

"Oh it did that all right. They reckoned James was going mad over it. Soon enough, it was proved.

"The King was obliged to open Parliament within the month. The King's Speech is prepared in advance according to the Government's say-so. Has been since the time of Charles the Second. The Monarch says what the Government aims to do in the coming session and everyone is very dutiful and quiet. This time, it all went wrong." Emptying his glass, the landlord roared for more and waited until it appeared to start. More sailors came in, this time from a French ship. The barmaid greeted them and there were lots of kisses all round. Popular guys, Alan thought, especially for supposed hostile forces. What propaganda had they been fed in Edinburgh?

"Where was I? Ah, yes, Parliament. Well, all went as usual. Black Rod did his bit and they all trooped through to hear the planned programme the Whigs had in mind. James seemed preoccupied and stumbled over a few words. No-one thought much of that. But, he became agitated when he got to the part about a proposed fishing agreement with Hanover. He got to the bit about Hanover and stopped.

"You could have heard a pin drop. No-one dared say a word. It was in all the papers. Well, James stopped and went sort of pale. 'I'll have no agreements with a bunch of heathen Protestants!' Bawled it out loud, he did. 'Their harlot entangled my own darling boy in a web of deceit to seize my throne! They are thieves and murders. They killed him for their own ends!' And so it went on. Scandalous, it was. We all knew the Hanoverians were horror-struck. They'd adored Arthur. There was extended public mourning throughout Hanover after the assassination. It was genuine. Well, they had to hustle the King out of Parliament, but the cat was out of the bag. All the continental papers were represented - "

"Hang on - " Alan interrupted.

"No, let me finish. It might have ended with a suitable diplomatic freeze and thaw after a year or two. But, some bright spark in the Royal Navy, who wanted to make a name for himself, heard about it. In the usual way of these things, the proposed fishing treaty allowed for trawlers from various European countries to fish in the British part of the North Sea and around Dogger Bank. In effect, it had been agreed. In fact, apart from the signature, it was already being observed. Trawlers from Hanover, Prussia, Denmark, Belgium and France were to be allowed to fish for cod and mackerel. They had been doing so for some weeks with no problem. After all, Europe has lived without major wars for nearly two hundred years. Exclude Italian Reunification from that.

"Then, one fine day, Captain Trotman Hawker took it upon himself to clear the seas for His Britannic Majesty with a bloody rowing boat."

"A what?" Hank asked, astounded.

"Don't take me literally, my young colonial friend. It was some tiny ship of no appreciable importance. I reckon he wanted to get 'is name in the history books. Well, 'e bloody well did that. The little bastard sank two trawlers. One was from Hanover, t'other was a Frenchie. What was 'is ship now? Ah, yes, the HMS 'Spiteful'. And, my God, she was!"

"Okay, okay!" Hank butted in. "So, did they declare war or what?"

"Well, I'd 'ave thought you'd've heard that bit. Where were you lads? On the moon?"

"Near enough. Tell us."

Lighting another snout, and ignoring the jollities of the sailors in the background, he continued. "It's short but sweet. The Hanoverians demanded that Hawker be handed over for trial - as did the Frogs. Normally, you'd expect the British to stand united on that sort of thing. You know - stuff the foreigners and all that. The trouble was, the survivors of the trawlers were landed at Harwich by the luckless Captain Hawker. The press were there, o' course. Photographers, reporters, the lot. The photos of those poor sods were summat terrible. One poor French lad 'ad lost a leg. A Hanoverian bloke was badly burned and they'd given him no medical attention at all. Well, you can imagine the effect of the pictures on the public, let alone the Continentals.

"The Government was caught by the balls. They tried to defend it and stand firm, but half the Cabinet resigned. They took ship to the Continent and joined King George and declared for Prince Henry. Then the Hanoverians and the French withdrew their Ambassadors and declared war!"

"It's a bloody nightmare!" Berrick expostulated. "No wonder the people aren't for James!"

"And we've been foxed," Alan grimly nodded.

CHAPTER EIGHT

They trudged back to their digs from the pub, sunk deep in thought. Hank was also silent, unusually for him. A blizzard was hitting the South-West with a vengeance, but they ignored it, though the streets were almost deserted.

The snow froze their feet in the inadequate leather boots they had been given in Edinburgh and, by the time they got back to a cheerful coal fire and hot coffee from their bustling landlady, they were chilled to the bone.

They took off their boots and extended their legs to warm their freezing feet in the glowing warmth, each sunk in a private reverie. In the corner, a grandfather clock chimed the hour. It was 10 pm.

"What I didn't get was how you got in tow with the Germans, Hank." Alan lifted a wary eye. "I mean. Why were you on a battleship of the German Navy? How the hell did you get there, and why?"

Hank nodded almost absently and sipped his coffee. "Yeah. I guess it may seem strange. The fact is, I've been here for over a year." He sat up a little and looked at them squarely. "Let me give in to you straight from the shoulder. Okay?"

They nodded. Berrick took off his wet socks, and theatrically bowed to Hank with a gesture to carry on.

Hank's face grew dreamy as he looked inwardly upon memories he alone had in this universe. "I was an only kid. My ma was on the game. She never knew who my pa was. Didn't care either. I was a mouth to be fed. Later ... a lot later ... I became her confidant when her looks faded and she ended up working at Albertini's Deli on Thirty-Fourth Street.

"I hung out with the guys. Got drafted. Did a stint in 'Nam towards the end. I was eighteen and scared shitless. Charlie wounded me here," he tapped his left shoulder, "an' I was invalided out. When I was fit for duty, we were pullin' out. So I went to Germany and then back to normal life. What you Limeys call Civvy Street." He breathed deeply. "There's a lot in that period I've left out, but let it pass.

"I spent the next few years doin' a little of this an' a little of that. Tried to be a rockstar. Failed. Tried to be a writer. Failed. Did a few hitches in the Gulf of Mexico as a roustabout on a two-bit oil-rig. Quit. Became a salesman and was successful. Became manager of the company. All looked good. I made good commission. Then, one day, I came back home early. I wasn't married, but I was livin' with a chick named Lucy. I found her and a big buck black son-of-a-bitch humpin' on the floor of the lounge.

"I beat the shit out of him an' her both. Turned out he had a fragile skull. Next thing I knew, I was indicted for Murder One.

"But I was away. Los Angeles, Las Vegas, Vancouver, Hawaii. Wherever it was, as long as it was away from Boston, I was there. They'd never get me." He drained his coffee and looked sideways at them. "Yeah, I know. Christ! This guy's a fuckin' murderer, you're thinkin'. Well, maybe I am an', there again, maybe I'm not. You see, Lucy was a doll. But, she was a real bitch too, y'know. Oh, shit! O' course, you don't know." He spread his hands placatingly. "When I met her, she was a street-walker. I pulled her outa that, set her up and got her a decent job as a receptionist for a local lawyer I know. A client of mine. I sold ... this sounds shitty....stationery to his firm. So, I got her in there.

"What I didn't know was that she had a sugar-daddy. An', by a sugar-daddy, I mean a fuckin' great big black SOB called Ibrahim Mohammed. A Black Power leader. She'd been his Ace of Spades, if you'll pardon the pun, in Chicago.

"We thought that a move to Boston was far enough to be safe. How wrong can you be?" He grunted in disbelief. "When I stumbled in on them, he'd been there for fifteen minutes. I thought she was all for it. Turned out he'd told her what he was goin' to do to her, then kill her. Then he'd wait for me an' fix me so I was done for killin' her. He'd lost a lot of bread from her flyin' the coop an' he was sore. I just didn't realise.

"Well, give Lucy her due. She pointed out to the authorities that I'd killed the SOB because I was savin' her life. One look at Mohammed's record would've convinced the authorities that right was on my side. She said Mohammed had beaten her. True. But not as much as I did, an' that shames me to this day. She said I fled outa fear I'd be executed for his murder."

"The long and the short of it was that they caught me an' I was put away for a lesser sentence. I was out in three years. Lucy had gone. There were richer pickings elsewhere. But Mohammed's buddies were after me. Nowhere was safe. I fled from city to city. But, soon enough, there'd be a black dude askin' questions of people, all very polite and nice. But you could tell from the shades and the porkpie hat who the guy was. They wanted to 'try' me. And I knew what that meant. I had nowhere to go.

"Then one day, another day, another town, I found myself in Pokemoke City, Maryland. Washed up. Broke. An' I was sinkin' a bottle of booze in a singles bar when a guy came over. I thought he was gay an' told him to beat it.

"'No, sir. I'm goin' to get you the best thing you ever heard.'

"'Yeah, yeah,' I said. 'I know. Take me somewhere, smashed out of my brain, an', before I know it, I'm a film star. 'Cept the film's a snuff movie an' a guy with a chainsaw will chop me up for the delectation of a highly questionable audience.

"'Hey, no way, Jose,' says the dude, lookin' downright upset that I should question his moral character. So, he starts talkin' an', y'know. I actually got to believe this guy.

"'You want a noo start?' He asked me, an' I kinda nodded.

"'Okay, fella, you got it. No strings, no costs. You'll be a noo man in a noo world where I can send you.'

"'Look, buddy,' I says to him suspicions arising again, 'I ain't interested. You dig? I got no bread, I ain't queer, an' I don't like the sound of what you're sayin'. It stinks.'

"'Okay, good buddy,' he says. 'I can tell a Vet when I see one. I'm one myself. They shipped me outa the Delta.' (That's the Mekong Delta in 'Nam, by the way.) 'I was with Cyrus J Phillips. You may have heard tell of him. Here's ma card. You want to follow it up? You make a few calls. I'm clean. I'm an okay guy. You keep in touch, you hear?'

"And then he left and I just, kinda stuck the card in my pocket. Next couple of months, I was in a job sellin' this an' that. Cars on commission, then insurance, then I was a store Santa. Thank the Lord I was. There I was, ' ho, ho, hoin' ', outside of Harvey's General Stores on Main Street, when a very sharply-dressed black dude steps up to me an' asks me if I've seen myself in the area.

"'This here's one bad dude,' he says, flashin' me a fake FBI ID. ' We've been huntin' this guy all over. You seen him, Mister?'

"Nearly swallowed my tonsils, I can tell you. But, when in the face of danger, derring-do, as my old company C.O. would say. So, I batted my eyelids at him charmingly and said, 'Oooh! Him! That bitch! He blew outa town last week for Baltimore. He thaid there were bad guys after hith ath ! That thon of a bitch. Can I interetht you in my ath, big boy?' An' I did a dinky twirl for him.

"'Goddam honky faggot! Get away from me!' And he was off. I had to go out back to be sick. The bastards were onto me again. Still, there were five days till Christmas, and one Santa looks much like another. So I kept the disguise. I headed for Harvey's and got to a phone. I dug out that card from my pocket-book and rang Cyrus J Phillips at the Pentagon. 'No, sir,' they said, 'he's at such-and-such a base in Idaho.' So I asked them to patch me through. Said they should say 'Comanche' to him an' refused to explain. It was nonsense in a way. But they love cloak-and-dagger stuff, so they did it. Of course, Phillips didn't know what it was about either, but he took the call out of curiosity."

'That you, Colonel?' I asked when I got put through.

"'General!' He says with a voice like gravel. I could almost see him with a great big cigar stickin' out of his mouth. 'Who is this?'

"'Comanche,' I said. `No need to know. You remember that set-to in the Delta, sir?'

"There was a kind of a silence for a few seconds before he answered. It was a slow, South Carolina kind of an answer. 'Were you in ma outfit, son?'

"'No, sir. I was in another one. But, I was there.'

"'So - what kin Ah do for you, boy?'

"'Well, sir, it's' - I hunted for the card again an' squinted at the name on it - 'it's a guy I met called JJ Gumper. Said you'd know the name an' suggested I should call you for an affidavit.'

"'Uh, huh. What kinda affidavit d'ya need, Mr No-Name?'

"' Well - uh - is he okay?'

"'Okay? Why in hell are you wastin' my time for? Okay fer whut?'

"'Just okay. I mean, is he a trickster, a headcase, a killer?'

"'Uh, he's a killer, all right.'

"My blood ran cold. 'Oh, shit!' I guess I spoke when I hadn't intended to.

"'Is he threatenin' you or somethin'?'

"'No, sir. He's made me an offer. I'm just leery of offers from guys I don't know. I don't want to end up in a snuff movie or lyin' in a gutter with my throat cut.'

"Well, that General laughed fit to bust. 'Tell me. What does this guy look like?'

"'He's big - six-foot-two, maybe six-foot-three, about two hundred pounds. An' it's muscle.'

"'Black or white?'

"' White.'

"'Any characteristics?'

"I thought back. 'Yeah. Well, I guess. He was chewin' a cocktail stick.'

"'Uh, huh. Well, that's your man. He's clean. If you want proof it's him, get him to show you his left shoulder. That's where he was hit.'

"'You say he's clean. What do you mean?'

"'I mean he's trustworthy. After 'Nam, he got Jesus. Kain't say I'm of his persuasion. I'm a Methodist. But ole JJ is as straight as a die. You see him, you give him ma best!'

"I was gettin' real jumpy by now. Any smartly-dressed black bastard had me wettin' my pants despite the disguise. Soon enough, they'd twig that I was one of the Santas and start checkin' us out too. I was too young to die but I thought that, in 'Nam, a lot of others my age ended up six feet under.

"I looked at the address on Gumper's card. He was callin' hisself 'JJ'. It was only three blocks. I ambled out, lookin' relaxed and feelin' like a cat on a hot tin roof. There was a blizzard blowin' hard by now, so I reckoned I was safe. I stepped out smartly. It was a simple route. One block west, hang a left for another block, then a right. I ducked my head down an' walked. It was cold enough to freeze yer lungs. You ever been in a blizzard in the Great Plains in the Mid West? No, I guess not. That's what it was like. Used to freeze folks solid, back in the Old West, if they were caught out in it. Prob'ly still does.

"Anyhows, I was into the next street an' trudgin' with ma bag of presents slung over ma shoulder, 'cause the snow was startin' to drift, when a shadow seemed to just solidify beside me. It was a black dude."

"I was real muffled up, you gotta realise, but he knew me. Y'know? Outa all the Santas in Pokemoke City, he guessed it was me. There was a gun stickin' in ma side. I guess I kinda stiffened.

"'Keep movin', honky,' he says - shouted, in fact. 'This here's a Smith & Wesson, an' it's silenced. It's your choice, white boy. Move or die!'

"Who the hell wants to die? So, I moved. Still goin' in the same direction, mind. I knew I was dead either way, an' my mind was workin' overtime. Where's he takin' me? What'll they do to me? Will it be slow or will it be quick? No. It'd be real slow. 'Eef I don't like you, I keel you - but eef I like you, I keel you slow.' " He imitated a Mexican accent and looked at them. Their attention was fully concentrated on his story.

"We'd passed the street I was to turn down to get to JJ's place, when it happened. All of a sudden, we was ambushed by a bunch of kids. Snotty-nosed little assholes. I'd kiss `em now, if I could. They sprung outa nowhere - eight or ten of 'em - an' pelted us with snowballs with stones in 'em. Caught Smilin' Boy right on the nose. O' course, he flung up his hands to protect hisself an' blinked. I didn't. I swung that bag of presents in a haymaker and knocked him flyin'.

"Before you could say Jack Robinson, I was off. The kids were peltin' merry hell outa my dusky friend. I was scared shitless, I can tell you. But, I was cunning. I stuck to the road. Didn't want to leave tracks on the sidewalk. Trucks an' cars were still comin' through an' I reckoned my footsteps'd get obliterated by their tyres.

"Anyhow, I hung a right into JJ's street and couldn't see the hand in front of my face. It was a real honey. I could reckon roughly where JJ's apartment lay, but, before I knew it, I plunged into knee-deep snow an' almost got run over by a truck. I was trottin' along, scannin' the numbers, when I heard a faint voice shoutin', 'I'm on your track honky. You kain't hide from me, white trash! An' when I turned, I could see a shadow in the lights o' that truck turn as the brakes squealed." He paused sipping his coffee and grimacing as it had gone cold.

"He didn't stand a chance. Y'see, he thought I'd gone the other way. He was lookin' away from me. What with the snow, I reckon he didn't hear the truck an' the driver didn't see him. He was still thinkin' how he'd almost killed me. Next thing I knew, the bastard was under the front wheels of the truck an' there was a lot of blood. I jus' kept goin'.

CHAPTER NINE

"JJ's place was in a plain building. I pushed the buzzer an' just blurted out ma name. Next thing, I was in an' up the stairs like a good ol' boy. JJ let me in an' checked the stairs before he closed the door.

"'Hey, man. You're shiverin' real bad. What gives?' He says. So I told him. He was cool, that guy. Sat me down an' gave me a tall glass of bourbon straight. Told me to get outa ma Santa rig-up, which Ah did 'cos it was soakin', what with the snow an' the sweat of the fear of death.

"While Ah was doin' that, he was on a cell-phone to someone, real urgent. 'Keep your eyes peeled. They's seen him an' one o' them black fuckers is dead meat. But they'll be others.'

"I said, 'I thought you was all gone to Jesus - what's all this bad-mouthin' black assholes?' - an' he says how Jesus didn't say nothin' 'bout black assholes, an' how they was Satan's seed. I didn't argue. O' course, I asked him to show me his shoulder like the General said, an' he did, so I relaxed a lot. I was safe for a while .

'So, what're we gonna do with you?' He asked.

"'You told me I could be a new man in a new place with a new start. Well - I need it. Those Black Power guys, or whatever they were, are out to get me.'

"'Okay, cool it!' He says, an' gets me to tell him the whole story, which I did. He sat with his eyes closed and listened. When I finished he said, 'You're a patriot?'

"'Sure as hell, I am,' I replied.

"'Tell me - what would you say if you could free America from colonial domination - like in the Revolution?' He asks, an' I blinked. Didn't know what he was drivin' at.

"'Okay. Just bear with me, okay? Suppose these here United States of America were still a British colony. An', suppose you were there with your knowledge an' abilities right now. What do you reckon you could do?'

"I thought maybe he'd lost his marbles, but he didn't look crazy. His old Colonel reckoned him okay. An', besides, I'd got all the homicidal negroes in the US after my blood. So, I gave him the benefit of my serious thoughts.

I thought a bit an' said, 'Well, one man on his own, it'd be tough.'

"'George Washington was one man on his own.'

"'Hardly,' I said, because I knew my history. ' He'd a nation behind him.'

"'Yep. But they needed a leader. Right?'

"'Okay. I'll accept that.'

"'That's why I chose you.'

"'Oh?' I looked pretty blank.

"'You won a Purple Heart in 'Nam.'

"Well, I wasn't one to brag. But it so happened that I had, so I admitted it.

" 'For tenacity, valour and leadership in the face of overwhelmin' odds.' Am I right?'

"I said that sounded kinda familiar an' he jus' grinned.

"'Yep. You act like it.' He placed his hands on his knees and sat back. He had the weirdest eyes, y'know? They glowed, sort of. He looked at me, but it was like he was lookin' through me. Then, he started talkin'. Told me about himself. 'Nam. Gettin' Jesus (in a Ku Klux Klan way, which I don't count). An' then his discovery, one day, that there was a whole universe out there we knew nothin' about.

"I started thinkin' - hey, we've got ourselves a fruitcake here. Next, it'll be little green men who're gonna fly us to Venus. But he jus' gave me a big smile an' a sleepy kinda look.

"'No. Afore you start sayin' to yo'self, this guy's nuts, he believes in conspiracy theories an' stuff, jes' hol' on an' pin back your ears.'

"So, he started tellin' me 'bout this Sioux squaw he'd shacked up with (seemed Injuns were okay, even though negroes weren't). She'd been - um - psychic, I think that's the right word. He took her back to that very apartment.

"Soon as she stepped in, she said that there were 'vibrations' in the place. Didn't mean nothin' to ole JJ. Th' only vibrations he got were from his Harley Davidson. She walked around the place, pokin' in cupboards an' up in th'attic.

"Then she got to this one cupboard. It was a wall-cupboard, built in, y'know? JJ said she just stopped dead and turned to him an' said, 'Open the door.'

" JJ said he couldn't as it was jammed. Always had bin. She stamped her foot an' said to 'get a chisel and to open that damn' door.' Fierce little thing she was, so it seems. Well, old JJ fished around for a while an' found a claw hammer and a knife. They pulled out some nails an' then he cut around the door. "Must've bin nigh on 100 years worth 'f paint to cut through," he said. But, in the end, they did it.

124

" 'Open it,' she said.

" 'Open it yourself,' he said, so she did." Hank stopped. "All her hair was stickin' up on end. So was his. Some kind've static.

"I need a beer. The Landlady's got a few.   This could be an all-nighter. Reckon she's got some whisky too. Fancy some?"

Alan and Berrick nodded.

"Beer would be great. Don't take long. I'm getting into this tale of yours." Alan said as Hank bustled away in search of refreshments. They looked at each other.

"Another doorway," Alan commented laconically.

Hank came back with an armful of bottles. He unscrewed one and poured them a healthy glassful apiece and then attended to his own. He took a long draught. "One good thing here is the beer. None of that cold piss you get in the States. It's got taste and a hell of a belt," he belched gently. "Now. Where was I? Ah! The cupboard.

"Well, JJ opened the door and peered in expectin' a few shelves and a lot of dust. Funny thing was, all the hairs on him stood on end when he was near that door. Plain weird, he called it. To his surprise, he found another room, larger than his and very clean. Said it looked like one of those places you see in a nineteenth century photo - curtains tied back, oriental rug on the floor and a smell of expensive cigar smoke in the air. But stale cigar smoke. He stepped through with his lady love and closed the door behind them. 'It was jes' part of the wood panelling,' he said, 'Ah got scaired we wouldn't ha' found our way back, but a push here and it popped open.'

" 'Okay,' I said, gettin' kinda pissed off, 'so you got inta the nex' door apartment. Big deal! Where the hell is this takin' us?'

" 'Hush the fuckup, will ya?' He said sharpish, 'I'm gettin' to that.' An' he lights up an' scratches his haid.

" 'So, we decided to explore. Ah went to the winder an' looked out. Ah couldn't believe it. We were lookin' out at NYC! But it weren't no NYC in our day an' age. It was like it was 1910 or somethin'. Ah reckoned we was on Fifth Avenue. Almost all the traffic was horses an' horse-drawn buses, 'ceptin' a few old bangers. But they was all pre-Model T stuff. I rubbed my eyes an' said to Miriam (that's my Indian lady friend) 'D'you see what I see?' An' she said, 'Yep. An' have you seen the flags?'

" 'Well, pardner, Ah was jes' plain dumbfounded! They was all Union Jacks - British flags! Ah thought we must be on a film set, so we went out an' checked for ourselves. Got some real funny looks too, 'cos of our duds. They all had collars an' ties an' top hats. We walked a few blocks an' it was all the same. I was feelin' really weird, man, y'know? So, I asked a guy for a newspaper. He was standin' on the corner. He told me it was a tanner an' I said, what in hell's a tanner? Looked at me as if I was plumb crazy. So I pulled a paper out of a garbage can an' brought it back with me. Then, we walked back to the apartment an' came through that door.' "And he pointed at it in the corner.

" He reached into a basket beside him and pulled out a paper. It was the New York Times and the date was just over a year before. You'd have thought it was a hundred years ago to look at it, tho'. The front page was nothin' but classified advertising. Readin' it, I almost threw up - not in revulsion - I just freaked man! It had pictures, photos that is. Grainy black'n'white, they were. It was the stories though. It had a Court page an' humble suggestions to His Majesty from His loyal American subjects. Cravin' a measure of dominion like Australia had. The Lord Mayor of NYC - can ya dig it? The Lord

126

Mayor was a guy who stood for President in our time ten years ago. Had his picture, waving to the crowds from some prehistoric car on Fifth Avenue. An' the crowds were all wavin' Union Jacks!"

Hank finished his bottle of beer and belched softly again before picking up a second. He looked across at the other two. "I told JJ he was fuckin' nuts tryin' to pass this stuff off as real. But he jes' looked at me real calm an' said he was going to dress for a visit an' said I should do so too. Threw me over a heap of ol' fashioned clothes. 'We'll have a real good time, my friend. Then we'll see who's telling you the truth.'

" I didn't reckon I had much choice. Play along with this guy and see what profit there might be for me in it - or wait for some homicidal black boy to blow my brains out, so I got changed. Kept my I.D. and such, though. I said 'Hey JJ ? What happened to your ol' lady?'

" He shrugged and smiled in a sad sort of way. 'She went over an' stayed. Joined her own people, I b'lieve. She sent me a letter. Where is it?'

" He dug into a drawer and pulled out an envelope. It had a stamp with a King's head on it an' was addressed to a number in Fifth Avenue - 1074, I believe. She said she was joining her own people, but she might be back some day an' not to wait for her. Seemed genuine enough to me.

" 'How'd you get this?' I asked. He jes' said he had it delivered in the post to the apartment on the other side 'f the door. Never had any other mail. No one seemed to use the place. He couldn't work it out. Reckoned it was some kind of function room. He hadn't stopped anyone to ask.

"Well, we was dressed by then so he says 'Shall we?' an' I said 'Why not?' An' he led the way through the cupboard door, the pair of us dressed for an Ante-Bellum Ball or Teddy Roosevelt's Swearing-In, all ma hair standin' up. An' there we were. I swear to you, my eyes were out on stalks, man!

"The room was big. It had wood panels and a big eastern rug all the colours of the rainbow on the floor. Your feet sank into it. You could smell old cigar smoke too, just like JJ said. It was when I went to the window that real astonishment hit me. Y'ever seen one of them old hand-cranked black and white films from eighteen-ninety something? It was that to a tee. But all the way up the street. There was no way this could be a set up. I was still in a state of shock when JJ took me out onto the street. It was totally different order of things. If y'know New York, it's always movin', never stands still. Here, it was the same, but one hundred years or so earlier. Remember, they had traffic jams in 1890s NYC - that's when the term was coined.

" We ate in a restaurant run by some Switzers. Everyone had American or European accents - but different. Less... harsh, mebbe. Mebbe the way they spoke before all the Eyetalians and Jews and such arrived. Here it was Anglos and Irish and a few Ethnics. Not many blacks. Those there were knew their place.

" I wondered how JJ could pay for the meal and he admitted that he did printing of fliers using his computer. Beat the pants off local competition for graphics and colour. But he was keepin' it low-key. Just enough to build up a nest-egg.

" We'd pushed back the plates after a real belly-buster of a meal and he says it's time for me to decide. Which universe do you choose, mister? Ours - or this one?

" I protested that I didn't know this one. How would I get started here? What would I use for money?

" 'No problem,' he says and pulls out a bag of gold sovereigns!

" 'There's £ 50 in this. That's a good six months' salary for an artisan here an' now. Should be enough to get you started. You're bright. You're a Vietnam Vet. You should know a bit about America by your age. You could become a frontiersman, an industrialist, a revolutionary. You've got a new life to live. Do it!'

" I felt like a kid abandoned on a street corner and left by his parents. Totally lost.

" I looked him in the eye. 'How an' why are you doin' it?'

" He looked grim for a moment then, he told me about guilt: his guilt, the American nation's guilt. About makin' things right. How he had found Jesus (his kinda Jesus) and he wanted this America to be even greater than the fucked-up one we lived in.

" 'I ain't no saint, though, and Ah ain't rich. This is all Ah' kin offer you. Take it or leave it.'

" 'What - now ?' I was gawping at him.

" 'Well - you know the way back and what's waiting for you on the other side.' He lit a ceegar and smiled at me. 'After all, Miriam's here so you ain't the only one from our side over here.'

" 'Yeah, but where in hell is she? Shit, man. You make a hell of a hard deal.'

" 'As I said, take it or leave it. Be who you want to be.' Then I thought back, away from that smoky restaurant to a time when I had been cut off from my unit in the Mekong. I'd survived there with a knife and my common sense against a bunch of little yellow men who were huntin' me an' who would have castrated me, crucified me and stuck my pecker in my mouth as I bled to death. And, I survived. Who's out to kill me here, I asked myself? I stuck my hand out.

" 'You've got a deal. I'll write and let you know how I do.' He grinned and gave me the money.

" 'I'll get the check," he said."

The three of them sat around the embers of the fire in the Plymouth digs, each lost in reverie. Doors to other universes, mused Berrick. How poetic!

"The question is, Hank, old son, how the hell do we get back home?" Berrick gazed at Hank in the flickering light of the fire, but he did not answer.

"I'm whacked." Alan stirred himself at length." Let's hit the hay and catch up on your other reminiscences in the morning. Okay, Berrick?" They left Hank to himself with a new bottle of beer and a fire which hissed and spat as snowflakes percolated down the chimney to immolate themselves in the glowing coals.

"We need to do something, guys." Hank greeted them in the morning as they staggered into the dining room to be faced with a breakfast of kedgeree which they avoided. A large quantity of sweet black tea brought some life to their bloodshot eyes and some colour returned to their grey complexions.

"Hung over, huh? That's the real ale everyone went on about back you know when," Hank laughed as the Landlady bustled about clearing the table and tut tutting at the untouched plates.

"You gentlemen need a good breakfast in this cold weather," she admonished fatly, "otherwise you'll fade away."

"Hank," Alan addressed the American, wondering how he looked so fresh and wide awake, "I think we should see someone who can give us an idea of what to do. We're just kicking our heels here and I'm not the passive type. Anyway, we need to find out if there's a way back for us. If you could get through too, there are clearly other portals, or gateways, or whatever they are."

"That's my boy! You too, Berrick? I have something interesting to show you."

"Sure. Let's get to it!"

They donned coats and galoshes, kindly lent by the Landlady before braving a day of dazzling brilliance and arctic temperatures. Within the minutes the fresh, clean air had cleared their heads and the mood of the two Scots was raised several notches.

"Where are we off to?" Berrick asked.

Hank pointed to a tram, a couple of hundred yards away.

"There. We'll take a tram. It's quicker and a hell of a lot warmer." He looked at his watch. "There's one due in five minutes."

In Edinburgh, Sir Ralph looked up from his desk as his Secretary came in and deposited a short message on his desk. Sighing, he donned his pince-nez spectacles and opened a brown envelope bearing his name marked 'TOP SECRET - EYES ONLY'. As he did, he glanced at the telegram he had received that morning:

"Confidential message from Swansea, 19.07 hours stop two civilians evacuated from Aerodrome earlier today observed boarding tramp steamer "Eurydice" at Swansea stop Left at 12.15 heading WSW stop ends. "

Puzzled at the unexpected delivery, Sir Ralph nodded his thanks to his secretary and waited until she had withdrawn from his study before he reached across the desk with one liver-spotted hand. He picked up the ivory-handled paper-knife and slit the envelope. His eyes scanned the brief text.

"Encoded message from Swansea, 01.34 hours stop "Eurydice" sank 23.47 hours last night stop believed no survivors stop"

Sir Ralph arose and crossed to the fire burning in the grate, screwing up the message and threw it into the blaze. Swiftly, it was consumed. As he watched it burn, the diplomat sighed deeply.

"Forgive us our trespasses...." he muttered, before, slowly and creakingly, he returned to his desk and other matters at state.

CHAPTER TEN

The tram smelt of oil and unwashed people. Those aboard shivered in the biting cold. The atmosphere was thick with pipe and cigarette smoke, making their eyes water.

"Now I know how non-smokers feel." Berrick muttered to himself, pulling his coat back as Alan sat down heavily beside him, his expression glum.

With a judder, the tram pulled away from the stop and conversation resumed around them as the frozen passengers paid their fares and swapped news and tittle-tattle. Hank was peering through the smog which had fogged the inside of the windows to see where they were going. With the windows steamed up, he had no idea of where they were. It was like finding your way whilst suffering from severe glaucoma. Street followed street and Hank merely peered through a little area he had cleared in his window to check where they had stopped.

"How much longer, Hank?" Alan grumbled, hugging himself to stay warm. The American merely grunted non-committally.

" I'm like the apocryphal man on the Clapham Omnibus," Alan continued, "except that nothing is clear to me."

"Pardon me?" Hank looked puzzled.

"Nothing, Hank. Just an allusion to English Law. Anyway, since you apparently know where we are, do you mind telling us where we are going?"

"Keep your voice down." Hank hissed, then continued in a normal tone, "I thought we'd look at the nearby countryside to get a breath of fresh air."

Coughing genuinely, Berrick said Amen to that and they settled to await their destination.

It wasn't long in coming as the tram came to a halt at its terminus within ten minutes. The last half dozen passengers descended and the three men, stretching and yawning stepped into the frigid air, smelling coal smoke from the row of turn-of-the-century villas which seemed to be the edge of Plymouth's development. Beyond, lay a country road, fields and trees. Berrick looked at the landscape and glanced quizzically at Hank.

"Well, we're here, but where the hell is here?"

Hank was not to be drawn that easily. Without answer, he set off into the country following the unmetalled country road at a cracking pace and the other two had no choice but to follow. The road surface was deeply-rutted and the snow had frozen as hard as rock in the cold. A crow cawed in the distance, emphasising the loneliness and emptiness of the spot so near a major town. Looking back, they could see Plymouth half-hidden in a pall of coal smoke. It looked peaceful despite a biting north-westerly wind which must have driven most people indoors.

For another twenty minutes, they trudged on, warmed by the exercise, but made aware of the arctic cold by the numbness of their faces and the way the harshness of the temperature made their eyes water. They encountered no one during the course of their brisk walk, only stirring some rooks from their perches to circle above them, wildly buffeted by the gale.

They had walked a good mile-and-a-half or more when they rounded a bend in the earth track they were following. A small copse of silver birches stood on a knoll ahead of them. Hank pointed as they walked.

"It's beyond those trees. Not far now."

"What is?" Berrick asked, but received no answer. A few hundred yards on, however, and he saw their destination. It was a large country house, hidden in a dell and surrounded by an ancient stone wall bewhiskered with ivy and encrusted with snow. The view should have been charming, but an obvious military presence gave the lie to that. The wrought-iron gates were closed and two sentries armed with Lee Enfield, bolt-action rifles, were marching to and fro before them, clad in khaki greatcoats, their breath fogging the air about them.

"They're British soldiers!"

"Sure are." Hank commented as they drew near. Alan and Berrick glanced at each other, perplexed. There was no time to ask what British soldiers were doing so far behind French and German lines, for they had been seen. The two sentries had ceased their marching and the rifles they carried were no longer at shoulder arms but now pointed menacingly at them.

"Halt!" Called one soldier with a corporal's two stripes on his arm." Friend or foe?"

"Friend!" Hank replied, raising his hands. Berrick and Alan also raised theirs, feeling naked and, strangely, guilty.

"Advance one and be recognised."

Hank advanced slowly until he approached the Corporal. The other soldier, a Private, still pointed his rifle suspiciously at Berrick and Alan. Hank produced some documentation and handed it to the Corporal who studied it carefully.

"Wait here. Keep your hands up!" He barked before trotting to a small cabin hidden beside the gate. He could be seen cranking up a field telephone and speaking rapidly for some time, giving descriptions of the three as he gave them a coolly appraising once-over. There was a wait, then the Corporal nodded, replied and hung up the telephone. Returning briskly, he waved the other two forward with a word to the Private who lowered his rifle with apparent regret.

"Apologies, gents. But orders is orders. You are to proceed through the main gate here, along the driveway an' present yourselves at the 'ouse," he pronounced the word 'ahse'.

"Thank you, Corporal," Hank nodded politely before leading the small party through the gate which the Private opened for them. They glimpsed artfully-clipped, snow-covered topiary and the odd blackbird foraging hungrily as they crunched up the gravel driveway.

Berrick glanced at Hank as they puffed their hot expelled breath into the air like steam engines.

"What was that documentation you showed him, Hank?"

"Oh, that? Just a letter of I.D. from our good Kriegsmarine Captain and a Commission as a Leutnant, a Lieutenant, that is, in their Navy."

"The Jerries must love you," Alan muttered.

"I guess. So do your boys - leastways, these ones do.' Hank grinned.

The house was grand in a Jacobean way. It was certainly far from palladian, but it spoke, nonetheless, of solidity and a squireish respectability. Warm, honey-coloured lights glowed from its mullioned windows and a plume of smoke rose lazily in the air from its tall, barley-sugar chimneys. Here lay peace and comfort, it said. Be you welcome.

The front door opened at their approach. Rather than the wing-collared butler replete in silver-buttoned cutaway that they had unconsciously expected, a thin, spotty-face youth in a khaki uniform and puttees ushered them in.

"G'nral Hannah's compliments, gents, an' would you be pleased to make y'rselves comf'table in the study. 'E'll be with youse presently.'" He led them through a small archway to a comfortably-appointed room with several hunting prints on the wall. In the grate, a fire painted the walls a cheerfully flickering red.

"That'll be an English rather than a Scots presently, I assume," Berrick commented as they stretched out their numbed fingers to the welcome warmth of the wood fire crackling in the hearth.

"It will not," boomed an Irish voice behind them, startling them. They turned to see a tall, imposing officer in immaculate attire, full dress, no less, standing on the threshold, waxed moustaches bristling beneath a jutting nose. The blue eyes that surveyed them were humorous nonetheless.

"It's an Irish presently."

Berrick grinned sheepishly and apologised.

"No, no. Just my joke, young man. Sit. Or stand if you prefer. It's perishing outside, and you will be cold, I'm thinking."

He walked into the room, a cavalryman to his jingling spurs and joined them at the fire, surveying them frankly but uncritically.

"It'll be a drop of the hard stuff you'll be needing after that walk, I'll be bound." He reached for a bell-pull by the mantelpiece, and gave it a tug.

"I only drink after nine am, sir," Alan exclaimed weakly.

"Then, you're in luck. It all of eleven o'clock already."

They warmed themselves companionably before the fire until a trolley loaded with decanters and glasses clinked its way in under the direction of an elderly man clad in civilian clothes and a long dark blue apron.

"Thank you, Farley. You may go."

The General held up the decanter of pale gold liquid with a questioning look.

"It's Irish whiskey with an "e". I like scotch, but right now it's milk from Kathleen O'Hoolihan's tit you'll get or nothing except some English piss like gin. What's it to be?"

"Irish," they replied as one.

Without ceremony, a glass of whiskey was handed to each. The General filled one for himself and looked at them with a strange smile on his face.

"A toast would be appropriate at this point. I'll make it."

They looked at him expectantly, glasses in hand. The General grinned and raised his.

"Damnation to this dump. Here's to Neil Armstrong, The Beatles, personal computers - and the real world!"

He swallowed his drink in one and laughed uproariously at Alan and Berrick's astonished expressions.

"What?" Yelled Berrick. "What ? Neil Armstrong....pcs ?" He gurgled to a standstill. The General smiled and poured another drink. He looked at Hank.

"Will you do the honours, Major Hansen?" He waved at the glasses Alan and Berrick had emptied without thinking.

"Yes, sir, General Hannah!" Hank was suddenly very military. His whole bearing had changed in a subtle way that was hard to explain. His bearing was, perhaps, slightly more erect. His speech more clipped and his manner more military. Hank replenished their glasses and returned them. Berrick and Alan looked at each other. There was a slight lifting of an eyebrow and furrowing of a forehead. Each read the other's thoughts. What was this all about?

"Sit, gentlemen, please." The Irish mannerisms had gone. The General was all British Army. Rational, analytical, pragmatic. As they settled in the comfortable armchairs, he began to weave a tapestry of words which explained the startling scenario in which they found themselves.

"First, gentlemen, I owe you an apology. So does Major Hansen here. We have not wished to deceive you in any way but circumstances here demanded an element of subterfuge. You will have gathered that I, like you, am from the world of jet planes, H-Bombs, pollution, IRA bombings and so on and so forth that we call home.

"You can imagine the reaction in certain intelligence circles in London, when we gathered that there were claims being made by one or two individuals that they had crossed into another time-frame. The claims were being made by a very solid citizen indeed. He was - is - in fact - a former senior officer in one of the Armed Services.

"Well, we've all heard the tales of "remote viewing" spying from the States. Sounded like utter twaddle when I first heard it. Then again, radio probably did before anyone heard it in action. So, we reserved judgement, brought in the old war horse, and listened to what he had to say." The General took out a packet of cigarettes and lit one. Blowing the grey smoke up towards the ceiling, he picked a piece of tobacco from his tongue and continued. "Well, we soon found that he had his head screwed on. Didn't beat about the bush either. He said he had discovered this doorway, when he was improving his old house. It 's late nineteenth century."

"Must be about the age of JJ's apartment."

"That's pretty old for the US, isn't it?" Asked Alan.

"Sure. But there are old places in New England and Virginia dating back to the first half of the eighteenth century and some very old places that are seventeenth century."

"Very interesting." The General commented.

"Pardon me, sir." Hank looked embarrassed, but the General merely grinned and continued.

"Architecture aside, the old war-horse took two chaps from Five down to check it out. They reported back that it was genuine. Now, the interesting thing is that the house was reported to be haunted. Does that make you think of anything gentlemen?"

"Good God!" Alan looked dumb-struck." Are you saying that many of our ghosts are actually real people crossing over to our dimension from here?" He paused to consider. "What an idea. But of course, it explains the old-fashioned dress of many ghosts. The women here wear long dresses and it explains the total disappearance of ghosts. Not all, maybe, but many, perhaps. They step through a doorway into this dimension."

"That'll confuse the psychics," the General chuckled, "to continue, however, the boys of Five made a report. They had "crossed over" and saw the obvious problems (and benefits) to look out for. At first, all they saw were benefits. This was a world in which Britain was - is - a major power. There are no nuclear bombs, there is little pollution. Minorities do as they are told. We have access to untapped energy - oil and gas - for example. Undesirables could be shipped to Darkest Africa and left there, the way it was done in the good old days. Oh, I'm not saying that this has happened, merely saying that it was mentioned in the discussion papers."

"And the disadvantages you mentioned?" Berrick raised an eyebrow questioningly.

"Ah, yes. I was coming to that. The disadvantages could stem from those who had come over from our dimension. They could be working against us from within. We reckon most of us have a double or a doppelganger living in this dimension. It makes things damn' difficult. Also, of course, if any of our rivals should hear of it -"

"But what about Hank, here?"

"I have a piece to say too," Hank grinned and nodded to the General who went on.

"You don't know, of course, how close we are to the US. Let's just say that our links are very, very solid and our co-operation is at a much more ingrained level than most people reckon. From our point of view, if America were weakened, the whole of the Free World is threatened. From the US point of view, there is only one power they can rely upon implicitly (except where issues of close national importance or prestige are concerned, but that is understood). It is ties of blood and belief in God and freedom. It's a common culture. We are family. We may disagree about things. We may be rude about each other and get in huffs with each other -"

"Like Suez," said Berrick.

"Give the boy a banana - like Suez. But, when the chips are down, we stick together like shit to a blanket. Here - let me top you all up."

While General Hannah refilled their glasses, Berrick spoke up.

"General Hannah. I hate to say this, but all we seem to be doing is sitting listening to life histories from Hank and political analysis from our time and the year now. What the hell are we doing here?"

The General seated himself before answering. He steepled his fingers and fixed Berrick with a steady look.

"You're the flies in the ointment, don't you see? Hank here is our barometer for bad weather brewing. You are that weather. So far, we had only found two access points - one in the US and one in the UK. You have now found access point two in the UK. That is bad news. How many others might there be?"

"God knows. However, we are here and we were entrusted with a mission -"

The General sat forward, a sudden interest written deep in his face. Softly he said, "You were entrusted with what?"

"A mission."

"By whom?"

"By an Official of the British Government in Edinburgh."

"Go on."

"Well, he seemed to be expecting us - or, more likely - our other selves. Certainly our clothes didn't seem to arouse any surprise on his part. In fact, he had us put up at the North British Hotel and rekitted us with suitable clothes overnight."

"Did he, indeed? And what was this mission, may I ask?"

There was a subtle change in the General's voice which Berrick noted. Even so, he decided the political concerns from his world overrode those from this twilight era.

"It's to draw France in on the side of the King and to split the Franco-German Alliance."

"And you agreed to this?" The General's voice grated alarmingly.

Berrick gobbled a bit, "Well it's the status quo. It's the establishment, isn't it? It may not be our Government or our monarch, but it's British. We saw no reason to say no. In fact, the whole thing was a novelty. At first, well, we were humouring someone we thought had a screw loose, to be totally honest. By the time the next day had dawned, we found otherwise. When we tried to make our excuses, we were escorted to the train at gunpoint. Then, we found that the people were being told outright lies. We felt that we were dealing with honest, decent individuals. We saw no signs of corruption or of an oppressive regime. What were we to think?" He had grown more confident as he spoke and his words were more belligerent when he concluded.

The General stroked his chin.

"Fair enough," he conceded, "I think you may have gathered that this is still not an ideal world - "

"We realise that. As I said, the Press told out-and-out lies about military victories when, in fact, they were roundly defeated."

"That's true."

"But that doesn't explain why you are apparently both on the side of the Franco-German Alliance, against British interests." Berrick stuck his jaw out as he tended to when angry or frightened and feigning anger.

Hank sighed and looked at the General. An honest imperceptible nod gave him the go-ahead and he turned to face them.

"This is ultra hush-hush. Do I have your word that you will not repeat this outside this room?"

They each nodded, mystified, before Hank continued.

"We've told you about the energy sources and such like. Okay? I told you about my reasons for escaping the US. Within certain limits that I won't clarify, that was true. I never really left the US Military, however. I am a card-carrying member of the United States Establishment. The General has not mentioned the fact that there's strong reason to believe that there are real forces at work here - on the British side - which endanger the security of our own dimension."

"What? From people with Zeppelins and biplanes?" Alan jeered, "Give me a break!"

"No. Hear me out. Why do you think you were sent on your mission by this Jacobite mandarin? Oh, sure, it sounds okay on first hearing. But analyse it. There a general ill-feeling towards Britain's monarchy. You've seen that people aren't unhappy about the foreign forces trying to overthrow the established monarchy. Why? Is it dynastic favouritism? Or is it more deep-seated?

"In the Lowlands, we believe there to be a research establishment that would be the envy of many governments in our world. We feel certain they are developing weapons of mass destruction there! They have also got modern troop formations on their side. And, who do you think controls all this? Not His Jacobite Majesty King James. Oh, no! It's a very strict group of extremists according to our sources. We know little or nothing about them. They are shadowy in the extreme. We are confident of their psychological profile, though, as a group. They are right-wing enough to stand side-by-side with Adolf Hitler. They aim to own this world, my friends. And, soon, they aim to own ours too!"

"Hold on. You're ahead of me. You say that the powers that be here know about us and our world. Yet, you say that they are being controlled by people from our timeframe. I don't follow you."

The General stepped in. "It's quite straightforward. You know the names of various ultra-nationalist British political groups. They're the successors of the BUF. We watch them like hawks. They're well-infiltrated by intelligence officers apparently devoted to the cause. These agents keep us closely informed of developments. These groups have contacts with lots of undesirable regimes and individuals - Ghadaffi, Saddam Hussein, renegade Russian soldiers and nuclear scientists. These people often have funding from wealthy sources. Some of these sources are linked to Nazi sympathisers. It is hinted that funds may even be coming from Odessa, the SS 'Pension Fund'."

"But they're Germans!"

"Of course. But, they share the same views. Get one sympathetic government in Europe and we'll soon have a plethora of them. They breed like rabbits."

The General lit up another cigarette, a sign of his increasing anger.

"We are more and more convinced that they have a gateway to this dimension, but we don't know where. We suspect that the ignorance of fascism as a political philosophy here is one reason why the powers-that-be have let these people in. To your mandarin, their smooth talk would ring a lot of sympathetic bells. Control the King, deal a stunning blow to the enemy and control the world. Meanwhile, sow the seeds of dissension among the people you are, ostensibly helping, to divide their ranks and give you time to let your plans mature. That's where you two come into it. "

"My God!" Breathed Alan, "I'm a fascist stooge!"

"You are that, old son," the General resumed the brogue for a minute, studying them both. "The question now is, what do we do with you?"

They looked sharply at him.

"That sounds ominous. What do you do with people?"

"Frankly," the General stubbed out his cigarette firmly, "if they're agin us, I kill 'em. If they are for us, I use 'em. Which are you?" All pretence had gone. The atmosphere in the room was brittle enough to shatter with a wrong word.

"I don't believe this!" Berrick expostulated. "Do we look like bloody fascists?"

"What do fascists look like, eh? They don't have Hitler moustaches and wear jackboots. They aren't all shaven-headed morons with inferiority complexes. Some German

Nazis were aristocrats. Some were scientists or artists. I want to know what you are."

He spoke flatly, matter-of-factly. He turned to Hank.

"You've talked with them, Major Hansen. Your opinion?"

Hank looked at them. They were both ashen-faced.

"Frankly, sir. I'd shoot them."

"What?" Alan stood up, "I thought you were fighting these bastards. Now you seem to be acting like them!"

Berrick stayed put. "I wished we'd never looked at that bloody flat," he muttered.

The General looked at Hank.

"Happy?"

"Yessir!"

"Thank you, Major. Relax, gentlemen. You won't be shot. I was pretty convinced anyway, but the Major thinks you are all right."

"Is that why he advocated shooting us?" Berrick asked, bitingly, clenching his hands together to stop them shaking.

"Yes. You see, your average fascist tends to fall into two categories: one, he goes into furious condemnatory mood and damns democracy, Communism or whatever and spouts shit or, two, he starts to blub. You two did neither. So, you are either bloody good actors or you're telling the truth."

Alan sat down suddenly, the strength gone from his legs. "What happens now?" He asked. "Can we go home?"

"No. There are things that need doing and we don't have the manpower to do them. Or, rather, we didn't. Until now."

CHAPTER ELEVEN

Three weeks had passed since their terrifying meeting with General Hannah and much had happened in the meantime. Alan and Berrick found themselves crammed into a stinking railway carriage heading north with a bunch of very hard, silent men who eyed them disapprovingly. They all wore standard British Army uniform of khaki tunic buttoned to the neck, baggy britches and puttees above solid, hob-nailed boots. They had had their luxuriant hair cropped very short in the style of all armies since the previous century. Hank, now a Major in British uniform, rode in the carriage in front with the brass which included General Hannah, Colonel Wildfowle and two urbane officers whose backgrounds they would not discuss. All were, like them, from, "the other side of the veil" as they put it.

Alan watched the flat countryside pass by. Lincolnshire, perhaps, he speculated. It was hard to tell. All place names had been removed by the retreating army and they were unsure of their whereabouts. He tried to stretch out his legs. They were still stiff from the enforced fitness training Hannah had insisted they undertake. He could do more now than he would have dared consider possible barely a month ago. His only experience of military life had been as a military cadet at school. At least he had known the drill of the square-bashing and saluting. Luckily, Berrick had had a similar schooling, so the emphasis had fallen on getting fit and learning to shoot accurately. It seemed that there had been some argument at a higher level about what type of rifle they should carry. Should it be the Lee Enfield .303 or the regular Nato 5.56mm lightweight SA-80 rifle of their own dimension? While argument raged, they practised with each. With only two days to go the decision was made to carry both. The Lee Enfields plus 30 rounds per man would be carried on their persons. The more modern rifles and ammo would accompany them in whatever transport they obtained at the railhead to which they were heading and at which they would disembark or 'de-train' as Hank put it. They would then make their way to the target. They had not yet been briefed as to the whereabouts of the target.

For long, uncomfortable hours, they steamed north, stopping only to relieve themselves and take food and the inevitable tea,' char and wads, ducks?' as a helpful lady asked at Leeds scene of the much-vaunted 'victory' of only a few weeks ago now. The evident friendliness of the English people they met made it plain that they were not seen as traitors to their country. Despite the long hours, conversation with their companions remained limited, nonetheless.

"Can't talk, see?" Said a Welshman. "We won't be 'yere for evah. This is Official Secrets Act, boy." He then lapsed into meaningful silence.

The others talked about past experiences and various conflicts - the Falklands for one or two older men, the Gulf for a number of others and Northern Ireland for all of them.

"At least we can shoot the boogers this time," one man groused, "it'll be hunter an' hunted. This time we'll be the hunters."

"Aye," a clearly Scots voice replied, "none o' this lookin' over yer shoulder an' feelin' the cross-hairs on the middle o' yer back a' the time."

"Too fuckin' true, Jock. We can nail these fuckers good an' proper!"

"An' then hame tae Pirbright -"

"An' shag Julie, the Soldiers' friend and get fookin' pissed - right lads?"

There was a chorus of agreement and the frost thawed a little. Harris, a Corporal with no regimental tags, like the rest, look cynically at the two newcomers.

"So - we've seen you two gettin' sorted out by the PTIs on the assault course. You don't look Army, though. Who, or what, are you?"

The next couple of hours were taken up by Alan and Berrick telling their tale. Initial disbelieving looks changed when they told the desperate Zeppelin fight and the sinking trawler.

"By fook - you didn't coom the tourist route did you, son?" Asked the square-faced Sergeant. He looked at the other nine of his section, sitting smoking and listening in the way that soldiers do when they are on their way into action. Listening and chatting to stop themselves brooding over the fighting to come.

"I reckon we've got a couple of virgins here, me lads. No, don't worry - I don't mean that sort," he explained leaning aside to Alan and Berrick, "I mean you ain't seen action. You might do summat stupid that could endanger my lads. Corp! You look after these two, keep their heads down, let 'em do somethin' useful, but keep them out of our hair. They'll thank you for it and by fook, I'll thank you for it." He looked at them with a professional eye, "You may think you're light on your feet, but you'd be like a herd of elephants if we've got a silent night mission to undertake. You will be on the rearguard detail. Keep your eyes peeled and lay low. Don't think it's not important. It could mean the difference between life and death if we're to escape after the action. If you screw up an' we're outflanked, we're all dead. It's not a holiday. If you fook up, we're food for the crows, so listen an' I'll give you some gen to learn what to do." He then gave them a point-by-point plan of how to do the job as the train rattled and steamed its way through the icy darkness outside.

Grey dawn was barely lightening the eastern horizon when the train juddered, clanked and creaked to a metallic halt. God alone new where they were. Alan awoke to find himself cuddled up against Berrick who still lay oblivious, his mouth open, peaked khaki cap over his eyes.

"Rise and shine, sleepin' beauties," the Sergeant bellowed. Other compartment doors were being opened noisily and a stream of regulars were filing into the corridor, glancing incuriously at this small group. Just another section , no different from their own. For they were also British soldiers . They wore badges of regular line regiments. The Green Howards, the Glorious Glosters, Yorkshire Light Infantry. Alan stifled a yawn and turned to the Sergeant.

"There must be a hell of a lot of British troops on this side, surely?"

"Aye. And more every day. James ain't popular, an' he's less so every day. People see the way it's goin', but, they don't know the half of it," he turned a humourless eye, "do they?"

They were in Border Country. The train had got as far as Lockerbie. Berrick recognised

this town. It looked undamaged by war but different from his recollection. The warm stone was a pleasant change from raw brick and blackened English cities scarred by industrial filth.

151

Here, the air was crisp and clean. The Sergeant drew them up in a line and marched over towards the General and the other officer with a parade-ground precision. His arm quivered like a spring as he snapped his hand to the brim of his peaked cap in salute.

"All present an' c'rrect, sah!" He bellowed.

"Thank you, Sergeant. Carry on."

The General's salute was relaxed like his demeanour. No one was fooled. This man was a fox, ruthless and devious. He had the charm of the old style officer and the deadliness of the cobra. He stood watching as the Sergeant formed the men into two ranks and stood them at ease before moving among them and handing out badges and shoulder-flashes.

"Each of you will sew these 'ere shoulder-flashes on neatly and wear these cap badges from 'ere on. You are the first Royal Leicesters. In case you are asked any awkward questions, we are retiring north in good order after bein' cut off from our pals in a skirmish with the Bosche at Carlisle. We sustained no casualties. We captured an enemy lorry with munitions an' are perceedin' to Perth to rest an' reform in a new regimental formation. Are you listenin', Bates?"

A private snapped to attention. "Yes, Sergeant."

"Well, you better be, son, or someone's goin' to stick that lovely antique rifle up your ARSE in another minute! D'you hear me?"

"Yes, Sergeant."

Glowering, the Sergeant continued. "We will take whatever form of transport we can obtain to make our way north pdq. Right now, that's Shanks's pony. All right? Then get on with it."

It was almost 9am when, wearing their new unit insignia and having consumed the inevitable 'char and wads' - or banjoes as the soldiers called them - they formed up and began their long march north, an antique lorry puttering on ahead.

Footsore and exhausted, Berrick and Alan slumped down by a small stream two days later when a rest break was called. They felt like a retreating rather than an advancing force by this time. The dust and dirt from the unmetalled roads had turned them all into scarecrows.   Moving as they were through the less populated parts of lowland Scotland, they had failed to find any means of transport other than their own feet.   The lorry had coped surprisingly well, chugging along ahead of them but its fuel was now dangerously low.   They hoped to find petrol in a nearby town which their maps indicated lay over the next low ridge of hills.

Alan lit up one of the Army-issue cigarettes that they had each received every day with their bully beef and bread. He blew the smoke out idly while Berrick cleaned his finger nails with a penknife.   There was little conversation.   The men rested or took a drink from their water flasks and smoked a fag.   There was an air of despondency about them.

"What the fuck are we doin' 'ere, anyway?"   One man muttered looking up into the dull, overcast sky. No-one replied.

Alan glanced at Berrick without comment and took another puff, his brow furrowed in puzzlement. He cocked his head and looked around.

"What's that?"

"What's what?"

"That noise. Listen."

They both looked about, searching the heather-clad hills for the source of the sound. Others who were not resting seeing them look up, nudged each other and nodded in their direction.

"There it is again, you know - I know it sounds crazy but -"

A grey, streamlined shape flipped over the hills to the north and zipped overhead. Seconds later, a loud roar deafened them.

"Christ! A jet! A Phantom!"

Alan looked appalled. "They've begun - and we're too sodding late!"

Everyone scattered and dived for cover. A second later, another Phantom roared overhead and disappeared in seconds with a further sonic boom. They lay in the bracken, shaken.

"Form up!" It was the General. He was visibly agitated. He turned and spoke urgently to Colonel Wildfowle and the two Lieutenants. A map in his hand was scrutinised. The Sergeant was called over and a brief council-of-war took place while the men waved midges away which, despite the season, still survived, even in the depths of winter. With a crisp salute, the Sergeant trotted back.

"Right, you lot! Gather round!"

They settled in a group, kneeling or sitting in the springy heather, some still anxiously scanning the sky for signs of any other hostile aircraft as the Sergeant unfolded a map of the area. "We're here." He said, pointing to an area surprisingly far north. "And here is the railway line to Perth. From there, we can get another train to St Andrews. It seems our pals have decided to use the site of what we know as RAF Leuchars. That's a guess - but those boys were flying from the north-east, not from the north. If you look at this map, you can see how we get there. A guess or not, the General feels that this is the place to aim for.

"You said we can get 'another train' at Perth, Sergeant," said the Scot, "are you aiming to hold one up to get us there first?"

"No, son," said the Sergeant grinning, "we're going to stick out a thumb and hitch a ride."

He was true to his word. With little delay, they shouldered their packs and rifles and marched two miles across rough moorland to a point where the railway line was crossing open country and turned the lorry south. For an hour or more, everyone sat around and chatted. One or two wildlife buffs spotted the odd hare or grouse. One of them claimed he had seen a fox and another a golden eagle, though the general opinion on that was one of scepticism.

At noon, they were contemplating brewing up some tea, when a distant whistle alerted them to the train's approach.

"All right, lads. Easy's the word. I'll stand on the line. If the train don't halt, I'll leap off and Henderson will drive the lorry onto the track and scarper. In the meantime, shoulder arms. We don't want to alarm the Servants of the GWR, do we?"

He squinted down the track. In the distance, an engine hove into view two miles down the line. It was pulling eight carriages or more.

"Let's hope they ain't carrying any real first Royal Leicesters on board," Berrick commented drily.

"Don't even think about it." Alan muttered.

They shouldered their rifles and stood up creakily. Their breeches were damp and they were decidedly cold. All around them, men were stamping their feet and slapping their arms around themselves like cabbies.

Gradually, the train approached, causing flocks of birds to fly up in alarm. The scene was idyllic. The brown moorland and bare hills were lit by a deceptively warm-looking winter sun. The sky was blue with billowing white clouds that wafted majestically overhead in a gentle breeze. As it approached, they could see the train was gleaming colourfully, its engine bright green, the carriages a chocolate brown and cream. Steadily, its engine chuffed up the gradient towards the point where Sergeant stood four-square in the middle of the track, right hand held high, the Union Flag held aloft in his left.

Slowly, the engine reduced power, sliding to a stop within feet of the Sergeant's gleaming ammunition boots. They watched him walk round to chat to the driver. The conversation was protracted as the Sergeant gesticulated and pointed to them several times.

"Christ," muttered the Scots soldier, "what's he daein' - tellin' him his life story?"

Whatever the story might have been, at length it was evidently accepted and the Sergeant waved them forward.

"All aboard, lads. Next stop Perth!"

The soldiers loaded the rifles on board plus ammo and several long boxes they lifted from the lorry whose purpose was not explained. The men piled on board also and with a whistle and a screeching of wheels, the steam engine began to gather way. There appeared to be no other passengers on board.

They all gathered together in a saloon carriage, ornately furnished and with a restaurant car attached. The General detailed a man to attend to tea and coffee plus cooking up a decent hot lunch from the excellent larder while they held a council-of-war.

"All our intelligence points to a lack of any reorganisation of the Stuart Government's forces. We know that the high technology of the fighter bombers they now have plus a suspected force of about battalion-size which we must assume are trained mercenaries could wipe out the Franco-German armies here and now. However, the King has no real control anymore. The tail is wagging the dog. The mercenaries must have held back until now to dictate their terms, so the Government has no real power left to contend with.

Hot tea and coffee were served with bacon and eggs and masses of freshly-buttered bread. When they had finished, the General swallowed the last of his coffee before speaking to them.

"We'll be in Perth in an hour and a half. Grab some shut-eye meantime. When we get there, we may need to commandeer another train, if we can't simply use this one."

Most of them were too keyed up by now to think of sleep. They played cards and smoked or gazed out of the window in idle curiosity at the countryside they were passing through. There were men working in the fields with horse-drawn ploughs while flocks of hungry birds descended on the freshly-turned earth in a search for juicy worms. Small towns came and went. Some were dominated by tall, grimy factory chimneys still belching black smoke into the clear, blue sky. Nearly every house they passed had a small column of smoke issuing from its chimney. Indeed, the very smuts and glowing cinders being blown hither and thither from the great behemoth which drew them noisily ever deeper into Stuart-held territory epitomised the steam-powered time into which they had been delivered.

They were getting used to boredom and inaction by now, although everyone was fretting.

"It's like the Task Force to the Falklands," the Sergeant commented "Bloody weeks getting there after frantic preparations and, then, BANG! You're in the thick of it!"

In the event, the arrival in Perth showed the extent to which the general security situation had deteriorated. They had seen isolated bodies of men marching hither and thither on their way north. There appeared to be no sense of panic, but, equally, no apparent overall control. In the town itself people went about their usual business and a few soldiers could be seen at the station.

When they eventually pulled to a halt, the General went to see the Station Master and Berrick wandered over to the kiosk to buy a paper.

"That'll be a tanner," said the comfortable-looking lady behind the counter, handing him the Dundee Courier. Its front page was nothing but advertisements, much as the London Times had been until three decades earlier.

"So, what's happening? Are we winning?" He asked with a friendly grin.

"Who knows, son? It isnae our war."

"Don't you care?" He asked.

"Ach, the Kings a'right, but he isnae in charge, is he?"

Pondering the accuracy of the comment, Berrick strolled back hearing idle conversations from other people on the concourse. Obviously, things were coming apart. People didn't believe the tales of super weapons with which the regime was endeavouring to bolster its flagging popular support. They had no faith in the Government any more. It would soon be every man for himself. He shook his head. Then would come the time for these mercenaries. No doubt they'd soon be reading about the effects of the Phantoms on the inferior Franco-German Army. Once they had shown their hand, the Stuart cause was dead. Indeed, it seemed moribund already, at least as far as the people were concerned. As to the soldiers from this time....he grimaced. They wouldn't stand a chance. There would be total massacres. Nothing now stood between the mercenaries and outright victory except for them. One carriageful of modern-day soldiers. How in hell could they - a puny force at best - expect to defeat this potent enemy?

He was still musing when he reached their train. He heard the sound of an approaching altercation .

"But I have no authority, sir! I beseech you to wait!" It was a soft man's bleat. The Station Master was trotting at the General's heels, wringing his hands. The General stopped suddenly, his bright eyes snapping dangerously at the anxious bureaucrat.

"No sir. The safety of the Realm is endangered. You have seen my authority. This train must take us. I don't care if your superior, wherever he may be, is unavailable. Doubtless, enemy forces are in control wherever he is anyway." He swung round aggressively. "If you don't do as you are told, I'll have you damn well shot - now!"

The Station Master positively wilted, especially when two or three of the special forces contingent appeared at the doors of the train casually cradling Lee Enfields in their hands. Making a desperate decision, the terrified little man nodded his head several times, swallowing heavily.

"Of course, General. Go ahead. My apologies, sir. I'll signal ahead for you."

"Do it," the General gritted, turning away and climbing aboard the forward compartment. "Dundee!" He snapped at the driver. "D'you have steam up?"

"Aye, sir."

"Then, don't hang about. Move!"

They didn't get to Dundee, however. It had not been the General's intention. There was, oddly, no direct line. They had to go south and link up with the Edinburgh line which took some hours. It was early evening when, with a splendid sunset over the Tay, the train halted at Tayport and they disembarked. They were still several miles from their destination. Everyone had rested on the journey, and despite an interest in visiting local hostelries for liquid refreshment, the General had gathered them round.

"Dawn is the best time for us to hit these people. We'll arrange transport locally. We'll do it quietly -"

"Sir?"

"What is it, Sar'nt Stock?"

"Why couldn't we use the train? It could take us to St Andrews, after all."

"It could have. Equally, it wouldn't be scheduled. These people aren't total idiots, don't forget. They won't be sitting singing songs around a campfire. They will be on full alert right now.

For one thing the locals must be wondering about the strange aircraft flying around. And for another, they will be aware that they've got opponents that are trained soldiers, albeit they are the best part of a century behind us in technology, but that wouldn't stop them from sending a small naval expeditionary force up the coast to find out where the Phantoms are based. These people are probably ex-military. They're trained. They'll have their eyes peeled. We need to sneak up on them."

"How should we go about getting transport then, sir?"

It was Henderson, the Scot. It was a reasonable question.

"With this." The General pulled out a small purse which clinked in his hand. "It's coin of the Realm. Sovereigns. Gold, in other words. Folk around here are conservative. They don't hold fancy views. Loyal soldiers requiring transport and prepared to pay for it will be accorded a positive response. Go to it!"

Indeed, if a ramshackle farm lorry, still redolent of the stink of the sheep it had been carrying two days ago could be regarded as suitable transport, they were, indeed, in luck. The Sergeant, disgusted by the manure-strewn vehicle ordered its immediate cleaning with soap and water. Not carbolic or any other kind of antiseptic, however, as the smell would carry.

"A soldier might wonder why a farm lorry smelt like a gents' toilet. Sheep and pigs ain't too choosy about that kind of thing. It might raise one or two questions too many."

It was dark by the time the sweating, cursing soldiers finished and Sergeant was satisfied.

"Very well, Sergeant. Carry on. We'll RV at the village of Balmullo outside St Andrews. We've found a car to get us there. We'll take two of your men - a driver and a guard. You follow on discretely. So, put the tarpaulin up to hide the men from curious glances."

An antique motor pulled up and a well dressed man stepped out.

"Here you are, sir. It's my pride and joy, so I'd appreciate getting it back in one piece. If King and Country call they will always get a loyal response from an old Black Watch hand."

"Much appreciated, Mr Smith. You look like a seven year man."

The gentleman laughed softly. "Indeed I was, sir. I was a captain. Caught a ball in the thigh from a Pathan at the Khyber. They invalided me out. Still get my pension, though. There you are General, I've filled her up. She's a good runner," he smiled engagingly. "By God, I wish I could come with you!"

The, General tapped the side of his nose. "Less said," he murmured.

"Of course, sir. Forgive me. Goodnight, then. And, good luck" The helpful civilian limped off into the night, pleased to feel part of some great enterprise and proud that he had refused any proffered payment.

"The old school," the General commented, softly, almost to himself, "you don't see too many in our day." He shook his head, coming out of whatever reverie he had been in. "Very well. C'mon lads. Don't dilly-dally."

He and Hank climbed into the leather upholstered Riley and MacRae and Freeman piled in too. The driver and guard muttering softly about "bloody Wells Fargo" before chugging off in an acrid cloud of petrol fumes.

"All aboard, lads!" The Sergeant sang out, "next stop sunny Blackpool by the sea!"

"I don't bloody think!" A voice at the back muttered darkly.

It had been nigh on seven pm when they left and it was nearly nine when they juddered into Balmullo, a small, one street village in North East Fife with a cargo of stiff, bad tempered soldiers on board. All had headaches from the foul exhaust fumes, but universal relief at their arrival made them forget the discomfort and their headaches. When they found that the General had organised a meal and a pint of ale for each man at the inn a mood of good cheer replaced their grumpiness.

MacRae, Freeman, Sergeant Stock, Thwaite, the taciturn Welshman and the others whose names they hadn't yet learned, tucked into steak pie and mashed tatties with gusto before supping their pint with relish. In a land in which beer was still the local product, they found the local unhopped brew was potent and satisfying.

"By 'eck the Real Ale Society'd vote this Brew of the Month," commented a small, ferrety looking man the others called Sparks.

"That's an idea," Berrick ruminated, "just think of it, trade between dimensions. British exports to the Britain. Kind of strange."

"I'll second that," Hank replied, "we've a lot of what they call microbreweries in Portland and Seattle. Same sort of beer. Lots of body, no fizz. Most Americans still drink, cold, gassy piss, but what you call real ale is making quite an impact these days. When you drink this you can see why."

He took another pull at his pint.

"Enjoy it while you can, lads." The General appeared silently and studied his watch, " I have arranged accommodation here. Now, it's 2200 hours, now. We'll be up at 0500 and off at 0530. You know your teams? You two gentlemen?" He looked and Berrick and Alan who nodded vigorously. "Good. This beer is your lot. Section leaders come with me. I need to cover our way out."

The others sat in silence or chatted idly over a cigarette while they were gone. Apart from themselves, the inn was empty. The General had insisted that the inn be off limits for civilians that night and the locals had complied without protest in an old world acceptance of authority.

After a few minutes more, they finished their pints in the golden light of the gas lamps, yawned and quietly headed off to bed.

CHAPTER TWELVE

It was before dawn when they were aroused by the Sergeant. He roared out the command to rise and shine and, sleepily, they tottered out of bed. Henderson passed them on his way to freshen up.

"Three things a man needs in the morning - a shit, a shower and a shave - I reckon we'll get two of them."

"What won't we get?" Berrick yawned.

"A shower, and what're the bets the shave will be with cold water?"

He was right. At least their brief breakfast was satisfying. The landlord had made porridge. Hot, with plenty of salt and fresh milk, it gave them full bellies. Fresh coffee, strong and dark woke them up, banishing the cobwebs of sleep.

Promptly, at 0530 hours they formed up outside the inn for a brief inspection by the General.

"Very well, men. We'll issue the NATO rifles and ammunition. Henderson, Freeman. You two handle the first Carl Gustav. Sparks and MacRae, you have the second. Each of you will be issued with four grenades.

"It's an hour till dawn. It'll take us half an hour to get close enough to launch our attack. The whole action should take no more than twenty minutes. We are after the aircraft, remember. The men only matter if they get in our way, but if you see a pilot, shoot to kill. Those men are as much a key to this affair as the Phantoms.

"When we have completed the action, we will retire to the sea directly north of the airfield. There we will be picked up by the light cruiser, Prinz Eugen and taken to London. Questions?"

There were none, however. Each man was issued with a rifle, ammunition and four grenades, before boarding the lorry, they trundled off into the dark.

In the darkness, the men were silent, though a number smoked. The noisy engine would have drowned out conversation, but Berrick worried that it telegraphed their presence to the airfield. As they neared Leuchars, however, he noticed that there were other farm vehicles about. He had forgotten how early country folk start their day. His worry lessened somewhat. Even so, the thought of the action to come loosened his bowels and was glad he was at the rear of the lorry as he slowly vented wind to relieve the pressure. The chill draft blowing through the flimsy tarpaulin dissipated the odour without offending the others.

They slowed to a halt and the Sergeant climbed down with Henderson, Freeman and two other men before the lorry jerked forward once more to continue further round the open site of the airfield. As a faint, false dawn reduced the darkness slightly, the two large hangers which housed the Phantoms resolved themselves from the field in which they stood. A long, straight stretch of tarmac gleamed wetly as it disappeared into the gloom. There was no visible defensive perimeter. For agonising minutes, they continued on their way. The General's car was nowhere to be seen.

At length, the motor ground to a halt in an isolated copse of trees six hundred yards or so from the field. The corporal

166

jumped down and, silently, the others joined him as did the driver.

"You two stay here with Wilson. When we come back our password is 'felix'. Y'got that?"

"Yes, corporal." They replied in unison.

"Right, anyone who comes near and doesn't know it, let 'em 'ave it. No prisoners. Okay?"

"Yes, Corporal."

"What is it, Wilson?"

They heard the snarling before they saw the patrol. Berrick realised why there was no perimeter fence. They had regular teams of guards with Dobermans to fend off curious locals. They kept silent as the patrol went by. There were two men, each with a pair of dogs. It seemed that the darkness of the copse obscured the lorry from view. A strong smell of aero-engine fuel permeated the air and Alan realised that the dogs must have found it confused their sensitive nostrils.

Tensely, they watched, crouching among the trees until the patrol melted into the dark. They all breathed more easily and the corporal glanced at his watch.

"Okay. Ten minutes to H Hour. Move out. You three keep watch. We're comin' out this way so I don't want any itchy trigger fingers. Understood?"

"Yes, corporal."

The small team left in absolute silence, their faces streaked with camouflage paint, their movements economical. They were watchful and stealthy as they moved out. One moment they were there, the next they weren't.

It was nail-biting tension for the three rear-guard men. Wilson detailed them to watch in the three directions away from the base. They lay on their bellies on the cold, wet grass while time crawled. Apart from the occasional sound of a breeze in the trees and the odd distinct lowing of cattle, there was nothing to indicate that this night was different from any other.

A sudden, brilliant flash lit the sky.

"Don't look!" Wilson snapped. "You'll lose your night vision."

Obediently, they looked towards their front, but the flickering light illuminated the entire countryside. A sudden, fierce wind tore at them as the roar of the explosion rent the night air. Then, another spectacular blast bigger than the first raised a huge flare making the whole are area bright as day.

"God Almighty! What was she carrying?" Wilson exclaimed.

"Not nukes?" Alan asked fearfully.

"If she was, son, we wouldn't be talkin' about it. Keep your eyes peeled for the patrols."

Again, a shockwave hit them, bending the grass and trees with its passage. They could clearly hear the sound of small arms fire and another, smaller explosion.

"Grenades," Wilson commented, "they've met resistance."

There came a series of whumph! whumph! whumph! explosions, but no great flashes as before. The fierce fires from the first two catastrophic bangs were building up though the smoke was being blown eastwards, away from them.

"What were those?" Alan asked.

"I think we've just fucked up their runway, just in case any of their birds are away on a hunt. They'll see the fires if they are, but where else will they have to land? Remember when the Vulcans bombed the airfield at Port Stanley all those years ago? They were denying the Argies landing. O'course they filled the holes in pdq but here I reckon they've less chance of doin' so if I know our cunning leader." He cocked his head.

"Keep yer heads down. Someone's comin'. Your side, Berrick!"

Squinting through his sights, Berrick saw a couple of shadowy figures running towards him. In the flickering back light of the fires, he couldn't make out any distinguishing features. They could have been wearing khaki or red for all difference it made. Both carried weapons and were scouting about anxiously.

"Wait!" Breathed Wilson.

The two looked to their left. They were about one hundred metres away.

"Are they ours?" Berrick asked softly.

"I don't know - wait!"

The leading man took something from his pocket and lifted it. Wilson lifted his night glasses to his eyes and squinted through them.

"He's using a walkie-talkie! They're enemy! Shoot! Now!"

The brief training they had received clicked into place. Berrick lined the two men in his sights . A drop of sweat trickled down his brow and ran into his eye. Pausing, he blinked, and rubbed it with the back of his hand. He felt a tremor of uncertainty as he settled again to take aim. A sudden change of wind direction brought him the sound of dogs snarling. Christ! He had seen them - they were Dobermans. His uncertainty vanished as he squeezed the trigger on automatic fire. Two brief bursts of four or five rounds a piece and the two men were scythed down. The dogs, now freed, turned, sensing the origin of the fire that had killed their masters and sped towards the three with their fangs bared. Breathing in a controlled manner and measuring the distance, Berrick exhaled slowly, sighting on the leading dog. He chose the single shot option. Crack! He swung across to the second dog, now barely twenty metres away as the first crumpled headlong into the long grass its skull shattered by the bullet. His next shot missed. The dog was on him. Its sharp teeth jarring on the bone of his upper left arm. He rolled, having now lost his rifle as Wilson and Alan rose to move to his aid. Rolling with agony as the frenzied beast tried to get at his throat, he tucked his chin down, yanking desperately at the bayonet clipped to his belt. It was buttoned down. With his injured arm he rabbit-punched the dog in the throat hard. It yelped and staggered back for a second before recovering and leaping forward in a blurred lunge for the kill. He felt the button pop and rolled to one side tugging at the haft of the blade. The dog, furious to have missed turned in fury and leapt, mouth agape giving a single surprised yelp as the blade stabbed through its soft throat and windpipe, deep into its brain, the momentum carrying it past Berrick, tearing the bayonet from his grasp and widening the gash in the Doberman's throat. The dog thrashed briefly, blood foaming at the mouth, its dying eyes rolling in disbelief at its death in the trampled, long wet grass.

"You alright, son?" Wilson was kneeling beside him looking in concern at the dark blood spreading from the torn, exposed flesh on Berrick's left arm.

"Yeah. I reckon so. I can move my fingers and - ouch! - flex the elbow. It's bloody sore though."

"Okay. Alan - keep watch!"

Swiftly and expertly, Wilson cut away the sleeve and noted the wounds on his upper arm. He swiftly tended to the injury, applying a field dressing. As he tied it off, he looked up and grinned. "You'll live, son. Nothin' much damaged there. You'll have a stiff arm for a coupla days, that' s all."

"Here come our lads," Alan murmured.

"Are you sure it's them?"

"No doubt about it. The General's in the lead. Couldn't mistake him. There are only six of 'em though. Must've lost men."

Seconds later, the General and his remaining unit staggered in calling 'felix' as they appeared.

"Is the lorry ready?"

"Sir!"

"Okay. All aboard. We need to go."

"No others to come, sir?" Asked Wilson, supporting the General who was visibly swaying on his feet.

"No. Lost three men. All dead. Never mind me. Start her up!" The General's voice was low. He appeared badly hurt, but ignored help, except for a hand to climb up with the others in the back. Wilson ran to the cab and started the ignition. With a roar, the engine caught and with a lurch, they were on their way, lurching and bouncing over the rough track, north to the sea.

In the murky light of an overcast dawn, the airfield could be clearly discerned. It was a scene of utter devastation. The two hangers continued to blaze fiercely. The runway was deeply pitted with craters rendering it useless either for take off or landing, had there been any aircraft to do so. Bodies lay scattered in the grass, some stretched out as though asleep. Others lay contorted in the rigor of agonised death. One or two bewildered survivors wandered around like lost souls or sailors adrift on an uncharted sea. An oily smoke blew fitfully over the scene and obscured it from view. The dark waters of the Firth of Tay heaved and shouldered their way towards the North Sea and sea birds hung on the wind or wheeled and cursed as the lorry ground to a halt by a small stretch of scrubby beach. Wearily, the smoke-blackened soldiers climbed out of the lorry. Gently, they lifted the General down. He was weak now, and the bleeding, small though the amount seemed to be, showed that he had been wounded in the chest.

"How is he, Corp?" Asked Wilson.

The Corporal, who doubled as medic shook his head. "Bad. If he manages to last, we can only hope the Prinz Eugen's doctor will help. There's extensive internal bleeding. He is strong but..." his voice trailed off.

"What time is the RV?" Hank was barely recognisable, his hair and face burnt by the fierce fires they had ignited. So blackened was he, that Alan only recognised him by his accent.

"Any minute now, sir. Are you alright? You look a sight."

"I feel it. I'm okay, just dog-tired like the men. I don't like being exposed like this, though. Set three men on point. Just in case."

"Sir!" The Sergeant detailed Berrick, Alan and Wilson again, being the freshest. They clattered up the rocks and took up defensive positions looking south and west. The countryside looked still and peaceful except a point partially hidden by trees, from which a black pall of smoke emanated. Lifting his

172

binoculars, Wilson scanned the scene. To the east, St Andrews looked serene, a little, walled medieval town with spires and famous golf links. Inland, isolated villages and hamlets. The only sign of activity was a couple of antique fire engines moving towards the airfield.

"Someone's seen the smoke. Only the Fire Brigade, though."

A faint shout came to them from the beach, whipped away by the stiff sea-breeze so only the sound could be made out. They looked down. Hank was waving at them, pointing. They followed the direction of his pointing finger and saw a sight for sore eyes. It was an immense grey battle cruiser rounding the headland, a German flag flapping at her stern. Wilson raised his glasses again.

"It's Prinz Eugen. Praise the Lord! There's hope for the General yet."

CHAPTER THIRTEEN

Berrick yawned and rolled over. A deliciously languorous relaxation was emphasised by the comfortable motion of the great fighting ship they had boarded only hours ago. In a half-awakened state, he reviewed the situation. For the first time in weeks, he was not in a position of stress. He had survived the journey in the airship and the subsequent sinking of the fishing smack. The rescue by the German battleship had introduced him to the realities of this curious world by introducing him to Hank. Then, there had been their brief sojourn in Plymouth, the meeting with the General and their subsequent training.

The most recent experience of the action at Leuchars seemed like a dream, or, perhaps, a nightmare. Yet, here they were, the main threat of superior air power overcome, now on their way south to Germany or wherever. He relaxed at the thought that it was all over. He went back to sleep swiftly, lulled by the rhythmic sway of the dreadnought as it ploughed through wave crest and trough across the deep grey of the North Sea towards its destination.

In a cot on the other side of the cabin, Alan slept more fitfully. Images of the burnt men disturbed him. He thought of the General fighting for his life two decks below in the ship's hospital. In his imagination, dark storm clouds were rising.

When they awoke, it was afternoon. A meal in the mess with a group of curious, but friendly German sailors who spoke very little English was followed by a debriefing from Hank. They covered the success of the action before he moved the subject on.

"Okay, men. First: the General is recovering after an operation by the ship's surgeon. Luckily, he specialises in the treatment of trauma : wounds and injuries, that is. As of now, General Hannah is recovering in the hospital. We are under reduced steam in order the lessen the motion of the ship. It's always a danger.

Second: the British North Sea Fleet is lurking hereabouts. The Imperial German Navy has units moving north to cover us, however. We should meet up around 0200 tomorrow.

"Third: as regards the general scenario, things look good for our side. We have troops in Edinburgh and Stirling. There is stiff resistance near Glasgow, however and there are the makings of a battle royal there. Imperial High Command is of the opinion that the object of this resistance is to draw in a large number of Allied troops. Then, they think, the mercenaries will be launched against us.

"Now, we believe the Mercenaries are only about brigade strength, but Cortes won South America with - what - five hundred men? It's technology that wins battles these days. Look at the Gulf War. We pasted the Iraqis before our troops even moved in. We don't expect anything like that level of input by the mercenaries . They don't need it. We reckon they may have a few tanks, Chieftains perhaps, and rocket launchers plus sophisticated gear that can target accurately. Chobham armour will deflect anything we can throw at them right now. Our men use antique trucks at best to transport supplies. The men march or go by train. They'll use APCs which are also armoured. They may have lost their air superiority, but they don't really need it. They can cut through the Franco-German armies like a hot knife through butter.

"Fourth and finally: our problem," he summed up, "is how we can overcome them. We are being reinforced by more men, but we don't have the means to get major items of equipment through our gateway. Dammit! We ain't even got a car through!" He looked frustrated, running his fingers through what little hair he had left. "We need ideas. Our intelligence gives up five, maybe six days before the balloon goes up, as you Brits say. Get your heads together and think." He glanced at his watch, "We reach the port of London at 0800. We'll have a conference when we dock. Dismissed!"

They sat on the quayside, Berrick on a crate awaiting uplift while Alan opted for a neatly-coiled pile of rope. They looked around. Vast areas of industrial warehousing advertised their world-wide trading links. Within a stone's throw were "Mulligan & Hearthew Calico", "Smith & Lefevre Cognacs and Fine Wines", "Great West Indian Trading Company" and so on. Upstream, the Tower of London and London Bridge could be seen.   Farther on, the smoke of the City made vision less certain, even on a sunny day like this one. However, St Paul's great dome could be distinguished as could other famous spires.

They smoked even though it was early in the day and thought things over. The chill soon drove them back aboard, however, for the sun cast an illusory warmth over the scene and the frost encrusting the box told the truth. It was bitter.

Back on board, they thawed out over a scalding mug of coffee apiece and mused.

"They can't get big stuff through," Hank said, "but the Mercenaries can."

"So, I reckon, we don't have time to find out where they come through."

"Evidently, so -"

"So, we have to suggest things that will be fast -"

"Like modern tanks and APCs?"

"Right. It needs to be powerful..."

"To cope with Chobham armour -"

"Amongst other things."

"Hmmm."

"Hmmm."

They talked for an hour or more until summoned to the Officers' Mess for a conference. Hank was more spruce than before. He had opted for a head-shave to obliterate the effects of partial hair loss. He was still rather blistered, but otherwise looked rested. The other survivors looked well. Wilson was chirpy. Thwaite was taciturn as usual. Henderson and MacRae forming a tight Scots duo said little. Sergeant Stock ran his finger round his collar, conscious of the discomfort of the studs at front and back which attached it to his shirt.

"Okay, men. We have a big problem. You know what it is. Any ideas?"

Sergeant Stock cleared his throat, "It seems to me, sir, that we need to have parts transferred through to this ... dimension... and assembled. If we get onto it fast, we could assemble our own APCs.... and tanks, even. There's no problem with shells and other ammo."

"Good point, Sergeant. We are doing that as we speak. Problem is," Hank scratched his head, "they won't be ready in time. It'll take a week, minimum, to assemble even half a dozen. Now, I know we have no idea how many tanks (if any) the Mercenaries may have, but we guess ten or twenty at least. Also, our portal is in this part of England and the battle is four hundred miles away in Scotland. We need to ship those mothers all that way over unmade roads. That increases the risk of engine failure, so they'll be late into action.

"What we need," he continued, "is something we can use in the right place in three days time."

He looked at the others. "Any other ideas?"

MacRae and Henderson looked up, Henderson deferring to his colleagues.

"We remember that the Yanks - sorry, sir - the Americans...."

"Don't worry about embarrassing me, MacRae," Hank grinned.

"No, sir. Sorry, sir. Anyway... in the Gulf, your guys used remote-guidance observation aircraft. Y'know the kindae thing. Like a kid's toy. You used 'em to watch the Iraqis. Well, we thought we could use an adaptation to do kamikazi attacks on the tanks and APCs - if they had enough explosives."

Hank sat up. "I like that, MacRae, Henderson. I like it a lot. Any other ideas, anyone?"

Berrick spoke in a quiet tone. Knowing he was in the company of professional soldiers, he was somewhat shy of their criticism.

"I seem to remember that the Japs beat our guys at the start of the war in the Far East by use of superior mobility. They bypassed our roads and strongpoints and attacked our rear by using troops on bicycles. It defeated us in Malaya despite our greater strength in numbers and armaments. It seems to me that the forces of the Franco-German armies are irrelevant to this conflict - that is, the one with the mercenaries - because they are totally outgunned and can easily be outmanoeuvred." He paused thoughtfully for a moment and then continued, "It seems to me that there are sufficiently potent armaments available to us either to knock out tanks or, at the very least, incapacitate them so that they are immobilised. A force of one hundred men armed with handheld missile launchers using cross-country motor bikes - the kind they use in motor-cross would be very difficult for tanks to deal with. They're very fast. They have a very small profile and they pack a hell of a punch. Let's assume a bad scenario of 50% losses. You still have fifty men picking them out and hitting their tracks at least and maybe destroying one or two. After all, isn't that what the American frontiersmen did to the British and Hessian forces in America during the Revolution? They used their rifles to pick off our troops at long distance. It caused considerable damage to morale and slowed up our columns. What we want to do here is the same. Slow them down till we can mount forces superior to theirs to attack them and, with any luck, tackle them at the other end to stop them getting more materiel through?"

Hank mused and looked at the others for their views. It seemed to strike a chord as nods from the others showed.

"The main problem is that we can't find out where they get their stuff from. I'll recommend the idea that you guys have come up with. They tie in with your "brass hats" on the other side more or less." Hank paused for a moment and looked squarely at them, "We have a different objective, however, gentlemen." There was a small ripple of interest around the room. The professional soldiers pricked up their ears and sat up to hear what had to come.

"It's pretty obvious. The whole campaign by the Mercenaries - there's no point in pretending that it has anything to do with the Stuarts - is dependent upon supply. They have the upper hand. We guess that their only real problems are a) finance and b) supply. Obviously b) depends upon a). If they have a large gate through to this dimension, it must be destroyed or captured. It's our task to find it.

"It seems obvious," he continued, "this gate is in Scotland, probably on the mainland. I don't see how it could be elsewhere. Equally, it's likely to be in the Lowlands, west of our territory."

"Glasgow," Hudson muttered. "It's a hell of a big place. Where do you look?"

"It may not be Glasgow. It could be one of the dozen towns nearby. We just don't know. But we have to find out. If we don't - even with your clever scheme - they could effectively annihilate the Franco-German Army. If they move south, we could be sunk. Understand this and listen good. If we don't beat these suckers, they could win this war, conquer Britain and Europe. My gateway in the States is small like the ones in England. Too small to do much in enough time to count. Also, America here is still basically New England. Most of the resources of the USA are west of there. Any effect there would be small."

In a small sign of his agitation, he lit a cigarette and puffed at it distractedly.

"If they can take over Europe, then this world and its resources are at their feet. Believe me, these guys make the

Nazis look like schoolboys. They don't want to conquer one world. They want to conquer two. If they win this battle, then chances are that they will infiltrate ours eventually. They could bomb, murder, intimidate and always have a safe haven to escape to."

"Jesus!" MacRae exclaimed. "Why the fuck are we the ones to do it?"

"Because we're here. Don't worry, we're shipping through troops, both Brits and Americans. They're comin' in by the score, but there's a subversive element at work. It's like Appeasement before World War II. People who won't or can't believe this is happening. There's too much pressure on our armed forces in the real world and they're cut to the bone. Also, there are too many freebooters with nasty right-wing views who don't have jobs. They're American extremists (Survivalists, they call themselves), British Fascists, Russian soldiers who haven't been paid for months or years, disgruntled white South Africans who want to have their land back with no blacks around at all. The list goes on and on. The truth of it is, it's gone beyond what we had originally thought. I haven't been hiding any of this from you, I only heard the news this morning."

Tiredly, he waved a flimsy at them, "This conflict may not just be confined to Scotland or even the rest of Britain. It's the world, boys. The whole goddam world."

Later, with a few hours to kill on shore, a small group of them, Stock, MacRae, Henderson, Wilson plus Alan and Berrick went uptown by tube. Despite the war it was business as usual in the sprawling metropolis.

"It's the largest city in the world in the here and now," Stock commented as the steam train lurched alarmingly round a bend as it headed towards Marble Arch. "It's like the movies, lots of ladies of easy virtue but no HIV. Even so," his voice was emphatic. "there's still syphilis an' gonorrhoea, so it's skins all around."

He drew a half dozen slim packs out and handed them around.

"Don't laugh, son," he said to MacRae who laughed to himself and raised a sceptical eyebrow, "if you don't 'ave one they'll give you one of theirs an' they're like bloody 'eavy dooty rubber tyres. You'll get more sensation usin' a bleedin' welly boot!" He cackled at his own humour before subsiding and looking at them more seriously.

"Listen. Any of you don't use this 'ere prophylactic an' you're on a charge - in our world, Get it? That means the stockade at best and Belfast at the worst. If you fancy 'aving the fuckin' Micks shooting yer balls or yer 'eads orf, that's up to you. An' that goes for you two an' all."

"Yes, Sergeant," Alan and Berrick nodded obediently. That threat was one at which they, at least, could raise a sardonic eyebrow.

A minute later the train pulled into the tube station. A stiff climb up a curving, iron staircase lead them out of the clinging smell of unwashed humanity. When they came out into the night air, however, they were glad of their heavy Army greatcoats. It was still bitingly cold, quite different from the London of their dimension.

Sergeant Stock sniffed the air.

"I can smell a pub, lads. Follow me!"

Like a nursery teacher leading her crocodile of five year olds the Sergeant ploughed across the road, causing a horse-drawn hansom cab to swerve and avoid them. A stream of cockney invective followed them into the steamy warmth of a low-beamed, homely English pub.

The locals were mostly middle-class and middle-aged. In the English fashion, they tended to ignore the incomers, concentrating on conversing with their own intimate circle or playing darts. One foaming pint followed another and the conversation became louder and more jovial. Alan was aware of the potency of the brew. It was a strong bitter from Kent, hoppy, as he had expected but lethal with men who hadn't had a drink for a month or more. He and Berrick still had their sea-legs in that department but the others were already well-oiled. As he watched them laugh uproariously at one of Henderson's tales from the NAAFI, he saw a young tough who had been drinking on his own finish his pint and saunter out. It was not his pinched, sallow face that drew Alan's attention, so much as the mode of leaving. It smacked of the surreptitious, as though he didn't want to be noticed, especially by them.

"Did you see that guy who just left, Berrick?"

"The skinny runt? Sure, why? What's on your mind?"

"Oh, nothing probably. Just something about the way he moved. No matter. I need a leak."

He stood up.

"Me too." Berrick joined him.

"Hey! Anyone know where the bogs are in this place?"

"Out the back, son," Stock answered, "watch out for any nice boys you might meet. That's where they have their love nests!"

The others laughed uproariously at the witticism as Alan and Berrick negotiated their way past various tables to the door at the rear of the pub. It was getting fuller now the evening was advancing.

Harry stood on a portly man's foot and apologised when he swore.

"Bloody soldiers! Why ain't you at the front?" He snarled.

" 'Cos we're back from the front." Alan replied belligerently, keeping going.

" 'ear that lads? 'E's back to front!"

"Christ! The wit of the drunk -" Berrick pushed the door open and stepped into the darkened yard.

"Where to?"

"Follow your nose," Alan advised, "an' make sure you don't step into something nasty."

Two or three minutes later they opened the door to go back into the now raucous and smoke-laden atmosphere. There was a real press of people to squeeze past.

"Must be half of London in here," grumbled Berrick, "I think we should find somewhere quieter."

"Bloody hell!" Alan yelled, "We'll need to do more than that!"

The reason for the press became suddenly apparent. A violent fight was taking place in the middle of the pub - and it was their lads who were in the thick of it. Sergeant Stock was staggering from a blow to the head from a bar stool which had split his scalp open. Blood flowed freely down his head as his protagonist dropped the stool and drew a vicious-looking knife from his belt. Alan deftly side-stepped MacRae who was pile-driving another crew-cut thug before him and grabbed a beer bottle by the neck. Without slowing his pace, he lifted it and cracked it hard onto the knife-wielder's skull. The man dropped like a stone. Something flew passed Alan's head, its passing breeze fanning his cheek. Startled, he turned. A man in a tight-fitting jacket with a waxed moustache grimaced and pulled another Japanese throwing wheel from his pocket. As he drew back his hand to throw again, a blur flashed past Alan's left shoulder and a bone-handled knife sprouted from the man's stomach. He doubled up, dropping the throwing wheel and fingering the knife jutting out of his belly, looked up in puzzlement. He mouthed an unheard question before sagging to the floor.

Berrick straightened from the deadly cast of the knife and yanked Alan smartly to one side as Henderson careered past from a haymaker he had taken on the temple. As the thug who had thrown the punch moved in for the finish, attention concentrated on the object of his attention, Berrick's size nine boot described a short upward arc into the man's groin. Screaming in agony as both his testicles caught the brunt of the British bootmaker's art in a steel-reinforced crushing, he fell to his knees, both hands clutching his privates and vomit spewing from his mouth. On balance again and finding the handy bottle still in his grasp, Alan smacked it hard against the thug's head, smashing the bottle and badly lacerating the man's scalp as he tumbled in a jumble of limbs onto the floor.

Almost as quickly as it started, it was over. Apart from Sergeant Stock's split head, they were only rather bruised. Around them lay one dead man still twitching, and six unconscious severely battered attackers.

"Move," said Henderson, "the cops will deal with this scum. C'mon sarge. Go, go go!"

CHAPTER FOURTEEN

It was dawn in the world from which Alan and Berrick had stepped mere weeks before. In the Cabinet Office of Number 10 Downing Street, the PM sat with a group of senior advisors. They constituted the Inner Cabinet, the Chief of the Armed Services, the Cabinet Secretary and Major Hank Stuyvesant.

They listened in silence to Hank's summary of the situation, their features tired from an interrupted night's sleep and rendered haggard now by the news he imparted. When he finished, the PM, a considerate man, when not defending his Government at the Despatch Box or before the all-seeing eye of the media pack, ordered coffee and sandwiches. He steepled his fingers in thought as the revivifying food and drink was brought in. A cup of strong coffee was carefully placed before him by the Butler who knew his dislike of food early in the day. As the trolley clinked its way out and the assembled personages, all male and all deeply worried, attacked the sandwiches or swallowed their coffee, the PM made time for himself by taking off his reading glasses and polishing them.

"You must be tired, Major."

" I'm okay, sir. I'm used to lack of sleep. Truth is, though, I spent most of yesterday sleepin' after the raid on Leuchars."

"I see you suffered burns."

"Nothin' to complain about, sir. Mostly superficial. "

Hank grinned. It made him seem younger. Even so, he looked tough dressed now in his civilian suit. Even the expensive

Saville Row tailoring could not hide the husky build of the career soldier.

"You have our sincere thanks for your gallant action, Major. Without the attack you and your men launched, God knows how things might have turned out."

The PM put his spectacles back on and took a sip of coffee and nodded in appreciation at the full flavour of the Mocha he favoured.

"Now, gentlemen, to business. We have notified the President of the report the Major has just given us. Autodictate has encrypted it via the terminal beside the Major's chair and it is, even now, being studied in textual form by the President and his advisors. We have a secure link with Washington. It's time we made contact."

He pressed a button on the table and glass shutters on the window closed, darkening the room. On the far side of the Cabinet Office, the wall retracted to left and right to reveal a large screen roughly six foot by six. As it lit up, a small group of men in their middle years could be seen in conference. The President, grey haired, though still with the vestige of youth in his chunky features sat behind his desk in the Oval Office.

"Good evening, Prime Minister."

"Good morning, Mr President. Do you have us on visual?"

"We do. I have been looking over the text of Major Stuyvesant's report. Major."

"Yessir, Mr President!"

Hank sprang to his feet at attention.

"Thank you, Major. At ease. Please sit down. This isn't a formal occasion. Good. Okay. I am proud of what you have done, Major. You and your men."

"Thank you, sir."

"We are all concerned at the scale of events as you describe them. Is it possible you could be mistaken? After all, the areas outside Europe you mention - Southern Africa, for example - are outside your area of empirical confirmation, are they not?"

"That's correct."

"How, then, d'you know that these people are actually in that part of the world?"

Hank looked thoughtful before he spoke. "Well, Mr President, let's say it's an educated guess, but no more than that."

"Thank you, Major. Prime Minister?"

"Mr President. May I suggest we speak privately?"

The President looked up his eyes seemingly locked directly onto the Prime Minister's. Wordlessly, he nodded and, unbidden, the advisors in each office arose and retired. Each remained silent until the last had left and they remained alone, face-to-face.

"Okay, Jim what is it?" The President asked, selecting a cigar from a silver-chased container on his desk. He lit it as he awaited an answer from his old friend.

"I think we have a mole, Ted. Are you clean at your end?"

"Checked and cleared immediately before this meeting and everyone checked before they came in. You?"

"Yes. Clean at this end." The PM cleared his throat before continuing, "We think we know the location in Scotland these mysterious people are using. Frankly, we're at a dead-end. When I say we think we know the location, what we mean is, we know roughly where they are in the other dimension or time-stream, call it what you will. All our enquiries at this end have come up with nothing. How about your end of things?"

"The same. Zip. So where does that leave us?"

"Up the creek if our boys can't sort these people out. Trouble is, we've only got rumour to go on. Prisoners captured by the Franco-German Army have been talking. They mention tanks - well, we haven't got any there and neither have they. The equipment all sounds like standard NATO issue. Obviously black market kit, probably bought from some arms dealer who's charged them an arm and a leg for it. The thing is - we're beat as to who these guys are and what they're after. They had the base at Leuchars and were flying out Phantoms. Not impossible when you think about it..."

"Shit, the Phantom's bin around for years. We had 'em in 'Nam, didn't we?"

"I think you did, so it proves my point. The equipment is pretty much up to the mark here. In our alternative time-stream, it's almost a century ahead. Devastating! It'd be the same with a handful of tanks. Mind you, one or two of our lads have been using their heads to think of ways of sorting them out.."

"That's good, Jim, as far as it goes, but I still don't know how these portals came to be in the first place. Can't we make them ourselves? "The President's expression was one of frustration. "If we could make one, we could make it big enough to get tanks through. As it is..."

The PM leaned forward decisively. The pressures of this business on top of another security scandal were clearly taking their toll on the President. Clear thought was hard when you had so many pressing matters of state to decide upon as it was.

"Ted - we have to move on both sides of the Pond. I understand that we have taken Edinburgh in the alternative time-stream. I've called up reserves, very discretely, to take over various duties in the military. Now that our boys have destroyed Leuchars, I don't see that air power is a significant factor in this conflict. Tanks are. The mercenaries (if indeed, they turn out so to be) have them and we don't know how. I'd like you to get satellites to watch all roads in Scotland for signs of large vehicles moving to any point where there seems to be no purpose in their going. They could be large container vehicles or even ships with loads which could contain tanks. Trouble is, we aren't sure that they are Western. With the Russians selling everything to anyone, they could be T72s for all I know. They'd still be bloody unstoppable. Can you do that for me?"

"Considerate it done, Jim. What else do you need?"

"Well, you'd be watching anyway, but we need to gauge the numbers they're getting through. How many tanks, guns and planes go through?"

"We are doing that. I'll keep you informed. You mentioned things we could do over here."

"Yes. I mentioned calling up reserves. I made an excuse that it's to free the Army of guard duties on military installations in Northern Ireland. As you know, we have had an increase in tension there recently. But we've enough troops to get by as it is. That means that I can spare two battalions of regulars to transfer. I'd like to ask you for the same number. Also guns - howitzers, rocket-launchers and all that, broken down to the smallest parts possible for reassembly on the other side -"

"But, if this is in the heart of Edinburgh, how are you going to explain it?"

The PM smiled tiredly. "Well, we have one advantage. There has been a recent increase in interest in Scotland as a venue for film companies. Also, as it's in the Old Town, it's not far from where the Military Tattoo is held annually. We can choose either or both options for an increased military presence. Covered trucks will come in full of men and supplies; covered trucks will leave later, empty, all this on a daily basis. Also, all locals out due to the need for a film company to make the place have verisimilitude for, say the forties or fifties. We don't need huge lorries so, if we resurrect as many as possible from mothballs and use them, we could lull people's concern.

I spoke to one of our men in the Heritage Ministry. He's scouting out a story for the media to swallow. We need an "Eagle Has Landed" type of story. One of your trusted movie directors would give added credibility if he were on site. He may even get a movie out of it courtesy of the Government."

The President blew a silent whistle. "I like it. That only covers the British end though."

"True. In the States, I suggest that you infiltrate a number of troops and specialists to set up Phase II. We need to take out the other centres of infiltration, if any. It'll be a long drawn-out process, so you'll need planes, tanks and ships. The gloves are off, Ted. You need to tell the Americans there to declare independence and get this thing off on a proper footing - and there's only one way - "

"Which is?"

"You'll have to get representatives of the British Government there to come over to our dimension and see what's in it for them to go it alone."

"No Boston Tea Party?"

"No. I think more of a Washington Soiree with trusted advisors and lots of smelling salts to help them recover from culture shock!"

Things were hotting up. After the attack at the West End Pub, apparently casual attacks were taking place on troops all over London. Half a dozen men were killed by stabbings or shootings. Over two dozen were seriously wounded. The Metropolitan Police were called in to investigate and, although unaware of the provenance of many of the soldiers attacked, were briefed as far as possible by General Hannah who greatly recovered after a period of rest in his own dimension.

"Gentlemen, we live in changing times as you are all well aware. I think it is fair to say that none of us greatly regret the passing of the old regime in favour of one which is, blessedly, free of corruption and more inclined to listen to the voice of people."

A chorus of "hear, hears" quietly concurred with this view.

"Now, you will be well aware of the recent phenomenon of isolated, but well-orchestrated attacks on some of our "special troops" by gangs of well-armed thugs. We, in the military, are convinced that these attacks are deliberately aimed by factions loyal to the Old King and that they are designed to create the maximum alarm and confusion to our cause. Let me add that we are aware of a build-up of technically superior forces in the Glasgow area which is aimed at the armies of our Franco-German allies with whom our own highly-selected troops will fight to cleanse us of the corrupt old regime. This could be a campaign designed to put us off balance. If they succeed and the suspected attack takes place without our men participating and you will understand that we are desperately concerned that there will be an escalation, these fiends may attempt a full-blooded attack on us. If they succeed, we may lose our chance of victory!"

Police vigilance increased and several small groups of thugs were successfully arrested and imprisoned without Habeas Corpus due to the War. Gradually, larger numbers of troops were coming through initially in England, while the scene was set in Edinburgh for a film set to be rigged at the Old Town site. Berrick and Alan were drafted north as early spring began to show signs of appearing. Crocuses were sprouting in Hyde Park and the open tops of omnibuses were now more popular with the public, at least when the sun shone.

General Hannah, no less, was there at Heston Aerodrome to see them off.

" Let's hope you can get our lads - and the Yanks - through. With them, we can crush the guttersnipes who are helping King James."

His brow furrowed as he held out a hand, "Thanks for your help, lads, even though we had to press you into service. You'll see it was all for the best."

They shook his hand and climbed onto the giant Zeppelin, grandly named the Prinz Georg. Here, the accommodation was sumptuous. No military vehicle this, but a plush, transatlantic model diverted from its usual Hamburg to Newark run for the use of senior German officers. As they slowly lifted off, a slight, blond man in an unusual sky blue uniform approached them.

"Messieurs? Let me introduce myself. I am *Capitaine Lebrun*, French Liaison Officer to the Imperial German Navy , who fly these technological marvels!"

They each bowed politely and shook hands. Lebrun politely offered them snuff which they equally politely refused, before they adjourned to a comfortable table by a window on the Observation Deck, to watch London disappear beneath them as they rose majestically to a height of five thousand feet. Smoke obscured most of the city, but they lifted into clear blue skies.

"I hope we don't get a visit from an unfriendly fighter," Alan commented dryly.

"Not a chance," Lebrun chuckled, curling his waxed moustache, "they have nothing in the air. Gentlemen, be assured. We are, as I believe you say in England, as safe as 'ouses."

"Aye," Berrick nodded, "we say that in Scotland too. But only when we're sure. And we're a sight more cautious than our English friends."

Lebrun was pleased to find that they were Scots. He recounted pre-war memories of a visit to Edinburgh, surprising them at the apparent amiability of Scots ladies and their evident susceptibility to Gallic charm.

Lebrun regaled them with tales of his conquests north of the border as they consumed a passable meal washed down with Alsatian wines and languidly watched the land pass slowly beneath them.

"D'you know," Lebrun asked, as they puffed at Cuban cigars and sipped cognac and coffee, "that these Zeppelins can cross the Atlantic in less than two days! *Incroyable*! Aeroplanes will never compete with that - or, if they do, you will be jammed so tight that you will be like cattle in a truck."

"You're right there, Lebrun. Just like cattle. No, this is the style to travel in," Berrick murmured, "comfortable, excellent cuisine and no jetlag."

Lebrun looked puzzled. "What is jetlag?"

Berrick came to, slightly. "Oh! Just a figure of speech. If you could fly across the Atlantic as fast as a rocket, you'd be there before you left, so to speak, because of the time difference. That's okay going west, but coming east you'd arrive at such a different hour that you'd be disorientated. Y'know, leave at lunch time and arrive five hours later and it's eleven pm. I mean you'd be ready for a cup of tea and it's bedtime. When you want dinner and feel tired it's five am-"

"Ye..s," Lebrun answered doubtfully.

"Berrick," Alan spoke in a friendly manner, "shuttup."

The journey north was leisurely, but not markedly so. They were due to land at three pm and by two they were crossing the Southern Uplands.

"Beautiful," Lebrun murmured looking at the heather covered hills and patches of forest which characterised the area. "So remote, untouched by Man."

"Don't you believe it, Lebrun," Berrick commented, "once this was all covered by the Caledonian Forest. The poor old Romans tried slogging through it. King Arthur fought the only battle we can actual attribute to a real location somewhere within it. It's all man-made."

A small movement below caught his attention. " Hey! Look! Down there - on the left. What's that?"

A small centre of activity could be discerned far below, but what it was could not be made out clearly. Lebrun called over a ship's officer.

"*Unteroffizier*? May I borrow your binoculars? Danke."

Lebrun focused carefully, pursing his lips.

"Well? What do you see?" Berrick, Alan and the *Unteroffizier* were looking at Lebrun in anticipation. He was concentrating for the nonce, however.

"Well," he drew the word out, "it is hard to tell. I see military men.   Not our side. Not *Les Alliés*. They have unfamiliar uniforms and.... that vehicle...*Mere de Dieu*! I have never seen the like!"

Unceremoniously, Alan prised the binoculars from him and gazed down with a muttered apology.

"*Was gibts*?" Asked the German, wondering what this pack of foreigners found so interesting in what looked to him like a bare wilderness.

"Shit!" Alan muttered, turning to Lebrun, his face ashen. "Tell the Captain of this thing to get out of here now! Fast! Don't ask him - tell him ! We have only seconds, for pity's sake!"

Perhaps it was his expression and bloodless aspect the inspection of the small group had caused that impelled Lebrun to knock the open mouthed *Unteroffizier* to one side as he dashed off the Observation Deck towards the Bridge.

"*Herr Kapitän*!" He yelled.

"What the hell?" Berrick asked.

"It's as bad as it can possibly be," Alan handed him the binoculars. "Look!"

Berrick stepped over to the window and peered down through the powerful Zeiss lenses. A small group of men in modern camouflage uniforms were gathered around an APC. It was state-of-the-art from their era. It carried British Army markings. He flicked the binoculars to one side. A group of four men were carrying something long - a box? - over to a fifth man. He held a long tube to which he was making adjustments. Berrick watched the men put the long box down and open it. A ghastly, empty, sick feeling engulfed him. One man was removing a long, pointed object from the box. The man with the tube was lifting it to his shoulder. The first man lifted the pointed object and put it into the tube.

"Christ! A missile launcher! Oh! Ye gods and little fishes! This thing's a hydrogen balloon, isn't it?"

Alan nodded mutely.

"How high up d'you reckon we are?"

"Two thousand feet maybe. We don't stand a chance. We're unarmed -" They reeled as the Captain, warned by Lebrun took sudden evasive action at the same moment as a small, bright flash caught Berrick's eye from the ground. Almost simultaneously, there was the blast of an explosion on the port side about fifty yards away. Hurling themselves to the floor, they just avoided the devastating blizzard of shattered glass which ripped through the Observation Deck, eviscerating the Unteroffizier and half a dozen waiters and barmen who, unforewarned, were cut down in an instant. Before they could get up, a faint pop-pop-popping sound reached their ears.

"Gunfire! Stay down, Berrick, for God's sake. We're well within range," Alan gritted between his teeth as he saw the carnage from his vantage point beneath the table. The Unteroffizier lay on his back, eyes open sightlessly, hands clutching uselessly at his open belly from which purple guts had rolled in an obscene confusion onto the plush carpet. A large dark stain was still spreading over the floor around him. Further on, a high pitched screaming sounded. It was reminiscent of a woman's voice. Horror struck, he saw a figure stagger from behind the bar, its face a mask of stripped skin and bloody bone. Two holes where eyes had been showed that the man had caught the full blast of the lethal shards as they swept into the peace of the Observation Deck. Staggering, the blinded man half-walked, half-crawled up the inclining deck as the vast ship completed her turn. He neared their table. The evasive manoeuvre was suddenly, abruptly reversed as the Zeppelin made a tight turn to port to avoid further missiles. The swift change of angle caught the victim by surprise, hurling him to the edge of the window which was no longer there. As suddenly as the window had shattered, he was no longer there. Only the urgent scream of aero-engines and the moan of the icy wind were to be heard.

Alan sat up, stunned and peered over the window's edge. Berrick joined him.

"D'you think -"

An explosion sounded above and behind them.

"What was that?" Appalled, they stared at each other.

"Look!" Berrick's finger was quivering with stress, but pointing down. They saw a great dark shadow racing over the heather, seemingly only a few feet away. Smoke could clearly be seen to be streaming from the huge hydrogen bag from which they were suspended.

"We've only seconds -" his breath came raggedly, yet his heart thumping slowly it seemed. Strange that. Everything slow. He turned to Alan who was saying something, but the wind had caught the words and blown them away unheard. He seemed excited. Why? Look down and see. Eyes tracking across and down. Shadow showing the fire gaining on the bag. Soon, he knew there would be a bang. A big one. It would blow them to Kingdom Come. But, something was different. What?

His head was muzzy, with a warm wetness trickling down his temple, Alan looking at him oddly, pointing at his head. He looked down and realised what was different. The view had changed. They were lower. Yes, but not just that. What was it?

Alan's words broke through his dazed stupefaction as he seized Berrick by the lapels, heaving him to his feet.

" - before it's too late!"

He heard the words even as he screamed in terror when Alan threw him bodily into space, kicking and cart-wheeling in the whistling wind. As he fell, the great ship passed slowly overhead, the searing heat from its burning envelope scorching his hair. A small something else, like a ball, fell out of the cabin in his wake and then the world turned and he gratefully moved into the welcoming arms of darkness .

CHAPTER FIFTEEN

An aeon, or, perhaps, mere seconds later, he was struggling for his life in freezing black water, trying to drag himself from a different and even more alarming embrace. He was stuck in mud, deep under the surface of the lochan he had briefly spotted in their burning passage. He could see little. Some weed trailed across his face, its slimy familiarity somehow obscene. A sudden brightness lit up the water he lay in and he realised it was no more than fifteen feet or so deep. His lungs were bursting now, and, the pressure made his head ache. He could feel the suction of the mud holding him down and remembered vaguely that the only way to escape quicksand was to swim horizontally out of it. Tentatively, he moved his arms and legs in a backstroke, the lazy kind he favoured in warmer climes under a hot sun. He felt himself move, slowly, too slowly. Keep calm, he adjured himself, don't lose it. He swam calmly, but steadily on, finding that the motion gradually freed him from the suction until, with his breath almost spent, he paddled up in desperation towards the bright patch of light that still moved on the surface of the water. His arms and legs were heavy, so heavy. He could feel his sapped will tell him to give in with good grace and accept his lot. ' Rest and be thankful, rest and be thankful,' ran the litany through his dulled brain.

He burst to the surface, lungs aching and gulped in the cold, fresh air treading water for an age before daring to open his eyes. The cold was eating into his limbs. He knew he had little time to escape before cramp hit him. He saw the lochan was a mere hundred yards in width and black from the muddy bottom. To his intense relief he was only twenty yards or so from the bank. Awkwardly, he swam, doggy style, his clothes and boots impeding his movements until he reached the bank and hauled himself out to lie, exhausted, on the springy heather. A smell of burning wafted on the breeze towards him. It was intense and carried a nasty overtone he didn't like. As he lay, cold and wet, he examined it, analysing what it was. Only then was violently sick, for it was the smell of meat cooking. It was the crew of the Zeppelin. He realised then what the bright flash had been as he emptied his stomach and continued to retch.

"Berrick!" A faint voice called from a long way away, "Berrick!"

He looked around, crouched on all fours. On the other side of the lochan, a dark figure was waving at him.

"Are you alright?"

Weakly, he nodded.

The figure of Alan staggered towards him, wet and bedraggled. He collapsed beside Berrick. "I'm shattered." He pushed himself up on one elbow and gazed at the little pool of black water which ruffled in the wind. One or two clouds whisked by overhead, their brilliant whiteness reflected momentarily on its surface before vanishing like passing thoughts. "If it hadn't been for that...." he turned his head back.. Alan was asleep already. He could feel utter exhaustion creep up on him too. Crawling away from the vomit, he found a place in the heather and collapsed in grateful abandonment to his body's demand for rest. He was asleep in the warm spring afternoon sunshine almost before his head reached the heather.

The patrol was professional. Armed with light 7.62mm rifles and trained to the highest military standards, they were carrying out a sweep of the area to check for survivors. The Lieutenant was sweeping the terrain with his glasses, watching for enemy activity when his walkie talkie squawked at him.

"Robinson here, sir. We've found two. They look like drowned rats. I think they're asleep."

"Asleep? Why d'you think that?"

"They're breathing. One of them has been sick. I think they jumped into a big pond up here."

"Righto, Sergeant, bring them down. We need to take them down to HQ to question them."

"Yessir."

A hefty kick in the ribs stirred Berrick. He rolled over, half-awake to see a young face peering at him wearing a military outfit.

"Wake up, Sleeping Beauty. On yer feet!" He glanced over, "Yer pal too. Up, both of you. My Lieutenant wants you two beauties for questioning. An' what Lieutenant wants, he gets. On yer feet!"

Groggily, they stood up, hands on their heads and, watched warily by the Sergeant who had wakened them, they were marched down the hill within two hundred yards of the blackened twisted wreckage of the Zeppelin as it lay, still burning at the spot where it had crashed.

The Lieutenant didn't question them there and then. They were piled into the APC which was large, empty and which smelt of diesel and sweaty male bodies. Three soldiers piled in beside them with suspicious looks before the Lieutenant and Sergeant joined them. The Lieutenant banged on the side of the vehicle and the engine started noisily. For the next half hour they bumped over rough terrain, Alan and Berrick being bounced around like peas in a drum. Suddenly, they were on a smoother surface and the Sergeant grunted with satisfaction.

"Half an hour, Tom?" Asked the Lieutenant.

"Near enough, sir. Shall I radio ahead?"

The Lieutenant nodded and took out a map, checking co-ordinates carefully and making a few pencil marks at precise locations. Alan glanced at Berrick, but found that he was looking inscrutable. With an exasperated sigh that was lost in a mechanical cacophony of the APC's engine noise, he settled and waited for them to reach their destination.

True to the Sergeant's prediction, it was half an hour later that they reached Charlie Zulu as the Sergeant had described it. They came to a juddering halt and the doors at the back were opened. The light was bright enough to make them all squint. A senior NCO, a Colour Sergeant by his uniform produced a quivering salute.

"Morning, Colour," the Lieutenant said, jumping down and returning the salute, "take our two beauties in the back for a couple of banjoes and tea, or whatever's on the go, and have 'em ready for interrogation at," he studied his watch, "1400 hours."

"Sah!" Bellowed the Colour Sergeant, "move these specimens out for food, if you please, Sergeant Hendry. They look like bloody tinkers! Get 'em cleaned up!" And, like the Lieutenant, he left them to it, marching away, his boots like black mirrors, his uniform ironed to knife-edged creases. Dutifully, the Sergeant and his men did as they were ordered.

At 1400 hours they were marched in plain military fatigues to an office in the large barracks in which they found themselves.

They had been fed an enormous meal of bacon, egg, sausage, baked beans and chips and were bloated. Despite the generous feeding, they were under the watchful gaze of two hefty MPs whose eyes were always on them.

"Strange bloody terrorists," Alan muttered as they clambered out their seats.

"Quiet!" Bawled one of the MPs. "No talking!"

The route to the Interview Room was through long corridors, past classrooms, all of them empty. The colour scheme was a pale green with exposed pipes and the lack of fripperies one might expect in a military building.

Ahead of them, marched the Sergeant and behind him the two armed MPs who kept faultlessly in step with him, denoting a thorough parade-ground training.

"Left wheel!" They marched into an office, bare and functional, a map of West Central Scotland on the wall. A desk and two officers sitting behind it were all that occupied the room.

"Prisoners and escort, halt! Right turn!"

They stood, side by side, gazing at the two seated officers. The Lieutenant who had commanded the section that had destroyed their airship was on the left. He looked young, but confident, the other, thinning on top, with a moustache, was older and heavier but with an indefinable air of authority. He nodded at the Sergeant.

"So." He started to fill the pipe with rough shag whilst casting a professional eye over the two prisoners, before popping the stem into his mouth and lighting the bowl. For a long moment, he merely puffed at his pipe as if trying to recall something, a faintly dreamy look in his eyes.

"So," he repeated, "this is the morning's bag, eh?"

"Yessir!" Replied the Sergeant.

"Mmmm. Evil-looking pair if ever I saw them. Killers' eyes. Both of 'em." He puffed away contentedly.

Alan bridled, "Look, you! We work for the -"

"Shut up!" Bellowed the Sergeant, his face puce with rage, "You will speak when you are asked to, an' not befoah!"

The senior officer took the pipe out of his mouth and waved the stem languidly in the air through the clouds of smoke.

"Thank you, Sergeant. I think I would like to hear who the prisoner claims he works for."

Alan stepped forward, a pulse visibly throbbing at his temple.

"Yes. I was about to say that I am currently employed by the British Army. I don't particularly care for this charade. We know who you are and we've seen how your bully-boys work. So don't try to pretend you are anything other than a bunch of thugs. We aren't impressed - sir."

He put as much irony in his use of the word "sir" as he could before returning a pace to stand beside Berrick again.

Before the two officers could react to this blunt statement, Berrick also stamped forward a pace.

"I second that. We know what fascist scum you are. You can't make it in our world, so you think you can here. Well, buddy boys, the Government is hot on your heels, you may have smuggled some of your thugs through to this world, but you are up against the combined forces of Great Britain and the USA, so forget your fancy airs. We are the official forces. You're mercenaries, so cut the crap - sir."

He also stamped back a pace and gazed ahead above both the officers' heads. There was a silence before the two officers looked at each other . The Lieutenant scribbled a note and passed it to the other who nodded and put down his pipe.

"I will ignore your outbursts for the moment, because you are either both utterly insane or completely deluded." He paused and gazed at them, his eyes cold, grey and very hard, "Understand this. I shall not repeat it. We are officers in the British Army, commissioned by Her Majesty the Queen and serving the Government of the UK. I don't know who you are working for, or who has told you that we are mercenaries, but, if you had been told such a thing, it is utterly untrue."

Alan and Berrick looked nonplussed. They turned and looked at each other whilst still standing to attention.

"Eyes front!" Bellowed the Sergeant.

Alan stepped forward again.

"Permission to speak, sir?"

"Very well. What is it?"

"You say you have commissions from the Queen. Who is this Queen you're talking about?"

The senior officer dropped his pipe, his face crimson with anger.

"Sergeant! Get these two out of here now!"

At the trot, they were ordered out and along the corridor again, their feet making pat-pat noises as the trainers slapped on the floor. The MP's boots clattered loudly in unison. In three minutes, they were confined in detention cells again, separately. The big steel doors slammed shut, the walls echoing the crash as they closed on the clinical white tiled cells. Each cell was eight feet long and four feet wide with a hard wooden bed, a thin horsehair mattress and a single blanket. A bucket sat in the corner for use as a lavatory. The only source of daylight was a small, barred window high up on the wall opposite the door.

Surprisingly enough, they each decided that sleep was a sensible thing to obtain. They stretched out on the respective beds, pulling the blankets over them and dozed off.

Outside, the two MPs made occasional checks on them. The Sergeant took off his cap and rubbed his forehead where a red mark could be distinguished clearly against the paler colour of his skin.

"A bloody cool pair. Must be trained terrorists. Anyone else would be shitting themselves right now."

"Most of the terrorists I've seen did." Observed the private, not to contradict the Sergeant, but simply to refer to his experience of six years in Ulster picking suspected IRA and UDA thugs.

"Fair comment, Jones, but these buggers don't need bicycle clips. Funny, that."

⍰

CHAPTER SIXTEEN

The two officers sat and smoked in the Interrogation Room. The older man, Captain Wykes puffed at his pipe and cocked an eye at Lieutenant Thompson.

"Terrorists, d'you think?"

"Dunno, sir. A rum pair, both well-spoken - privately educated I'd say. A hint of Scots accents would you say?"

"Mmh. Could be. SRA perhaps?"

"Well, sir, I can't think who else they'd be. Unless they're locals. After all, they've got a King."

"No. Can't be. They were on a German Zeppelin, don't forget. They said nothing about being prisoners."

"Mind you, sir, there's that bad business at Leuchars. Whoever carried that out as sure as heck wasn't one of these World War One Johnnie outfits. The damage definitely made by explosives from our patch."

"Yes...I hear the bullets in the bodies were standard NATO issue too, not the .303 variety the British forces here use. Remember, the survivors are sure the commands their attackers gave were in English. Also, the ammo doesn't fit the stuff the French and Germans are using."

"Terrorists, then?"

'Exactly. And there's only one thing to do with them."

Berrick was shattered into wakefulness as the door of his cell was thrown open with a crash.

"On yer feet! Move!"

A none-too-gentle hand pushed him over on his hard bed. The brilliant light had been switched on and its glare blinded him. Shielding his eyes, he sat up, still fully dressed. The blanket was roughly pulled off him and he was hauled to his feet.

"'Shun!"

He stiffened to attention. "By the front, quick march! Left...left...left, right, left."

They were seemingly in a hurry. His brain was still coping with being awake. Was it day or night? Lights were on, when does it get dark? It's spring...so maybe it's 8pm? He passed a window and through its tall, square-paned frame, he saw that it was evening. Blinking his eyes blearily as he kept the step of the smartly clad MP in front and very aware of the other behind, he suddenly realised he was alone. Where was Alan?

Before he could ponder that, he found himself back in the Interrogation Room. It had a classroom odour, hard to define but instantly recognisable. Perhaps he hadn't noticed it first time around because the officers were smoking, or at least, the older one was.

"Pris'ner an' escort, left wheel! Halt! Right turn!"

"Thank you, Sergeant." The Sergeant turned and looked sternly at Berrick standing before him, barely awake. IRA thugs had shat themselves under that steely gaze. Berrick, however, merely looked back at him steadily. The Colonel blinked. Damn! Impertinent little bastard had a nerve!

"D'you know the penalty for fifth-columnists in the uniform of opposing forces?"

Berrick raised an eyebrow, still coming to terms with being awake. Too soon to be afraid.

"No. But I'd expect you'd know, being one. And you can forget your high and mighty bloody airs, mister," he went on without letting the Colonel continue. "We've seen you bully-boys in London trying it on with our lads. Skinhead thugs, the lot of 'em. Your days are numbered, so stuff your kangaroo court. The British and US Governments are onto your games. You're up shit creek, pal."

Fighting down his near apoplexy the Colonel jumped to his feet and leaned heavily on his desk with both hands staring down at Berrick.

"D'you realise the seriousness of your position? I can have you shot now, out of hand. Why d'you persist in your idiotic attitude when you know you are up against the force of law and democratic government?"

Berrick looked incredulous, his eyebrows almost disappearing into his hairline.

"Spare me, for God's sake. Look - you must think I've lost my marbles if you think I'm so confused that I don't recognise a con artist when I see one. Hasn't anyone told you that we haven't had a monarch on the British throne for over one hundred years?"

The Colonel sat down abruptly. For a long moment, he seemed to be communing with some inner muse. As if off-handedly, he caught the Sergeant's eye and nodded to the door. For long moments as the prisoner and his escort clattered noisily away down the corridor, he just sat. The echoes were distant now as Berrick was quick-marched back to his lonely cell and the Colonel picked up his pipe and chewed the stem. Not wishing to break in on his CO's reverie, Lieutenant Thompson went over Berrick's statement in his mind. Did he seem to be mad? Was he under the influence of drugs or hypnotised? No, to both. Equally, it was obvious that he was worlds removed from reality. Thompson stopped and looked at the Colonel.

"Call the second prisoner."

"Sah!"

Alan was in a pub with Nils and Harald, his old Norwegian buddies from the Department of Engineering. They were drinking and laughing over the spitting image "plot" of "The President's Brain Is Missing" when she came in. In the background, the jukebox was playing Hotel California and the usual hubbub was a background murmur. The three of them paused and looked up from their beaten copper topped table. Alan went so far as to put his pint down. She was tall and slim with shoulder-length auburn hair. Her lovely face was pale and her finely-etched mouth was smiling lightly at the effect her appearance had caused. Her eyes, blue, or perhaps grey, scanned them before passing on to search the busy tap room. Alan looked down from her compelling features to see a slim figure in black, skin-tight leggings beneath a royal blue mohair jersey. A small broach in a whorling, silver Celtic style glinted above the gentle swell of her breast.

"My God!" He breathed. "I think I'm in love."

"Join the queue, " Nils grunted, "this calls for a viking raid."

"On the contrary," he rejoined, rising to his feet and in doing so, attracting her gaze once more. "This calls for a civilised approach."

As he stood, he realised how tall she was, nigh on six feet, the top of her head the level of his eyes. Her eyes twinkled in a smile. He was about to speak when a man gently brushed by with a muttered word of an apology to him.

"Darling," she said as he embraced her, his long dark curls tangling with her russet locks. The man dwarfed Alan. His build was impressive. An opponent to avoid tangling with. The man turned and smiled at him ironically -

The crash of the cell door banging back on its hinges awoke him. The wash of white light brought him suddenly to wakefulness.

Three minutes later, he was standing at attention before the two officers. There was a long silence while the Colonel sucked on his pipe stem and looked at him. When he spoke, his voice was gruff.

"You are a renegade and a traitor. The penalty for that is death in Conditions of War."

"You're full of shit. "Conditions of War", my eye! You're making excuses, chum. What you really mean is that you want us out of the way before the Sword of Damocles drops, right?"

"Wrong. You will be tried by a Court Martial and found guilty. You will then be shot."

"Well, I expected no less." Alan replied ironically." In the back of the head?"

"Before a firing squad in accordance with Military Law." The Colonel was becoming irate.

"Look. Cool down, Mister. I see you've accorded yourself the rank of Colonel -"

"I was granted that by Her Majesty the Queen. My Queen and yours."

"For Christ's sake, will you cut the crap? I don't know who this "Queen" of yours is! We're fighting one bunch of royalists under His Majesty King James The Whatever Number he is. Unless you have popped out of some time-warp where ex-Queen Victoria is still on the throne and you guys have reached our technological level a century or more early, I think I'm dealing with a bunch of cranks."

The Colonel sat back looking puzzled. The Lieutenant narrowed his eyes as though trying to work something out. Alan sighed theatrically.

"You do give the impression of soldiers, I'll grant you that. But, there again, most of your men will be former regular soldiers, won't they? Remember "The Dogs of War"? Remember Callan in Angola? Yeah - I can see you do. He applied military discipline too, didn't he? Excessively, perhaps.

"You seem to be the same, but, come on, be rational, please, for your own sakes if not mine. We know you're sneaking men and weapons in from Scotland in our time, we just haven't found out where yet. But, it's no secret, that Commonwealth Forces are coming in as well as US forces. We have the entire resources of the Commonwealth of Great Britain and the USA to mount against you. You know you'll be the cause of much misery and death and you won't win in the end. Give up!"

Alan was no longer standing to attention, he had been pleading with them like an advocate summing up after a trial. His judges, however, merely looked puzzled. It was the Lieutenant who spoke after receiving a nod from his superior.

214

When he did, it was with a marked Army accent. "Are you trying to convince us that you represent - or serve - a British state which is a republic?"

It was Alan's turn to look blank. "Hasn't it been plain that I am a soldier of the Republic, if you wish to call it that? You must be well aware that it is officially called the Commonwealth, surely?"

A tinge of doubt now coloured his speech, nonetheless.

"The only Commonwealth of which I am aware is the one formed after the nations which had been part of the British Empire gained their independence after the War."

"I'm sorry - which war are you referring to?"

The Lieutenant looked exasperated and was about to reply when the Colonel lifted his hand to still him.

"Tell me, young man, if you would, what is your knowledge of events since 1900? Just a summary, please."

He motioned the Lieutenant to sit and leaned forward over the deal table. Alan scratched his head.

"Well - I'm not a great historian but - here goes. Mmm, 1900? That should be when Lord Curzon was President Of The Council, I think. Queen Victoria was assassinated by a Fenian in 1867 and her son, Edward was such a tearaway that no one wanted him. The Royal Family were very unpopular at the time and there was a feeling of, "now or never" and Gladstone pushed the bill through Parliament.

If you go forward to 1900, we had the Boer War, if I remember. We won of course. I don't remember a lot after that except Rights for Women and all that. The Home Rule Bills for Ireland and Scotland were passed in 1914 or 1915, I think. There was a lot of trouble in Europe at that time. Russia became a Bolshevik Republic in 1917 after the war they had with the German and Austro-Hungarian empires. They were trounced. It had something to do with the Serb who shot the Hapsburg Crown Prince in Sarajevo.

"The Italians elected Mussolini in the early Twenties as a Fascist. The Italians were hacked off at the airs of the Austro-Hungarian after their victory over Russia. He seemed okay at first, but he got imperialist ideas about Abyssinia in the Thirties.

"It seemed everyone had an empire except Italy, so they wanted to create one, just like the Romans.

"Franco became leader of Spain at the end of the Thirties after the Spanish Civil War. He was another Fascist. Russia was a bloody mess. We tried to counteract the Bolshies along with American, German and French armies, but somehow they got their way and set up the USSR. Got a nasty dictator called Stalin. He signed a treaty with Kaiser Bill but launched an attack in '41 when the old Kaiser died.

"Luckily a guy called Einstein fled the German Empire just as war was threatening in 1940 and got to the States. The German Chancellor, Adolph Hitler had turned out to be a rabid anti-semite and the Jews left in droves, though Hitler had other plans for them. Luckily for them, the Kaiser kept Hitler in check and the Jews escaped from Germany. They reckon that's what cost Germany the War - and Hitler his life.

"Well, the Russians beat the Germans with the help of the French and they divided Germany between them. France got Alsace-Lorraine back and the Americans developed A Bombs in 1952. Peace broke out.

"France got Alsace-Lorraine back, which they'd lost in the Franco-Prussian War in 1870 odd and the Americans developed A Bombs in 1952. The US had had the aim of rivalling Britain in the role of the World's Policeman ever since Teddy Roosevelt was President in the 1890s or 1900s. They'd had a war with Spain and won Cuba and the Phillipines. Now they had the A Bomb - or was it the H Bomb? I forget - with the help of Brits who they had tempted over with generous offers of US dollars, they were ready to try it out.

"It all came to a head in 1953 in Korea. The USSR moved south to gain a hold on the Far East between Japan, which had kicked their arses back in '03 and China, which they were infiltrating with Communist insurgents under a guy called Mao. They reckoned that taking Korea could swing it in their favour. Trouble was, the Japs not only owned half of China, they also owned Korea. They're pretty fierce fighters, the Japs. The Russians had a hard time of it initially, but they had the good old Russian Steamroller of overwhelming numbers. They just kept pushing. Naturally, being devious bastards, they did it under the guise of a North Korean Army, using Communist Koreans who had fled to them from the Japs, so they could say they were merely 'helping' the natives.

"The Japs got worried. They had intended to rival the Americans in the Pacific as a great power and had made no pretence of it. Now, though, the boot was on the other foot. They were under intense pressure from both Communist China and the Russians. They were stuck and outnumbered by a factor of six to one.

"They had a big powwow with the Yanks and made a treaty at Anchorage in '53 called the Mutual Aid Agreement. They'd allow Chiang Kai Shek, the anti-Communist Chinese leader, who they had been fighting, to join them against the USSR and the Chinese Communists in exchange for certain guaranteed territorial rights on the mainland of China plus Taiwan if and when they won. Of course, this wasn't just good neighbourliness on the part of the Americans. The USSR was also claiming back Alaska from the States. The Americans had bought it in good faith in the nineteenth century from the Russian Czar for peanuts, but its material assets were and are enormous. They were making a statement.

"The Russians backed their argument by sinking an American ship and over six hundred people had drowned, though neither the passengers not the crew were Americans. Of course, the Americans had the ultimate weapon, but the Russians didn't know it and now, the US had a reason to go to war.

"In the autumn of 1953, US forces, backed by the British, despite our beginning to pull out of the region, what with Indian independence, landed in Korea. We were there to back the Japs, but the Russians were pushing them into the sea. There was a long, bloody set-to and, this time, we pushed them back. All looked well, but, come March 1954, the North Korean and Russian forces counterattacked. It looked as if our boys and the Japs, were doomed. They were fighting like tigers. The ordinary Jap soldiers had been taking heart from the democratic changes the Anchorage Agreement had forced on the Japanese Government and it was now a clear battle of democracy versus tyranny. The Russians had squeezed the Allied forces into a pocket on the south coast that was barely twenty miles wide when the US Government took a fateful decision. They decided to use the H Bomb. They took out Seoul and Pusan in two separate attacks which devastated both cities.

"It was all over inside a week. The North Koreans surrendered and the whole country became a protectorate of a new body set up by the US, Britain and France called the United Nations.

"Later, of course, came Vietnam, but that was in the sixties and seventies. It was more of a grass-roots type of war. By then, the Chinese Communists had beaten the Japs and kicked them and Chiang Kai Shek out to Taiwan. The Russians had become members of the UN and had developed their own H Bomb, so things were more level-pegging than in Korea. The US went in, of course, but it was a disaster. We had all but given our Empire away by that time, so we kept out of it."

"So," said Colonel Wykes, "what's the current status quo?"

"Well, France is the dominant European Power. They set up an EEC and drew West Germany in as the other half of the Axis. America became the dominant power elsewhere in the world and we were left on the sidelines until we joined the EEC in 1979. The communists folded in the early Nineties and Germany reunited. We're in a state of flux, I suppose. But, I'm only telling you what you already know, surely?"

The Colonel shook his head wonderingly.

"If you are telling us the truth - and for your sake, I pray you are - then, we are faced with an appalling situation."

"In what way?"

"Because you say that you represent the British Government's forces. Correct?"

"Correct."

"Well, chum. So do we. But they seem to be different governments."

Alan's mouth was dry. He licked his lips and swallowed hard.

"Y'mean you're from another time-span too?"

"It looks that way. You mentioned renegades in this area, well, we have come across some thuggish types who have appeared in the Glasgow area. We've banged them up in clink. Haven't had time to do anything with 'em yet. Are you saying they are from your, ah, dimension?"

"Not at all. They're locals. Thugs taking advantage of the uncertainties of the current situation."

"Those are the sort we caught."

The Colonel opened his tobacco pouch and, absentmindedly, filled his pipe.

"So," he lit the pipe puffing at it industriously and filling the room with fragrant smoke, his gaze distant, as though deep in thought.

"I'll need proof that you are from where you say you understand?"

"Yes...sir. That seems reasonable, and I can provide it, but -"

"But?"

"We seem to be on opposite sides."

"We do?"

"Well. After all, you're here defending the Stuarts' territory."

"Ah! The Stuarts," he laughed gently, "or should I say the Stuart? King James died two weeks ago. He had syphilis, y'know. Poor man was out of his mind. Sad really, I suppose. We merely moved in when we discovered this place because we understood that British territory was under attack by combined French and German attack. We weren't defending them. We're quite separate, y'see?"

"No, sir. I'm afraid not."

"I think we need to talk and we should do that over a drink ....and with your colleague. Officers' Mess. Oh - and your proof. I'd like to see that."

Half an hour later, having been allowed to change back into their now cleaned and pressed uniforms, Alan and Berrick found themselves in the atmosphere of a more familiar type of environment. A bar, manned by smartly-dressed staff. They recognised the drinks at the bar.

"Christ. I'd kill for a pint of Deuchar's." Berrick exclaimed as they checked through the large manilla envelopes containing their possessions which had also been returned to them. "I haven't had one since we were last at The Jug ."

" It feels like a lifetime ago! I'll have one too," Alan agreed. "When was that?"

"I dunno. Oh - hang on - I do. President Steel had just told our dear PM to shove it when he suggested that all official documents should be produced in Scots only. Must have been January?"

"That's right!" Alan laughed "What a blinder."

The Colonel looked bemused, "You have a PM in Scotland?"

"Of course. Don't you?"

"Ah, well, no, as a matter of fact. There's a lot of humphing in Scotland at present, but our Government is still London-based."

"So, how does Scotland decide on its separate legislation?"

"Well," the Colonel waved his hands about vaguely, um. Through the Scottish Grand Committee."

"And where's that?"

"At Westminster."

"Doesn't sound very democratic."

"Oh, it is. Only Scots MPs take part."

"They have the final say, then?"

"Oh, goodness me, no. The Parliament of the UK decides that in the end."

Alan and Berrick glanced at each other as they quaffed their beers. Alan raised a sceptical eyebrow.

"So English, Welsh and Irish MPs decide what legislation should apply in a country they don't live in?"

"Well, uh....you see. That is to say..."

"I reckon you guys are sitting on a powder-keg if you don't mind me saying." Berrick smiled briefly before changing the subject. "You were going to tell us where your people stand in this strange situation."

The Colonel was wrong-footed for a few seconds by the topic of conversation and buried his face in a large g & t before he got to grips with the change of topic.

"Right. The current situation is an imponderable. We had reports of strange goings-on through one of the weird magazines that UFO freaks and Nessie-watchers read. There was talk of people (unnamed, of course) who had found their way into another dimension or time, as it appeared. Five - MI5, that is - looked into it as they do in such circumstances and, bingo, it was true. They sent in a team. Two set up bases in Glasgow by the gate to our own dimension while others did a recce to the south. I believe they used microlite aircraft to gain data in the form of pictures. They carried out on-the-spot interviews and collected physical data before reporting back.

"The details we received were alarming. Britain had been successfully invaded by a combined Franco-German force which had taken much of England. Wales was being invaded and British forces were falling back on Scotland. We couldn't tolerate that. Our Government is fairly paranoid about European influence in the UK from the European Union of which we pretend to be a part. So, Tommy Atkinson got his marching orders. We came here about a month ago to find utter chaos reigned. No overall control, units wandering around with no idea of their purpose and the command structure in shreds. We made contact with the civil authorities in Glasgow and, thereby, with the Court in an attempt to force a change in the balance of power. We even managed to set up a small strike group of four jets at Leuchars. We built a runway in days, but within seventy-two hours of their being established they were taken out."

"I think we need to update you on that, Colonel." Alan proposed nervously. "We were actually part of that action."

"WHAT?" The Colonel's roar silenced the Mess. "You were part of that group of murderous thugs - ? "

"No."

"Whaddyou mean, no? You just said you were."

"Colonel. We were part of a British Army Task Force sent to attack an outpost manned, to the best of our knowledge, by mercenaries who were in danger of imperilling our Army and our Allies. We had as much knowledge about you as you had about us. The only people we could conceive of who might have that level of technology were the extremist neo-fascists and their hangers-on. You can hardly blame us for attacking people who were attacking us."

The Colonel blew out his cheeks.

"I don't damn well like it. Not one bloody bit. Still, it seems to clarify things somewhat."

"Doesn't it, though?" Alan replied with a gleam in his eye. He took a swallow of beer.

"So," Berrick probed, leaning forward and tracing a vague shape in the damp ring his beer glass had left on the table, his eyes gazing at the faint light reflected from the moisture. "What great plans do your people have?"

"I can hardly see that I can tell you two matters of state like that! I don't even know that you are who you say you are," the Colonel lifted his glass and swallowed a large mouthful of his drink. "Before we go any further, I want to see that proof you spoke of." His voice had a hard, sceptical edge to it.

Alan glanced at Berrick and nodded.

Berrick opened his manila envelope and slid out his proof set of 1993 coins.

"What are these?" The Colonel squinted at them.

"It's a proof set of euros minted at Stirling. They're British, so I'd appreciate you not handling them. They're not meant for general circulation."

Lovingly, he indicated the coins set out in their airtight, plastic casing.

"That's a fifty euro piece. Pure gold. Isn't it beautiful?"

Mutely, the Colonel nodded.

"It's got President Steel's head on the obverse for Great Britain and a unicorn on the reverse for Scotland surrounded by fifteen stars for the nations of the EU. English ones have the three leopards: Welsh ones have a dragon. The smaller value coins here are pure silver."

"Superb craftsmanship." The Colonel held up the plastic packet and scrutinised it closely. "I used to collect coins myself, when I was a boy. These really are stunners!" He studied the detail of the coins. He noted the date:1993 and the head of President Steel, a face well-known to him in his own time, instantly recognisable and the words 'Brit Omn Def'.

He shrugged. "Yes, I agree. They are beautiful. It just seems so...implausible. I don't know..."his voice trailed off.

"No less implausible than your having a Queen seems to us, "Berrick answered.

"No, ahem, I suppose not."

"So, fundamentally, Colonel, we're on the same side," Berrick lifted his gaze and met the Colonel's directly, a strange, quirky look in his eyes. "So, what the fuck are we doing fighting each other? Tell me that."

"A palpable hit, Colonel, you'll agree," Alan added.

"All I will say is this - make contact with your people -"

"General Hannah."

"Very well with... ah... General Hannah... and arrange a meeting on neutral territory..."

"Where the hell is neutral territory to be found?"

"Eh?... ah... I haven't thought... no, you're right. Arrange a meeting at..."

"Let's say Antonine's Wall, shall we? It's open, visible for a long way and in the middle of the country. Each side to be accompanied by two armed guards with back up of one tank and a platoon of infantry."

"What about your European friends?"

"Well, Colonel. They don't want to take over the country. This is an old-fashioned dynastic conflict. They want the old King's grandson to inherit. Unless you want your Queen to take over, I think everyone has the same end in mind. The troops loyal to King James won't dispute it. They've no-one to put up in contention and, besides, they 're in total disarray. The French and Germans will be happy, the new King will be happy. Dammit, Everyone will be. What the hell are we fighting for?"

CHAPTER SEVENTEEN

A week later, on a warm spring day, two small parties arrived at a point on the ancient earth rampart erected nearly 2000 years before by the Roman Emperor, Antonine, to guard the Northern frontier of the recently-expanded Empire. It had lasted only eighty years or so, but it still stood, less obvious than the more southerly stone wall erected in the name of the Emperor Hadrian, but significant in that it was a high-water mark of ancient and now modern military achievement.

Two officers, accompanied by the agreed pair of armed guards approached each other under two flags. Incongruously, each carried the white flag of truce and the Union Flag of the United Kingdom and of the Commonwealth, respectively. The group which approached from the west was one of six men. That proceeding from the east consisted of four. From a distance, agreed early in a series of radio exchanges, two tanks sat squatly in their camouflage, a platoon of professional soldiers taking up defensive positions in the surrounding landscape, their rifles and machine guns at the ready. Their officers' binoculars scanning the terrain for any sign of treachery on the part of the other side.

Alan and Berrick, dressed in the uniform of the Royal Greenjackets kept in step of the Senior Officer representing HMG's Armed Forces in the "Caledonian Conflict" as they quaintly and, perhaps, rather disparaging described the events in this other Britain, this might-have-been land.

The wind, soughing over the open farmland, brought the scent of freshly-awakened plants as the seeds quickened under the warming sun and fresh, green shots thrust out of the still, cold soil.

Private James Merridew squinted along his sights at the soldier, similarly dressed, who was keeping a watchful eye on him. Neither of them was aware of the coincidental fact that the soldier he was prepared to kill at a moment's notice was also Private James Merridew. Had they stood side by side, their own identical mothers could not have told them apart.

Although many of the soldiers on each side were different individuals, Lieutenants Piers Fortescue both observed the meeting of the two parties through their binoculars and kept their platoons' sergeants informed of the progress of the parley and handover of Alan and Berrick. A small amount of concern was generated by the animated discussion which took place. They saw actual gesticulations by both negotiators which they took initially as signs of argument. Little did they know that each had been to Glenalmond College. At the same time, they each knew their alter ego.

"Dermod, my God, you old bugger! Didn't know you were a General! How the buggery did you manage that and what are you doing with this lot?"

"Lachlan? But you're on exercise in Kenya, aren't you? How the blazes are you here and what are you doing on that side?"

When they realised that they were old friends and yet that they had never met before, they simply collapsed in laughter slapping each other on the backs to total bemusement of their respective guards until one of them looked hard at one of the two on the Republican side.

"'Ere, John. 'ow come you're over there an'," he turned to his companion, "an' over 'ere beside me?"

Slowly, the soldiers from both sides drifted forward, led by their officers, rising from their positions, coming down to the rendezvous. As many of them recognised their doppelganger, there were emotional meetings and heart-felt handshakes, astonished recognitions of self/other-self and a total relaxation of military discipline.

Alan and Berrick, watching the astonishing spectacle, lit up cigars and stood back.

"Well, that's a sight for sore eyes, ain't it?"

"Alan, you've put it in a nutshell. The question now is, how will two British Governments get on, two dimensions apart and what will they do with this one?"

A fortnight later, they found themselves at Scone, ancient coronation place of the kings of Scots. The young Prince Henry arrived with a guard of honour composed of troops from both Germany and France and was met by a combined ceremonial guard of soldiers of the Commonwealth and of the United Kingdom. In recognition of the strangeness of the occasion, each half of the British contingent was composed of the doppelgangers of the other.

As the soon-to-be-crowned King approached, the Union Flags were lowered simultaneously by the flag-bearers, Privates Ewen Brown of the Black Watch.

The Prince came to attention, saluted and then inspected the Guard with General Hannah and General MacKenzie, before proceeding to the solemn enthronement.

A large crowd of members of the public, the men in flat caps, some in plus-fours, the women in flowery bonnets, mutton-chop sleeves and full-length dresses waved and cheered from the sidelines as the new King of Scots and Monarch of Great Britain and Ireland emerged, crowned, to acknowledge the crowd, before entering the State Coach and proceeding to Perth.

There, before another large cheering crowd and after the Loyal Greeting by the Lord Provost and Council, he took a train to Edinburgh and hosted a Coronation Ball at Holyrood Palace. It was a glittering occasion at which by dint of their catalytic involvement, Alan and Berrick were present. The ancient palace from which King James VI had proceeded south to London in 1603, never to return on a permanent footing, was livelier that it had been for those empty centuries. The dancers, the flower of British aristocracy, meritocracy, wealth and armed forces danced the night away with an infusion of the up-and-coming, the young, the intelligent, journalists, bankers, company directors, writers, poets and singers. The human wealth of the United Kingdom was there, revelling in the joy of the occasion .

His Majesty, King Henry's Lord Chamberlain banged his white staff on the floor as midnight approached.

"My lords, ladies and gentlemen, his Grace the King." There was a buzz at the use of the Scots honorific rather than the English "His Majesty".

The King was in good humour, dressed simply, a blackbird amongst peacocks, his soft voice hard to hear as he did not choose to bellow as had the Lord Chamberlain. The hubbub quickly subsided, however, and his voice, clear and baritone rose over their great number to the far corners of the ballroom.

"....we have had a period of national division of late with brother pitted against brother and father against grandfather,

grandfather against grandson. Not at least in my own case. During that terrible and divisive time, we discovered that we are not alone in this world of ours. There are others with similar outlooks to our own who are guardians of this land we call Great Britain..."

"Neatly gets over our being republican," Alan smiled as glanced at Berrick.

"... and to them we tender our thanks for ending a conflict which my father's untimely death..."

"Fortunate, I'd have called it," Berrick muttered wryly.

"...had made meaningless. I have, therefore, ordered that our Government hold talks with the governments of our cousin, Queen Elizabeth and with that of our fellow countrymen of the Commonwealth to initiate a Great Conclave. By pooling our natural and human resources, we hope to further the aims of civilisation and understanding for the benefit of all!"

For Alan and Berrick, the next quarter of an hour was a dazzling whirlwind of activity. With various noted military men, French, German and British, they were chivvied into line by a liveried Master of Ceremonies who whispered instructions into the ear of each before they were ushered forward. Various honours were bestowed upon them. General Hannah went down on one knee and bowed his head as King Henry knighted him for his services. General MacKenzie was made a Knight of the Ancient Order of St Andrew. Then Alan was ordered forward. He bowed, being now in civilian dress, as was Berrick.   His starched collar was tight and uncomfortable and he felt sweat drip down between his shoulder blades as the King awarded him the Order of St Cuthbert which consisted of an enamel gold cross to be worn around the neck and a pale blue sash worn across the left shoulder crossing his body to the right hip. In a daze, he bowed and exited left as instructed. Having joined the other, equally stunned recipients of awards, he watched as Berrick was awarded the same order.

The recipients of awards were served chilled champagne by an attentive waiter and not a few hands trembled with emotion, spilling more of the vintage wine than they drank.

Alan and Berrick joined General Sir Dermod Hannah in a breath of fresh air outside to calm their nerves as the Ball recommenced.

"God! I was more scared in there than I was in the Falklands," the General commented, lighting a cigarette.

Alan and Berrick lit up cigars and joined him on the terrace, feeling elated and yet drained at the same time. For a long minute, they stood in the darkness of the Palace grounds and gazed up towards Salisbury Crags, looming over them in the night. As midsummer approached, they could see the spectacular rock formation that dominated the old town quite clearly, for the northern sky was still a limpid blue for all that it was ten o'clock at night.

"What now, Sir Dermod?"

"Sir Dermod! By God it has a certain *je ne sais quoi* about it, though, wouldn't you say?" The General laughed softly as he dropped his cigarette and crushed it beneath his spurred boot in a shower of sparks.

"You boys have done your job and received the thanks of a grateful nation. Time for you to go home, I think. Back to - what is it you do?"

"We're estate agents."

"Back to helping people buy houses, then."

"And that's it?" Berrick asked, unable to grasp the idea that he was, once more, master of his own destiny.

"Sure an' I can't use youse anymore. Mebbe we'll meet some day for a glass of good Scottish malt at the NB." The General was back to the blarney again.

"And this world. What of it?"

The General put a finger against his nose, "Under wraps, where we're from. It never happened."

"But people will ask! Hell, my business! It might be bust! We haven't been there for months! There'll be no cash in the bank to pay the bills..."

"Hell's teeth! I hadn't even thought of that!" Alan groaned.

"Oh, you'll make out all right. Goodnight, lads. And thanks." The General shook them each by the hand. He looked at them sharply, all trace of drunkenness vanished. "Never a word. Understood?"

Nodding amiably, he returned to the Ball. Berrick looked at Alan and shook his head.

"Lets get pissed!"

"Alan! You always know the solution."

⸮

CHAPTER EIGHTEEN

Four hours later, they tottered out of the palace with the last hundred or so guests of the Ball. All were well-oiled and most were merry. Leaning against each other, their collars unbuttoned, they watched a line of hansom cabs and the odd motorised taxi draw up to the entrance to take on board the last of the cream or was it the dregs of British society?

Alan staggered out and leaned against one of the two lamp posts which were occasionally resolving into one and then becoming two again. It was quite disconcerting.

Berrick weaved his way blearily to his side and slapped him on the shoulder.

"Where are y'going to?"

"To that bloody flat. If I'm gonna be pished, I'll be pished in my flat an' not in a world where I was press-ganged!"

"I'll second that..."

Arm in arm, they wandered up the High Street, weaving from side to side, falling over, usually together, sometimes not, tripping on the cobbles and barging into lamp posts which gave off faint luminescence.

"This's it, innit?" Berrick asked, peering into a gloomy passageway.

"Whoa, neddy. Wassat Berrick, old chum, ol' buddy?"

He clapped a hand on Berrick's shoulder and, swaying gently peered myopically at the close.

"Wait just a minute, ol' chap." Berrick looked puzzled. "This is the right place, but iss not, if you follow me."

"Can't say I do," Alan screwed his face up in a forlorn attempt to compute the deep meaning that Berrick was trying to communicate. "No, definitely not. Run it past me again." He swayed alarming for a moment. "Gotta have a fag ."

He tried to light it with little success, while Berrick muttered to himself hiccupping.

"Nev' mind. Let's go up the stairs. Oh - wait a sec, Berrick. Damn, Don' you 'member?"

"'Member what, ol' horse?"

"We din' come out of here. We came out of the ol' duffer's place."

"Ol' duffer? What ol' duffer? Ah! Oh! That ol' duffer. Oh, well. Best toddle on down to his fine 'bode, hadn't we?"

Berrick collided heavily with him and they collapsed together in a tangle of limbs and muffled curses. They picked themselves up carefully. There were few noises from the streets around town and not a soul was to be seen as they swayed carefully down the close to the Canongate. They turned left to head back towards the Palace and tottered the few hundred yards to the house they had last seen some months ago. Now it stood silent as a tomb, its smoke-blackened walls and blank windows testimony to the change in the power-structure in the land. It had the empty feeling of an abandoned shell.

"It's funny, really."

"What is?"

"Y'know, Alan, we went into the flat and came out down 'ere, 500 yards away."

"Funny place, the Old Town......They're always finding something they didn't know existed before. What's different about a time-tunnel that's five hundred yards long?"

"Dunno. I've never seen one before that was five yards long let alone five hundred. Y'know, ol' chum? It looks awful deserted, that house."

"Deserted?" They swayed uncertainly in the wash of a slowly setting moon casting its eerie, borrowed light over the huddled, medieval town. The house remained stubbornly inscrutable.

"Yup. Absholutely. Let's see whether there is anyone in, shall we?"

Alan banged hard on the door. They heard the sound echo hollowly before Berrick also knocked hard on the door. Stepping back in as sober a manner as they could manage and swaying precipitately, they looked up at the blank windows of the first floor, but there was no answering gleam of light.

"I don' think anyb'dy's in."

"I reckon you're right. Try the door. Silly idea, I know, but it might be unlocked."

Gingerly, Alan turned the great wrought iron ring of the door handle. Stiffly, it turned and a loud "click" sounded. The door swung open silently to reveal a gaping, black emptiness within.

"Spooky!" Alan breathed, sobering.

Berrick also found his inebriation lessen as he contemplated the dense silence of the house.

"Whaddayou think? Go in?"

"In for a penny..."

"Exactly. I want to get home. Away from this antiquated hell hole!"

"Snap!"

They ventured in on tiptoe. The black and white tiles on the floor were familiar. Alan took a box of matches from his pocket and struck one. It was waxed, so it burned slightly longer than usual. They looked around in the light of the small steady flame.

"It's empty!"

"It is deserted," Berrick breathed, "C'mon. Let's get moving. These old houses give me the creeps."

They walked through the door which led to the public rooms of the house. Berrick used his own matches as well. Everywhere, there were signs of a rapid evacuation of the place. Odd items had been left, here an antimacassar, and there an ashtray. Otherwise, nothing but bare floorboards and dust. Lighter marks on the walls showed where pictures once hung. A sense of sad emptiness permeated the place. Their footsteps echoed loudly as they climbed the creaking stairs to the small landing they had found themselves on when they came through from the flat. Now, it was dark and empty though the blue carpet remained. Already, a stale mustiness pervaded the air. They almost jumped out of their skins, hearts pounding as a faint scurrying from a corner startled them. The dim light of a match showed a faint gleam of a pair of red eyes.

"Rats!" Alan shivered. "Time to move on. It's more like the set of a horror movie with every passing minute."

With a curse, he dropped the lighted match and sucked his thumb and index finger.

"Damn! I burnt myself!"

"I wouldn't worry - look - there's light coming in through the windows below. It'll be dawn soon. Time for a new start."

"Time to file for bankruptcy, more like."

They hurried over to search for the panel hidden in the wall. In the gloom, Berrick felt for a button or a switch but found nothing.

"Are you sure this is the place?" He asked.

"Yes. But I don't remember a button being here before. Remember, the door opened inwards onto the flat. Maybe a push would do it?" He belched softly. "Pardon me."

Alan knocked on the wall. It sounded solid. Slowly, he moved along to his right knocking softly every six inches or so. There was no change in the sound. "It's all bloody solid!"

"It can't be. I distinctly remember that we came through here - we were pretty woozy, mind you - there was a staircase on our right. On our right. Yes, of course! That means we came in over here. Look at the wall... d'you see?"

Alan walked over to join him as he detected a faint glimmering of light from the room below. The moon had set now as the soft luminescence began to penetrate the still gloomy chiaroscuro cast on the wall by the balustrade behind them. The sun was near the horizon. Another day was dawning.

"Here." He pointed at an apparent flaw in the decoration revealed in the light. A suggestion of a vertical line could be seen in the wallpaper. It was more of a hint than a statement, but sufficiently distinct for him to ignore the rest of the wall.

He tapped at the wall tentatively. A distinct hollowness could be distinguished.

"This is it! It must be!"

"Go for it!"

Alan put his shoulder to the wall and pushed. At first, nothing happened. He redoubled his efforts and felt a slight give. Heaving hard and with Berrick now lending an enthusiastic shoulder, suddenly the wall gave. A doorway reluctantly revealed itself with the sound of a loud crash and piercing shrieks.

They staggered through and into the bedroom. A large wardrobe lay on the floor and in two beds, tousled-haired young women, puffy-eyed with sleep, were sitting up in a state of shock. They were clutching their downies to their breasts and staring in sleepy dishevelment at the two drunk, very formally-clad men who had invaded the sanctity of their bedroom. Their screams were deafening and both men clapped their hands to their ears.

"Please! Ladies!" Alan bellowed and regretted it as his head thumped with the sound. "Ladies! We only came through a door. We didn't know you were here."

"That's completely right. Absolutely." Berrick concurred with a vacuous smile.

"What door?" The most self-possessed of the girls asked, pushing her blonde hair from her eyes. Berrick, seeing her, started in surprise, swung round and cannoned into Alan, almost knocking him off his feet, "Watch out!" Alan grumbled, "I'm feeling delicate."

"Sorry. My fault." He mouthed silently at Alan, indicating the girl with a covert jabbing with his thumb. Ignoring his agitation, Alan grinned toothily at the girls and attempted to disguise his drunkenness.

"This door." He gestured vaguely in the direction of the shadowy corner from which they had emerged.

"Here!" Berrick showed them by pushing the door to.

"Oh!" She exclaimed, pushing her long blonde hair out of her eyes. To Berrick's discomforture, one of her breasts was close to peeping out of her nightie, but he couldn't drag his eyes from the sight.

"I didn't know there was a door there." She went on," smiling up at them both. "Where does it go?"

"Eh... well..."

"Just into the stair in the next close," Alan replied quickly, kicking Berrick's ankle.

"Ouch! Oh, that's right. Just into the next close." He bit his lip. Alan's boot was a solid triumph of the British bootmaker's art.

"And we knew the girls who were here before you, y'see?" Alan improvised. "And they let us get away through here when our landlord came by at odd times..."

"Exactly," Berrick broke in, "at odd times like dawn when he's after our rent. And we're just back."

"- from a fancy dress ball and he wants his dosh-"

"- and we don't have it."

"Can you help us get away girls? Please?"

"Please?"

By now, the young women had shrugged themselves into dressing-gowns and combed their hair back with their fingers.

They had also climbed out of their beds and approached the two interlopers gingerly, as if they were wild animals whose reliability was dubious. Showing what good citizens they were, they lifted the wardrobe and stood it back up against the door while the girls muttered to each other.

At length, the blonde girl turned. "Well... all right. Just this once, you understand, Mr..?"

"Oh, you bet! I'm Berrick Kildrum and this is Alan Cruickshank." Berrick grinned toothily. "Ah... I didn't catch your name?"

"Oh! I'm Candice Melville. You look as if you could do with a coffee."

After the third cup of coffee Candice had made for them, they were shaking with relief at the return to normality .

"I hope you don't mind if... well..." Berrick stammered to a halt, blushing, "would you like to get together for a meal or a drink some evening this week as a token of my apology?"

She laughed. It was a pleasant, musical sound and it brought a smile to his lips. She shook her head slightly, but not in refusal, more in amusement at him. "We'll see." She glanced significantly at her watch. "I need to get up for work later this morning. Give me your 'phone number and I'll ring you if I decide that you've bowled me over with your charms. But no promises. Understood?"

Berrick grinned. He then gave her his phone number and asked for hers. As she was about to close the door, he bent forward and gave her a quick peck on the cheek. She feigned shock and shooed them out. With a cheerful goodbye and a grin, Berrick then joined Alan who had been standing champing on the landing and they went back down the dusty stair they had first climbed several months back.

Candice closed the door and leaned against it. He was nice, but he wasn't telling her the truth. She knew that. The local area code of his phone number was north of the Castle. In the New Town. Why should he have said that he lived in the next close? Sighing, she lifted the 'phone and spoke softly for a minute before replacing the handset.

CHAPTER NINETEEN

It was with a measure of culture shock that they returned to their own place in time. The car they had come in had gone. Alan groaned. "Some bastard's stolen it!"

"More likely it was lifted to the Police Pound in Leith and it'll cost you more than it's worth to get it back."

"Don't remind me. What shall we do...Christ! I don't even know what day it is."

"Well," Berrick counted off on his fingers, "the Ball was in parallel time so let's assume the days and dates were the same. Okay?

"So, we went to Holyrood on Tuesday evening," he ticked off his fingers, "got drunk and went, the following morning, that is this morning through the Gateway. Right? So, it's Wednesday. QED."

"Smartarse."

"Well, now that's sorted, let's go to the office, shall we?" Berrick asked brightly.

"What office? It'll be empty with a pile of bills and demands knee deep behind the door."

"Let's see, shall we?"

The walked down the Mound with the early morning bustle just beginning around them. It was a fine, early spring day with the blue sky and a gentle warmth in the sun's rays. It took them twenty minutes to reach Northumberland Street. Alan suddenly stopped.

"Hang on. You live here."

"So I do. I'd almost forgotten."

"Why don't we look in on your humble abode. Your dreadful flatmate should be about."

"Well, I suppose so. It's a bit early for the office to be open. It's only.." he glanced at his watch, "...six thirty. Yeah, let's get some tea and toast."

"Lead on, MacDuff."

It took only four minutes to get there. Berrick felt his heart begin to beat faster as they reached the gate leading down to the basement flat he owned. The small, front yard looked tiny enough.

"Hey. The curtains are drawn in Drew's room. He must be in!"

"Well, come on. Let's see, shall we?"

Quietly, they stole down the stairs, almost guiltily and reached the front door. Alan suddenly looked aghast.

"But, you haven't got keys!"

"Whaddayou mean?"

Berrick pulled out a small keyring, "I've still got my keys. I kept hold of them, whatever I was wearing. It's a sort of link with home, I suppose. Anyway, let's go in."

He unlocked the door and went it, Alan closing it behind him. Quietly, so as not to waken the tenant, they walked along the passage which ran the length of the flat to the kitchen at the rear.

Within five minutes, they had made large, steaming mugs of coffee and a stack of toast which they thickly buttered before repairing to the sitting room. Closing the door, Berrick switched on the TV to catch the early morning show. For several minutes, they simply luxuriated at being where they belonged. They learned about the latest happenings of the world but not a word was there about the involvement of the Government or of British Forces in any struggle in another dimension.

"It's as if it didn't happen," Alan commented. They had taken off their ties and jackets plus the medals they had received and were feeling relaxed and tired.

The sitting room door opened. Round it, a tousled head appeared sleepily.

"Oh! Hi, Berrick. Late night or early morning?"

Berrick turned, "Hi, Drew. Late night actually. Did you miss me?"

The head disappeared as Drew headed to the bathroom. "Miss you? Christ, man. I wished you'd go out more. You bloody live in front of that TV."

They heard the bathroom door shut and the sound of the shower being turned on.

Berrick shook his head tiredly.

Alan cocked an eye at him "Why are you shaking your head?"

"Oh, I don't know. I haven't been here for months, but you'd think he might have noticed, wouldn't you? Anyway, I hardly watch the thing usually. Just an odd comment, I suppose."

They watched the headlines at seven thirty as the sound of Drew's shower ended. They heard the bathroom door open and the sound of him walking back to his room.

The few words of conversation reached them, followed by an exclamation. Footsteps of someone wearing shoes came along the passage to the lounge door. They were watching a feature on "Baywatch" in a half-awake way when a familiar voice snapped them back to the present.

"Hello, Alan! How the hell did you get in? And who's that with you?"

Berrick turned round and stared. His jaw dropped as he saw himself standing at the door with an inquisitive look on his face.

"G-G-Good God!" he stammered. His doppelganger appeared equally stunned.

"Good Grief! It's you! I mean, me!"

For a long moment, they stared at each other while the idiot babble on the box continued in the background. Alan, although equally stunned was the first to break the spell.

"Look, Berrick...ah, "Mark II", if I can call you that? Sit down, old man. You look as if you've seen a ghost!"

Gingerly, Berrick Mark II acquiesced wordlessly. He was pale. Numbly, he sat on the vacant armchair and began to search for words.

"I'm really awfully sorry..um..y'know... taking your place..."

"I couldn't thing of anyone I'd rather have do it. Good God!" Berrick repeated, "This is amazing! I mean - you're me and - well, I'm you. Bloody hell! Tell me, Berrick, uh, how's the business? I guess you've been to my office?"

"Oh, absolutely! My pal Alan has been doing the same, by the way. He'll be there at nine, so he can have the benefit of the surprise too, Alan."

"And things are okay?"

"Bloody marvellous! Market's booming! We've got a fantastic deal with one of the Health Trusts to sell off redundant buildings on the South Side and Alan has made in-roads into the landed estate market. We've done pretty well."

"And... how do I put this?" Alan fumbled for words, "what plans do you have?"

"Ah. Yes. That's....difficult. You may not know the score family-wise where I come from."

"No. No, we don't. Haven't the time to look up our nearest and dearest. Why?"

"Well, I'm afraid that..." his voice quavered for a moment before he continued. "Ma and Pa died in the flu epidemic five years ago. I'm alone. It's the same for Alan - Mark II, as you would call him - as well. We've been sons to your parents while you were away. I don't know how you excuse it -"

"Don't," Berrick said, "I understand. But that doesn't answer the question, does it?"

Berrick II leaned back into the settee and blew out his cheeks.

"Frankly, I far prefer this world to the claustrophobic old one I came from. It's exciting and innovative. A century ahead of us. The environment's purer, of course in the old world and there's much less over population, but it is dull."

He glanced at both of them quizzically, "All right. Let me be straight with you. I don't want to go back. neither does Alan. We want to stay here."

"Okay," said Alan, "I....that is, we....understand. The problem is quite straightforward. How can two of each of us survive unnoticed in this rather small city?"

247

They mused for a long period punctuated by Drew's voice at the door shouting 'See you!' before he went out, banging the door behind him.

"London," said Alan.

"Eh? What about London?" asked Berrick.

"We open an office in London. We make it a family concern. There are different property rules in the two countries, so we needn't overlap. Of course, you two as our 'brothers' would need to use different Christian names - middle names, perhaps?

Berrick glanced at his doppelganger." Mine's Robert. What's yours?"

"Robert." He replied and they both laughed, identically.

Alan chewed his thumbnail tentatively.

"Y'know, that could work. We'll need to put it to your Alan."

Half an hour later, Alan II summoned by a phone call, left the office and drove round to Northumberland Street. After the same initial shock and surprise, he also put his mind to the suggestion.

"London, eh? Well - why not? How do we deal with the passport situation if we decide to have a Caribbean holiday?"

"I hadn't thought of that," Berrick replied, "but I know a man who can wangle it."

They sat together in the lounge, looking at each other curiously. How does it feel, after all, to see your very image sitting across the room from you? Superstition held it that to see yourself in living form was a premonition of your own death. Each of them could feel that atavistic fear at the back of their mind despite having their feet firmly planted on solid ground.

Alan broke the awkward silence which had followed Berrick's assertion that he could pull strings to give them each separate identities.

"Look, Alan," he suppressed the nervous giggle that tried to force its way into his throat at the incongruity of talking thus to himself, "I don't know how to put this -"

"I do," replied his alter ego. "You want to know what I've been up to with Tanja, don't you?"

Alan sat upright and blinked in surprise, before cursing his stupidity.

"Of course. I should have guessed that you of all people would know. So, tell me."

Alan II looked at him calmly, that familiar line of concentration, or was it amusement? between his eyes. "You know that she'd have thought I - you, that is - was/were nuts if I'd started talking about where I'm from, don't you?" He sighed. "We'd better tell you about our experiences on arriving here in your world." He sipped his coffee and sat back in the chintzy sofa, one leg crossed over and resting on the other knee by the ankle. Berrick II blew his cheeks out and raised his eyebrows. Semi-mockingly, he held out a hand, theatrically in Alan II's direction. "Gentlemen - Mr Alan Cruickshank!"

CHAPTER TWENTY

"I'd like to know what the hell we're doing here, for one thing," Berrick hissed at Alan. "That old duffer seems to believe we're some sort of undercover bods like the Scarlet Pimpernel. Where did he get that idea from?"

Alan shrugged irritatedly," I've an idea that there's an agent on the Continent who shares my illustrious surname. There aren't many of us, so he may have us confused." He took a heavy half-hunter from his waistcoat pocket and studied it abstractedly. It was nearing ten-thirty am. He glanced up at the large oil painting that dominated the hall of the Sir Ralph Fairbairn's official residence. It was old-fashioned and in a very formal style. He ran his finger round his collar.

"Why can't they make these damn' things comfortable?" He grumbled to himself.

Berrick laughed softly. "You're never happy unless you're grumbling, are you?" He looked at something he held in the palm of his hand with some interest, still chortling to himself.

"Spare me the analysis, please." He raised an eyebrow irritatedly at Berrick's renewed merriment before he too grinned. "What have you got there? No. Don't tell me." He held up a hand." It's a Marie Antoinette livre of 1788, 'condition extra fane', " he put on a ludicrously affected accent.

" Like hell. It's actually a James IX groat in very fine condition, if you must know."

"You're wasting your time. It'll never do you any good. Mark my words."

Seeking to change the subject from one of Alan's favourite topics, Berrick looked around conspiratorially. "Fancy taking a peek about the place? Sir Ralph won't be ready for ten minutes or more and I'm getting bunions on my corns walking backwards and forwards on this bloody wooden floor. Besides," he held up a small black lump. Alan's mouth opened in a silent 0.

"I thought this bloody war had disrupted trade with the West Indies?"

"True. I just had a little saved up for a rainy day." He produced a small pipe from his waistcoat pocket.

"Let's have a wander while the old boy gets into his corset to meet us. I must admit, I'm puzzled as to what a senior Government official can want with two underpaid solicitors in the middle of a war."

"Maybe he wants to buy back all that territory we've been losing to the Frogs and Squareheads."

"Listen, Rick. Don't even hint at that sort of joke when we see the old fart!" Alan said, thoroughly alarmed as they reached some stairs which spiralled upwards attracting their interest. "People have been thrown into jail and worse for saying that sort of thing!"

"Don't worry. That wasn't for public consumption. Come to think of it, neither is this. If anyone knew I had it, I'd have half of Edinburgh wanting a smoke. You know, I'll bet you that this is almost the only kif in town."

They went up swiftly and silently, pausing at the pale blue first landing they came to before ascending once more. A passage led from the top landing from its pale orange colouring into the recesses of the old house, the darkness of the passage only increasing its mysteriousness.

"What's that smell? Incense? Something else, too. Patchouli, perhaps. Just a trace. What a strange place this is. Why would a Government official have such exotic smells floating about his residence?"

"He'll be an old India hand, I expect."

Berrick nodded as he puffed at the pipe before passing it over. As he did so, he took a slim leather case from his jacket pocket and opened it. He took a cigarette out and lit it before offering one to Alan who shook his head. Silently, they enjoyed the elevating effects of the kif and regretted the war which had led to supplies drying up at every source ('even Forsyth's don't have any,' the senior partner of his legal firm had tut-tutted only the previous week). Soon, too soon for them, it was used up. Only a small amount remained in Berrick's greased-paper twist and that would be kept for some future occasion, he had decided. He peered over the banister.

"Well, there's no sign of the frump who showed us in," he said. "Let's explore up here a little. Wow! What a buzz I'm getting! Hey, Alan?"

His companion was attempting to blow smoke-rings and humming 'Greensleeves' in snatches in-between.

"Come on. Let's see what's down the passageway."

"'Lead on MacDuff....thou marshall'st me the way to Duncan's chamber..'"

"Shakespeare would be spinning in his grave at such cavalier misquoting of his play. Hullo. A door."

"How unusual."

"Shut up, Alan. It is unusual, now you come to mention it. Look...d'you see?"

"See what, old chum, old horse?"

"A keyhole."

"A keyhole! Of course." A look of puzzlement came over Alan's face. "Sorry, old chap. Can't quite put that together and make any sense out of it. "What so speshul 'bout a keyhole?"

"What do you see at funfairs, chump?"

"Eh? Funfairs? Oh! Got you. Ha ha! Yeess."

"Well?"

"Eh?"

"God, Alan. You're bloody hopeless when you're stewed. We look through it like 'What the Butler saw'. Understan' ?"

"Got you."

Berrick knelt in a mildly wobbly way while Alan stopped the wall from falling over with only one hand and lent silent moral support.

"Well...I can see a flat."

"Ooh, eeh."

"Sarckie bastard. Look for yourself. It's a bloody funny-looking place too. Or mebbe that kif was a trifle stronger than I thought." Admittedly, the strains of 'Goodbye Dolly Gray', the hit song of the War were running through his head, but, even so, the place did have something odd about it. Blinking his eyes in the semi-darkness of the corridor, Alan abandoned the charitable act of single-handedly supporting the building like some latter-day Samson and sank gently to kneel beside

Berrick as though in an act of worship. He, now, pressed his left eye to the keyhole and peered around.

"Iss different. Very...I dunno...relaxed?"

"Thass it. Relaxed. Informal. Not like this place. You ever feel the lust to get out and about? Go to America or something where they don't wear these bloody uncomfortable wing collars all the time?"

"Why?"

"Just a thought. Thinkin' aloud, y'see?" He peered through the keyhole again. "Bloody funny, though that place. It's like a picture of a house in another country. See that box on the dresser? What's that for? And that one over there...the big one with the dark glass plate on the front of it. I mean...what is it?"

A certain recklessness caused by the uninhibiting effects of the drug in their system may be the attributive cause of their next action. It was to push open the door. After all, there was not a soul to be seen and no one to argue that the room they had peered at through its keyhole was anything other than just another room in the same building. Something about it made it clear that it was different in some subtle way. Boredom and curiosity had gripped them in the somewhat straitjacketed era in which they were born. It was not a boredom which could be dismissed by becoming a soldier or seaman. It was a boredom bred of social stagnation. The prospect of a meeting with Sir Ralph did not excite them. Rather the contrary. It appalled them. Any excuse to take their minds off the thought that the old fox, noted for his cunning in the capital, had some devious and, potentially lethal scheme in which they featured filled them with alarm. An appeal to the inquisitive side of their natures was bound to succeed, especially when they had had their inhibitions lowered by strong kif.

A heave with their shoulders and they were into the room almost before they knew it. In the murky daylight in the room, they blinked their eyes for a moment, peering about them.

Quietly, Berrick pushed the door to. It was clearly a cupboard door and was held shut by paint alone. Guiltily, they looked at each other. Alan put his finger to his lips. Berrick nodded. They hadn't made a lot of noise, but in a quiet flat, it had sounded loudly. Silence reigned, however. Satisfied that no one else was around, they looked in some perplexity at the contents of the room. A small set of black boxes on a table in the corner puzzled Berrick. He studied it closely. Various buttons and dials confronted him with apparent instructions.

"Whaddyou think this is?"

"God knows." Alan stood, hands on hips and gazed blankly at the instructions. He saw the word 'START'. Hesitantly, he lifted a finger and, cautiously, he prodded the button. A faint sound issued from the machine. He looked at Berrick in puzzlement and shook his head. He turned away.

A voice suddenly bellowed," Help! I need somebody!" and some strange, very loud music of a kind they had never heard before erupted, accompanying the man's voice, reiterating his cry for help. They leapt physically in the air and threw themselves into opposite corners of the room, ducking behind chairs and peering nervously round to seek out the person who was doing the shouting. Slowly, they realised that it was music. What music though! It was utterly unlike anything either of them had ever heard before. It was raucous, it was sung by someone whose voice was untrained, but it was compulsively attractive. They both made the quantum leap at the same moment.

"It's the machine!"

"It's a phonograph!"

Gingerly, they crept out from their refuges and came closer to the machine wonderingly.

"Incredible!"

"Astonishing!"

Soon, they had discovered that this room was no ordinary dwelling. It had entertainment devices they had never even dreamt of. The box that talked to them was a big surprise, causing them to sit down from sheer astonishment. The kinema machine - they could think of no other name for it - had them in raptures. It seemed that they had only been there a few minutes, but a time check came on before STV's next news bulletin.

"One o'clock! Jesus! The old man'll kill us." Alan said in sudden apprehension.

"The old man be buggered," Berrick replied irreverently," haven't you been watching that whadyoumaycallit or is your mind elsewhere?"

Alan turned to him, a look of puzzlement on his face. "What are you driving at?"

"It's obvious, isn't it? We aren't in our own time."

"Not -" Alan's jaw dropped." You mean we're in - the future?"

"That's exactly what I mean. This isn't the here and now. This is, oh, two, mebbe three hundred years ahead of us. You saw that flying machine a minute ago. It was streets ahead of the aeroplanes we have. And the cars! Wow! Some of those machines..." his voice tailed off in silent admiration.

Alan struggled to his feet from the embrace of the soft armchair. "If that's true...."

He didn't complete the sentence, but walked out of the room as if in search of something. Puzzled, Berrick turned the machine off and followed him.

"Alan? Alan? Where are you going?"

"Out."

"Out where?"

Alan paused dramatically, his hand on the front door. He smiled conspiratorially.

"Out there." He pointed. "Wherever, or whenever it is. And stuff the Sir Ralphs of this world. Or is it that one? There's only one way to find out."

He pulled the door-handle after unsnibbing the lock and turned.

"You coming?"

"Try to hold me back." Berrick grinned.

They came out onto a dusty landing. A foostie smell was evident, but many tenements had worse. Softly, they stole down the stairway, noting the nasty lighting which would have made a healthy twenty year-old look like a corpse, but pressing ahead with the task of getting out before anyone observed them. In a minute, they had reached the ground floor and, with a measure of relief, they now walked to the front door. Alan was about to open it when Berrick caught sight of a scrap of paper lying on the floor.

"What's this?"

"Probably a piece of rubbish. C'mon. I want to see this world of the future."

Not thinking, Berrick stuffed the scrap of paper into his jacket pocket and followed.

As he sipped his coffee, now stone cold, Alan recalled their initial impressions. The weather was chilly and there was a haar blowing fog like smoke up the street. They appeared to be in an ancient part of Edinburgh - for they recognised the style of architecture - and correctly guessed that they were in the Old Town.

They muttered to each other in the High Street as to which direction to take. They finally plumped for the uphill direction and went off noting differences almost at once.

"Look at these yellow stripes along the side of the road. I've never seen them before. Have you?"

"No."

A bus went past followed by a stream of cars, headlights switched on in the gloom. They stopped dead and stared at the strange, futuristic vehicles slowly pulling out to overtake the bus which had ground to a halt to let a passenger descend. It was a little old lady who looked at the two men standing, stock-still and open-mouthed at the cars as she walked past, fishing in her handbag for keys.

"You're too bloody early in the year fur fancy dress! The Festival isnae fur months!"

They turned to speak to her, but were met with her front door slamming shut in their faces.

"Fancy dress?" Berrick looked down at his clothes, from his elastic-sided boots to his fancy waistcoat and frock-coat. "What d'you reckon they wear here?"

They were shortly to find out as the haar gradually dissipated and the greyness of the day was relieved by the occasional patch of blue in the sky overhead.

For an hour, they wandered about the city, getting odd looks and sniggers from passers-by. They were unable to comprehend the scale of the changes in the city they were so familiar with. When a roar came from overhead, they saw a large airliner banking as it turned to land at Edinburgh Airport.

"We did it. We did cross over into the future." Berrick smacked his hands together. "It's better than I ever dreamed it could be. Look -"

A young man with a baseball cap set on his head back-to-front zipped past them on a skateboard while, by contrast, a pair of policemen were proceeding up the High Street on horseback.

"It's fantastic."

"Yes," Berrick replied." We need to be practical, though. Is our money good here, d'you reckon?"

"Only one way to find out. Let's ask."

They crossed the street at St Giles' Cathedral and walked down to look in the shop windows. It took several before they found one that quoted any prices. Indeed, it was a cafe that gave prices.

"Well, that does it. What does 75p mean?"

"God knows. I'm getting hungry too."

Now, slightly dispirited, they wandered around the area and counted out the money they had on them.

"I've two sovereigns and a couple of half-sovereigns. The rest's just seven bob in silver and a few coppers."

"I'm a bit better off, then. Ten quid in sovereigns and three and six in change," Berrick replied thoughtfully, his eyes narrowing. "Remember my hobby?"

Alan laughed. "What - coin collecting? A fat lot of good that's going to do for you in this situation. You haven't got your collection with you, surely? No, I thought not. So where's that going to take us?"

Berrick smiled and nodded over the road. Looking over, Alan saw a small shop. It had escaped his attention until now. It was a coin shop.

"They may use different coinage, but I bet gold is still valuable in the future. What do you think?"

They had decided to be cautious and only to offer the shopkeeper a half-sovereign and , then, only for its gold content.

"How interesting," the latter had said when he was offered the coin. "Jacobite coins were never a speciality of mine. I hadnae realised that they minted them in exile. Quite, quite fascinating." He looked up at Berrick, who was feeling decidedly nervous at the mention of Jacobites. If the Royals weren't the House of Stuart, then what was the social structure in this time? The proprietor studied him with a beady eye. "Where did you get it?"

"Ah...oh, y'know. I'm um, just back from the Continent."

"Ah! I see," the proprietor beamed, "Italy?"

Berrick nodded jerkily, wishing the man would just shut up and get on with deciding what, if anything, he was willing to pay for the wretched thing. Sweat was forming on his brow and upper lip, not to mention under his arms. He could feel the slow, cold trickle as he replied as coolly as he could, "oh...briefly, yes. Yes, I'm sure I did."

"That must be its provenance. Nice workmanship. I pay for good stuff like this. I know keen collectors, if you take my drift."

"Take your wha....oh, yes, I.....take your drift, as you say. Ah, how much, Mr.." he studied the little name board the proprietor was wearing on his breast, "Mr Wainwright?"

"Bill, please!" The proprietor reached out and offered his hand. Nonplussed for a second, Berrick wiped his hand on his trouser-leg unobtrusively before subjecting it to a mauling by Mr Wainwright's huge paw. Berrick glanced out of the window into Cockburn Street where Alan was pacing up and down nervously awaiting the outcome to the meeting.

"I just need some ID. Purely a formality, you understand," smiled Mr Wainwright.

"ID ?" Berrick asked blankly.

"Identification. You know. Who you are, where you live. That sort of thing?"

"But I...I don't think.. "Berrick searched feverishly through his pockets for anything he could offer in this world that would be accepted as evidence of who he was. Besides, what evidence of personal identity did people where they were from carry around with them? They left that to Johnnie Foreigner and his undemocratic regimes. He pulled a handkerchief out of his left hand pocket and wiped his brow with it. Putting it back, he pulled another from his right and a piece of pink paper, square in shape fell onto the glass showcase which lay between them. The proprietor seized it with a small cry and had it under the

261

light to scribble down details before Berrick even realised it was anything other than the wastepaper he had absent-mindedly put into his pocket earlier rather than leaving it as litter in the doorway to the tenement.

"Mr Berrick Kildrum, 23a, Northumberland St.."

"That's me!" Berrick exclaimed.

"I should hope so. It's your driving licence." The proprietor said in surprise. "Who else's would you use?"

"Oh...that is to say....I mean...m..m...mine, of course. I thought I'd lost it. That's all."

With a grunt, the proprietor handed it back over. "Just regulations, son, because of the gold content, y'understand? It willnae last much longer. Just till May. Anyway, I owe you a decent amount for that piece. I didn't say how much, did I? Silly bugger that I am." He smiled at Berrick as he opened his electronic till. "I owe you two hundred and fifty pounds, unless you want it in euros."

Not liking the sound of euros, whatever they were, Berrick opted for pounds. At least they sounded familiar. He received a healthy stack of tenners and twenties plus the driving licence and bade the proprietor good day.

"So, you managed to make out all right, in the end ?" Berrick asked his twin, bringing in Alan's third cup of hot coffee since he had started to tell the tale. "Your throat must be getting dry."

"Mmm, thanks, Berrick. I'll call you that to distinguish you from Rick here. Say, Rick? Can you carry on for a while? I could do with a break."

Berrick II grinned." Always was a skiver. Isn't that right, Alan? OK. As he was saying, coin collecting would never do me any good..."

It was the driving licence that did it, of course. The money was extremely useful. Once the two found themselves in a world so far ahead of them that it literally made their heads spin, they knew that they didn't want to go back to meet a doubtlessly enraged former diplomat kept waiting for the whole morning by two small-time domestic property conveyancing lawyers. The problem they faced was where to live. Finding a driving licence in his own name made Berrick nervous.

"It means that someone else called Berrick Kildrum is stalking the streets of this fair city too.

So? If nothing else, we must meet this Mr Kildrum."

"Why?"

"Why? Because, he will be grateful for the return of his driving licence for one thing. For another, I'd like to see this other Berrick Kildrum."

"What are you driving at, Alan?"

"Haven't you noticed anything? All right...besides the coin shop ...yes, yes and the driving licence. I stand corrected. No. What I mean is - everything is not just familiar, it's the same. OK, OK. Add a century of two of development, but, otherwise, it's the same. And, that being the case...you follow me?"

"Ye.e.es," it was clear that Berrick was lost.

"Who do you think might be a friend of Mr Kildrum?"

"Oh!"

"Oh, indeed. If we want to make it in this world of the future, perhaps our namesakes will be a help -"

"Maybe they'd think we were madmen."

"Maybe so. Maybe. Well. There's only one way to find out."

Berrick pulled the small driving licence out of his pocket and studied it. "Northumberland Street. A nice address. More expensive than I can afford. Yes, Alan, I think I'd like to see this...other Berrick Kildrum."

Having had their food and washed it down with hot coffee, they strolled back round to Cockburn Street and down from there to Princes Street. At every pace, some new wonder drew their attention. Girls were extremely immodestly dressed. Some were even exposing their legs to public gaze and, apparently without embarrassment. They blushed at seeing such sights even while they were excited by them. The streets seemed to be cleaner in one sense, for there was no sign of horse manure to be seen. By contrast, however, there was more wastepaper in the gutter, though it was not an excessive amount. Indeed, they passed a crew of men clad in coveralls accompanied by a huge behemoth of a machine which quite frightened them initially by the grinding mechanical roar it made as it lifted bins made of some unknown substance, seemingly like rubber, yet harder, into its vast maw. Swiftly, they walked by, ever conscious of the speed of the motor cars which swished past them with quiet engines and comfortable-looking passengers.

At the foot of Waverley Bridge, they passed an office and glanced in as they passed. To their puzzlement, several people inside seemed to be avidly watching screens akin to the one they had noticed in the flat earlier.

"Is it an entertainment house?" Alan asked rhetorically, glancing around.

"No. It seems to be a business."

"D'you think they've reached some sort of utopian state where the moneyed classes spend their days in idle pursuits, would you think?" Berrick asked.

"No. Surely not. It's so...aimless."

They reached Princes Street and shortly thereafter were heading down Dundas Street in its steep, headlong rush downhill towards the Botanics. Their footsteps slowed as they turned into Northumberland Street. They gradually approached the basement stair which appeared on the driving licence.

"Is this a good idea, Alan? I mean...this fellow may be convinced that I'm an imposter if I tell him I'm Berrick Kildrum. He may call the police and then what may happen to us, eh?"

Alan paused and chewed his thumb thoughtfully. He nodded. "It's a risk, I'll grant you, but what else would you suggest?"

Berrick cursed. "All right. I suppose I'll just have to go for it. It gives me the heebie-jeebies, though."

"I know, old man. I know." He brightened up. "I'll be there with you, don't forget. If this other fellow says he'll clipe to the rozzers, I'll crack him over the head. How about that for an idea?"

"Spare me that, please. " Berrick clattered down the stairs and forestalled any further discussion on the matter by banging hard on the doorknocker.

For a long moment, there was silence. He banged hard again and looked at Alan questioningly.

"I don't think -" he began and stopped. A loud slamming of a door inside sounded. Swallowing hard, Alan nodded at him. "Give it your best, Rick."

The door swung open and a young, skinny man with spectacles on was blinking up at him.

"Ah..." Berrick ventured, suddenly tongue-tied.

"Oh? It's you. Forget yer key, did you? Hey, Rick! I dig yer duds. Where'd ye get them, eh? C'mon in. I'm just about away to work. I've changed shift this week, so you're lucky you caught me. Hi Alan!" He turned and went back in, leaving the door wide open and both men standing, staring at each other.

It had been very awkward at first, pretending to be the other pair. They had sat around in the lounge as Berrick had no idea which room was his. They explored once Dave went out. Berrick went into a room which looked appropriate and discovered clothes which fitted him perfectly. Photographs showed Berrick smiling out at them in lifelike colour, not tinted black & white as they were accustomed to seeing. He was the image of Berrick. Another photo showed Alan grinning with a large glass of beer in one hand and a very pretty, dark-haired girl holding his other.

"Trouble." Alan muttered.

Berrick changed into something more normal for the place and Alan found some trousers which weren't too long and a sweatshirt. They felt that they could fit in more easily, though the disturbing physical likeness of their two namesakes made them extremely nervous. Digging around, they found a sheet of paper from a local solicitor's firm listing properties for sale under Berrick's bed. Alan pointed out an address which was familiar to them both. It was the flat in the Old Town where they had found the driving licence. Maybe their alter egos had

had a similar experience to their own. They laughed together at the embarrassment of not having any idea of how to operate anything in the place. Well, they hesitated. Perhaps not everything. They both knew how to switch on an electric light and flush the loo, but it went little further than that.

"We were anxious that you were going to come back at the end of the day and demand to know who the bloody hell we were. Then, about six pm, we got lucky. " Berrick went on. "I found a spare set of keys. Dave was out, so we'd had a good nose around to familiarise ourselves. You can imagine. We couldn't boil an egg! "

They had found it all rather overpowering, trying to come to terms with the technology of a century ahead without any kind of handbook. They fused the kettle by switching it on without putting water in, they burnt the toast and flooded the floor with the washing machine. The burnt toast caused the smoke alarm to go off and the Fire Brigade appeared and tramped about the house looking grim and checking wiring. Pretending that he'd been away a long time and forgotten how to use half the appliances in the house, Berrick said, "I've been away, you know. Out in the Empire. Africa." He smiled at the lantern-jawed fireman whose expression of incredulity was shown by the total disappearance of his eyebrows in an upwards direction.

"The whit?"

Berrick went very pale, realising that he had said something very stupid or something controversial.

"Africa?" He ventured.

"Aye. Africa. Ah ken Africa. Ah didnae ken we still had an Empire there!"

"No. Of course not," Berrick laughed squeakily, "but they still haven't developed, you know. A bit backward. No electricity -"

"Or gas -" Alan added.

"No - nor gas."

"It's nae wonder darkies eat their bairns." The fireman commented drily.

They got him to give them, grudgingly, a swift 'acclimatisation course' on how to use their domestic appliances without sudden death resulting. He left later muttering something about limp-wristed fairies, which puzzled them both mightily. They hadn't realised that such superstitions would have persisted so far into the future.

In fact, they were as absorbent as sponges over the next few days. They read the papers, watched TV, listened to the radio and went to the library to look up the encyclopaedia in order to understand the place they were in. It was with a distinct shock that they found that the year was the same as their own. The change of the nature of government was the only cause to which they could attribute that. Otherwise, why was their world not like this?

After a day spent in deep research, Alan discovered where he lived and, also, where both of them worked. It was with considerable trepidation that they both went round to the corner of Royal Circus on the morning of the second day and tramped down the stairs to their basement office.

Alan recognised the pretty, dark-haired girl at reception the moment he crossed the threshold.

"And where have you two been for the last two days?" She demanded. "I've got clients climbing the bloody walls because you both swanned off and left me to handle it. "You, Alan

Cruickshank and you, Berrick Kildrum, both owe me a big lunch.. I don't know what you'd do without me."

Alan hobbled over to her with a big smile and gave her a big hug, she reacted by pulling him away towards a smaller room to one side, waving a little to Berrick with her free hand as she did so. This, it seemed, was normal.

"Don't I get a kiss, then?" She said, but Alan had almost beaten her to it, smothering her with half his face until she had to fight him off to come up for air.

"What happened to you? You're limping." She looked concerned.

"It's a groin strain. I was.....hang-gliding with Rick and I fell off."

"Fell...hang-gliding? But you always told me you were terrified of heights!"

"I did? Oh, yes, yes. Of course I did. Well, you can see why now, can't you?"

"And how long...excuse us, Rick," she pushed Alan's door to in Berrick's face. He grinned and strolled over to the other room. Judging by the small pile of books about coins on the desk, it was his. He pushed the door to and sat down, swinging his feet up on the desk. He was beginning to like this place. They were starting to fit in.

Two days later, Berrick and Alan met General Hannah in the NB for a drink. It had taken several telephone calls to nail the old warhorse down and both Berricks and Alans had had to separate lest the secret be out. Berrick II and Alan II went for a

269

quiet week in Mull while their alter egos put the problem to the General.

"It's damned irregular, so it is. Y'know that of course. Mmm. I'll need to rattle a cage or two. Y'see, we thought all the traffic was one way, from this world to the other, not vice-versa. Now, I'm afraid, the Gateways have been taken over. Those we had heard of in Russia, China and so on? Unstable. Closed off early. The talk of large military formations going through were just so much talk. They are closing off. Whatever the anomaly that caused them was, it seems to be coming to an end now. The scientists can't explain them yet. At least, they can't in terms I understand. They're now fully under Government control. Yours was anyway. The girls in that flat are actually Armed Forces, despite appearances to the contrary. If you had been anyone else, they'd have piled you straight back through the gateway or they'd have blown your heads off."

He waved a hand to shush them at that.

"Don't worry, lads. They were told to expect you. But only you. As to your friends..."

He let that statement hang in the air for a moment, swirling his whisky around in his glass for a moment before continuing. "Can you tell me how they got through?"

"Same way we did, but before us." Berrick omitted mentioning that they had used another gateway.

General Hannah regarded them over the rim of his glass, his disbelief plainly evident.

"Well, it's all academic now. In days, maybe hours, the gateway will be pinched off and we'll be back on our own again. Looks like they've missed the boat. It might have been better if...." He took a swallow of his whisky.

Alan sipped his own thoughtfully.

"What about our lads.. and the Americans.. over there?"

"Withdrawn quietly. The place is pristine. Apart from your alter egos, the two worlds are separate again. At least, they will be when the gateways close off."

"Something that has concerned me, General," Alan studied his drink thoughtfully, before looking up, "Why did the military move in once it was realised how much in advance of the Other Land we were. You must all have known they presented us with no material danger?"

General Hannah looked uncomfortable momentarily. He took a swallow of his whisky before looking them straight in the eye.

"There are some things a soldier needs to do. Orders is orders."

"Hasn't that been the excuse all through the centuries?" Berrick asked him challengingly. His gaze was hard and direct. The General met it without blinking, however.

"True. We live in a difficult world. Those may not have been as sophisticated as ours, but problems are problems. This is one we felt we needed to overcome. Military intervention seemed appropriate."

"For whose sake, General?" Berrick asked. "Theirs or ours?"

The General smiled tightly. He raised an eyebrow interrogatively.

"Now, you don't expect me to give you answers that are too direct, lads, do you? My concern is the security of the Commonwealth. We saw potential for that security to be undermined by goodness knows who, or what. Look at it

271

sensibly. We had found one and…… with your discovery, two entrances to this country 'by the back door'.

"Ordinarily, you expect us to be the ones defending the status quo. In this instance, however, we took a look at the evidence that confronted us and found, as Major Hansen showed both of you, that the feeling of the population at large was in favour of the Usurper, not of the Incumbent. We became even more concerned when we found evidence of a similar level of technology to our own being employed, so we thought, on the part of Stuart cause. This was, of course, our friends from the United Kingdom of Great Britain and Northern Ireland in the other parallel universe. Now, the fact that we had assumed that we would find ourselves fighting against antipathetic forces to our own meant that we were, perhaps, somewhat premature in our analysis of this situation when we launched the attack on Leuchars. However, in the fullness of time, we discovered our mistake, and put it to rights. An unhealthy regime was overturned and the right guy got the job!" He sat up a little straighter. "It could easily have been a hostile army from a regime in which Adolph Hitler had won their Second World War and we might have been fighting for our lives against a politically hostile empire whose sole aim was to overcome us and subject our entire world to total, abject slavery. We were lucky, that's all."

"I suppose that's true enough, but we were forced into your Army, sent on a highly dangerous mission and subjected to murderous attack on one occasion in a pub in London," Alan commented.

"Ah, yes, I remember hearing about that." the General replied, lighting up a cigarette and breathing the smoke out through his nostrils. "That was not the work of fascist bully-boys from our day and age. Indeed, it was not the work of our esteemed fellow-countrymen from the Realm of Her Majesty Queen

Elizabeth either. In fact, it was merely a brutal attack set up by a group of East End thugs with whom a certain Sergeant Stock, whose name you may recall..."

"Yes, we remember Sergeant Stock," Berrick replied.

"... had been associated with in various nefarious activities during his free time once he and some other regulars had established themselves in London. Sergeant Stock is, shall we say, an entrepreneur. He saw various business openings which he proceeded to exploit, thereby putting several of the local East End hoods' noses out of joint. They saw Sergeant Stock as a rival and set out to remove him from the scene on that particular night. Unfortunately for them, they had reckoned without the somewhat more sophisticated fighting techniques of our time, thanks to the teaching of low cunning combined with various forms of oriental unarmed combat taught to our troops. As a consequence, they came off worse."

The General stubbed out his cigarette and smiled at them before polishing off his whisky in a smooth swallow and standing up.

"No, don't get up. I'll do my stuff for your new-found 'brothers'. The other world will go its own way now and we'll go ours. Best that way, I think."

He turned to go and stopped. He patted his breast pocket.

"I almost forgot. This if for you."

He held out a small envelope to Berrick who took it with a puzzled expression. With a nod the General left unobtrusive in his civilian dress.

Berrick opened the envelope and read it. His expression a puzzle.

"Well? Spit it out. Who's it from?"

Berrick handed it over to him, shaking his head. Alan read it himself and laughed and laughed. "We are relieved from charges of desertion from the Army. Desertion....!"

CHAPTER TWENTY-ONE

A week later, they arrived on Mull in the rain. A wind was lashing the western shore and big breakers were crashing spectacularly on the beach. A fine salt mist was blowing inshore as they left their car and walked the last hundred yards or so to the small cottage they had rented for a month for their 'brothers'.

They ducked behind the sheltering wall .

"Shall we?" Berrick asked.

"Yes. They'll be anxious, I'm sure."

Berrick rapped loudly on the peeling wooden door and they waited. Alan gazed out to sea, remembering the night cooped up in the tiny boat the Stuart Government had put them aboard. He remembered, also, how it almost became his tomb. Involuntarily, he shivered as though someone had stepped on his grave. His ruminations ended as the door creaked open and Alan II stood there, surprise on his face.

"Well! You're a sight for sore eyes, I can tell you!" Ushering them in, he turned and called, "Rick! Look who's here!"

A very different figure came clattering down the bare stairs from the smartly-dressed Berrick of Edinburgh. Seeing their surprise, he grinned. "You find me *chez moi* at my ease, gentlemen. No smartly-creased trousers. No suits and ties either. It's an old pair of moleskins and tennis shoes. A fisherman's jersey keeps much of the smir off. As to the rest, who's to notice except Alan ?"

Indeed, the change to a shaggier, bearded beachcomber was matched by Alan. They had not noticed the changes in him as well. He was wearing an lumberjack check shirt and old pair of jeans which were liberally daubed with oil paint. A brush was tucked behind his ear and it was plain that they had interrupted him in his work.

"Sorry. We didn't realise you'd be busy!" Alan exclaimed.

"Busy, my eye! We're enjoying ourselves. I haven't had so much fun in years. "Replied his namesake. "I never knew I had so much to say on canvass before. Don't you ever get the urge?"

"No. No, I can't say I do. A pint and a good curry seems to suit me OK."

"Enough chat," Berrick II said, intervening in a rather obvious manner to avoid any disagreements, "How about some tea? Or would you prefer something stronger?"

They walked into the sitting-room which was bare-boarded and painted an austere white. A fire was already burning in the grate. A freshly-gathered pile of driftwood was heaped to one side. Above the mantelpiece hung a mirror. Otherwise, the room had only two armchairs covered in a faded green covering and a large, sagging sofa piled with cushions. The most apparent aspect of the room from the moment one entered it was the stunning view out towards the west over the storm-wracked, foam-flecked restlessness of the broad Atlantic. As they watched, a thin and watery tendril of brightness fought through the phalanxes of cloud which were the scurrying, amorphous escort to the sea's heaving cauldron. It was a skirmish, no more and the clouds closed once more against the small lance-thrust of warmth which had struck through its monopolistic impenetrability only to be swiftly and silently vanquished.

The light in that room was bright, though the day seemed gloomy enough. By the window stood an artist's easel. The work on it was only half-completed. It was the headland jutting out into the sea a bare quarter-mile down the coast, its rocky contours disappearing in a flurry of wildly-crashing waves and wind-flung spume as they watched.

They sat down and nodded their appreciation at the tea Berrick II brought in on a tray.

"Lapsang suchong!" I didn't know Mull stretched to such dainties!" Alan commented drily.

Berrick II grinned. "My fault. I'd never tried it before getting here. I bought it at one of those big stores in Edinburgh."

They ate shortbread and drank their tea in a pleasant torpor brought on by the long journey and the tranquil atmosphere which they found in that room, despite the contrasting nature of the sea. Alan II's painting had a deep fascination for Alan who had never imagined himself expressing such a view of nature and, perhaps, by implication, of life itself. For the picture was a deep grey and green colour showing the conflict between wind and wave whilst they also combine to beat down and destroy. Tiny on the distant horizon, a small vessel was in trouble, broached by the power of the immense seas, her crew helpless. Yet, by comparison, in the foreground, a small figure was collecting the driftwood from the dunes and another man, whose dog was gambolling about him was collecting flotsam and jetsam. The sea takes and the sea gives back. The colour of tiny flowers like sea-grass brightened the foreground of the painting. Inshore, the sea became a pale green where it washed over the clear sand. Somehow, despite the subject being a storm, the picture gave a very positive feeling as Alan studied it closely. Someone was speaking to him.

277

"Sorry?"

"You were miles away." Alan II grinned at him. "Did you find yourself there?"

He found himself nodding. "In a way, yes. There's hope in that picture, for all the sky and sea are so lowering - threatening - if you like. There's life in it showing that for all the tragedy that there is, there is also hope."

"Bravo!" Berrick cheered. "Public house man turns art critic. Read all about it!"

"Fuck off, Rick!" Alan replied amiably. "I can read too."

The storm had abated by early evening and they decided to have a crack at setting up a barbecue. The wind had died back and, gradually, a fitful brightness began to prevail. Within half an hour, their decision could be seen to have been a good one. Fresh mutton was the most readily available meat on the island and that was their fare, washed down with a rough Italian wine they had brought with them.

"So, what does your source have to say about us, Alan?" Asked Berrick II. "Are we up the creek without a paddle ?"

It was Berrick, in fact, who put down his plate of lamb and baked potato. He paused to wipe a smut blown from the barbecue into his eyes before reaching into his jacket where it lay, thrown across the trunk of an ancient fallen tree. He pulled out a bulky, brown packet and tossed it over.

"See for yourself." He picked up his plate and concentrated on his food for a moment. When he looked up, Alan II was smiling over at him. In his hand, he held two passports.

"So, it's Robert Cruickshank and Fogo Kildrum! Jesus! Don't your family use normal names like the rest of us?"

Silently, Alan and Berrick raised their glasses.

"To our future," Robert lifted his and clinked it against Fogo's. Slowly, in a blaze of reds and purples, the sun set and left them to the glow of the wood fire, its glowing embers eddying this way and that in the breeze.

General Hannah was half-way through his office door at Redford Barracks and already looking forward to a quiet weekend's fishing on the Tweed when his telephone rang. Leaving the door ajar, he crossed the spartan office and picked up the receiver.

The conversation was brief and, at his end, monosyllabic.

"Very good, sir."

General Hannah severed the connection with the MoD in Whitehall and sighed.

"Who'd be a bloody soldier?" He asked himself rhetorically.

He did not hear a footstep on the stairs outside his office as Hank paused on his way to his own office on the third floor.

The General paused in thought and Hank, sensing something was not right, melted into the shadows. General Hannah consulted a tiny pocketbook. His finger ran down a short list of names and stopped. He grunted in satisfaction. Picking up the 'phone again, he punched a long sequence and waited.

"Hullo, Winston? Listen, me old horse. There's a little job I need done and your boys are best placed to do it. Have you got a pencil and paper? Good. I'll ask you to note this down and then destroy it once committed to memory, all right?....Excellent. Yes, yes, I know about that. I'm sure we can arrange some form of quid pro quo."

Swiftly, he gave details of the location and a description of what he wanted done.

"...got that? Good. Report back to me and only me."

He put the 'phone down and pulled out a packet of cigarettes. Lighting one, he stared out of the window of his office towards the Pentland Hills, so soft and serene in the gloaming. It was beautiful and restful.

Savagely, he ground out the cigarette in the ashtray and put on his peaked cap. There would be no rest for him. Not now. Not for a long, long time.

CHAPTER TWENTY-TWO

In late September, with the leaves on the trees that shield St Cuthbert's church from Lothian Road just turning Autumn gold, before a congregation of Scots Presbyterians from the groom's family and English Baptists from the bride's, Alan passed the ring to the minister and Berrick and Candice plighted their troth to each other. The church was packed. Its elegance was highlighted by a carved frieze of the last supper behind the altar. Everywhere were smiling faces. Many were those of soldiers who had been with them when they were in the Other Land, as they had begun to refer to it among themselves. General Hannah was there, as indeed, was Hank, smart in a US Marine Corps uniform. Alan raised an eyebrow enquiringly when they met. From a humble major, he appeared to have scaled the heights to have become a full Colonel.

"Congratulations, Hank. Promotion?"

"Aw, hell, Alan. You know me. Next week, I'll probably be a private again."

"Well, you know, you do tend to meet a better class of person there."

The bride looked stunning, dressed in a full-length cream silk wedding dress. Berrick wore a dark suit in an Edwardian style which Alan's echoed.

As the wedding party descended from the Vestry where they had signed the register before the required witnesses, they passed through an arch formed by the lifted swords of Henderson's and Macrae's regiment, the Scots Greys, all

281

dressed in full fig, tight brightly-coloured uniforms retained from the time of Waterloo. Press photographers, who, naturally, were unaware of the cause of the presence of so many military men for a mere civilian were merely told that Berrick had retired from the regiment some time before, but remained close to his former comrades-in-arms.

As they came out of the arch, they were showered with confetti by the guests. This caused squeals of delight from Candice before they climbed into a open-topped, horse-drawn carriage. Soon, they were on their way to a splendid wedding breakfast at the North British Hotel, still presiding over Waverley Station.

A new future beckoned them both and, eagerly, they accepted the challenge.

Far away on the island of St Kitts, sweltering under a Caribbean sun, Robert Cruickshank and Fogo Kildrum saluted them as they watched the ceremony on the Internet.

"And now our paths diverge. "Robert said.

"We go our own ways. Now, we each have a brother and a new life to live."

"There's no time to waste then, is there?"

They turned to the two blonde Swedish girls they had met only days ago and, briefly, their eyes met. They were the only two from another world. A world now gone.

"How about a swim, girls?" Fogo asked.

Robert switched the computer off and, as it cooled, they walked down the sandy path to the sea.

Hidden in the dunes, Winston Beattie lay, sweltering in the afternoon sun. He was peering through a pair of high-resolution binoculars. He grunted quietly to himself with satisfaction and reached over to the high-powered, bolt-action rifle that lay beside him. Squirming into a more comfortable position, he brought the sights to his eyes, aiming and adjusting the focus to the distant, dancing figures silhouetted against the dazzling blue of the sea. Resting the stock against his cheek, he sighted carefully and breathed in and then softly out as his finger gently began to pull the trigger. The hard pressure of a pistol pressed to his temple froze him.

"Not today, Winston, old chap. I'm here to update you." The voice was pure Sandhurst, but the face behind it was West Indian. "Put the rifle down, there's a good chap. You and I are going for a little walk."

Beattie did as he was told, moving very carefully, in case the pistol was fired. His skin was very precious to him and he could tell that the man holding it, as steadily as a rock, was a professional. He stepped back, hands raised, palms forward.

"What now?" He asked, his throat dry.

The other man gestured with a small movement of the pistol and Beattie shrugged and turned.

The two figures in single file went over the lip of the dunes and the sound of booming surf drifted in from the sea.

THE END

FOOTNOTES

Page 37   LMF - Lack of moral fibre (ie cowardice).

Page 48   Haud yer wheesht - Shut up.

Page 48   Tak tent – Pay attention.

Page 48   Dinnae fash – don't worry.

Page 49   Bide a wee – wait a bit.

Page 49   Whaur's ma sark? – where's my shirt/jacket?